I0678799

Unwanted Sidekick

Pam Kumpe

Pam Kumpe

DEDICATION

To Josh
Thank you for coming to my rescue.

To Nora
Thank you for helping me learn scriptures,
and for your kindness.

To my daddy, WC Dunn
Thank you for living life like Silas.
Thank you for being "Big Jake" to my heart too.
And thank you for loving like Marion Kane Raike.
Your love was like syrup for my soul.

Pam Kumpe

"I have told you these things, so that in me you may have peace. In this world you will have trouble. But take heart! I have overcome the world."
John 16:33 NIV

DISCLAIMER

This is a work of fiction. Names, characters, businesses, places, events and incidents are either the products of the author's imagination or used in a fictitious manner. Any resemblance to actual persons, living or dead, or actual events is purely coincidental.

The Sanders House / Washington, Arkansas

Muddy Steps

I never thought I was unusual until someone called me a delinquent. I never thought I was abnormal sitting by my daddy inside of a boxcar riding the rail, either. And I never longed for a mama more than I do right now. Since Tin Can Mahlee decided not to be my mama—since she ran off again—since criminals make poor mamas—I'm on the road to change her mind.

Crush shoved me, zapping me from my daydream, drilling me as he straddled the mud puddles. "Tin Can Mahlee's wanted for murder and she's in hiding. She doesn't want you to find her. She left you when she ran from the law in Jefferson, Texas. Once a hobo, always a hobo. She doesn't need a little girl hanging around."

Not looking at my unwanted sidekick, I kept pace with the thunder in my heart and the clashes in the sky. "Stop it. She's scared. She needs reminding—of how much she needs me. And I'm not little."

"She's the one who scares others. You will only remind her of how she needs to get on down the tracks."

"I know my Mahlee. She's hard like a jawbreaker, but once you know her, once you live with her, ride with her on the rail—well, she's … she's hard, but she's mine." I sighed. "I do love her. I do!"

"Shoelace, you never listen to anyone, and she never listens to anyone. You are a runner like her. I should leave you and go home to my brothers. You are harder to figure out than trying to swallow ten jawbreakers. I can't reason with you."

7

"Then go home. You have somewhere to live. Mr. Marion has set you up in the boy's home next to his house. Get out of here. Go sleep in your dry bed." I spun around, flapping my lips, and fumbled to keep my kitty from falling, and my satchel on my shoulder.

Crush softened his words. "I'm riding boxcars to see the country. I can go home later. I'm tired. Flat out tired!"

"Then, hush at me. Hush. Do you hear me?"

Meow. Meow.

I cuddled Tink beneath my coat. "Crush, you're soaked in the mind if you think seeing the country comes from being with me. I'm dumping you one day, you'll see. And you don't know what it's like to want a mama."

"Are you going there? Have you forgotten my parents died in a flood two years ago?"

I licked a drop of water from my top lip. "Sorry, I didn't mean to say anything about your ma and pa. I miss my Mahlee." Changing the subject I asked, "Why does it have to rain now? We're so close to Washington, Arkansas. Close to finding Mahlee."

My letters jumped from my insides like a waterfall of sorrow, joining the leaves and debris storming across the muddy road. Keeping the ugly words from spilling from my gut made my tummy ache, and the exhaustion and hunger wrapped itself in growls and grumbles from my mouth with words I should stop saying.

The worry and wonder, and the sadness and empty feelings leaked like an explosion from my broken heart. It felt like a bomb in my chest was ready to blow. I repeated the sad words to myself: *Not everyone searches for a hobo-mama who is a wanted killer.*

Unwanted Sidekick

The water poured like buckets from the sky and rolled down my face. I considered spitting at Crush, but since he has slugged me in boxcars for weeks, I swallowed my last bit of slobber.

The rain splashed on Tink's orange ears, and she wiggled, hoping to be free from my grasp. "Stay put, little one. You'll get soaked." I clutched my satchel, sure the walk from the train depot in Hope, Arkansas, had to be hours behind. Might only be minutes though—but when you're starving, every step is one closer to fainting and one more step to who knows where.

I purposed to keep moving down the road, staying to the side, next to the grassy weeds, away from any cars, although we haven't watched one pass us by.

Crush shoved me from behind on my right shoulder, his push firm on my bones. "Keep walking. You're slacking off. You're the one who picked this highway. We were dry on the train. We should have stayed inside until the storm moved out. We've jumped trains, and ridden in boxcars for days and days, getting on, barreling off, changing boxcars, hopping on another set of tracks, making choices and changing our minds. We were dry inside of the boxcars."

"Whatever. You don't have the say over me, or what I do."

Crush moved closer to my side. "I'm older than you. I'm nearly grown. Old enough to drive, remember? I'm smarter than you. Wiser too. You act like you're so tough, but you're only eleven. You're a kid who cries when things get hard, or in this case, wet."

"I'm not crying. I'm wiping rain from my face. I'm not a kid, either. I've seen horrible things you've never seen. I've gone through more. I watched my daddy fall into a river from a coal car and die in Memphis. Die! Did you hear me?"

"I hear you. Everyone can hear you."

"I've fought with the Phantom Killer in Texarkana, and argued with a doctor in Oklahoma who was a drunk, he had holes in his heart. I stood over my grandma Elsie when she died on a train too. I've broken bones, and I wear more scars on my head and arms and legs than anyone. I'm a messenger of hope with wounds!"

"Hope? You are a messenger of storms and fly in like a tornado. The town behind us is called Hope, but you—"

"What do you know? I saved my best friend Taddy from two men in Oklahoma. And I saved all of your brothers from living in a shack. I ... I ... did things no girl should have to do. I've ..." My tears rushed from my eyes, like a dam breaking from behind a wall of sadness, and my tears joined the flooded waters surrounding my feet. I collapsed to the mud puddle of lost dreams, toppling to my knees.

"What now? Why are you kneeling in the road?"

"You should go home, Crush. I'm trouble. I'm lost. I don't know where Mahlee is, or where she's gone. I know she sent those papers to Marion Kane to give him the property for the orphanage, and the envelope had a return address with the words Washington, Arkansas. If Mahlee is anywhere, it's there. I have to see. I have to try."

"Mahlee's long gone. She's off somewhere in the woods or in jail by now. She's not prone to staying in one place, you said so yourself."

Sobbing, I countered Crush with my hate, hoping to drive him away. Hoping he'd go home and leave me alone. Alone is what I do best, unless Mahlee is with me. Otherwise, alone is alone. No one can hurt me or make me sad, or leave me, if I'm already alone. The rail has made me calloused, rougher than a little girl should be, but more grown up on the inside than I wanted to be too.

I shouted at the wind and at Crush. "So we've taken the wrong train a few times, and now we're here on another trail. Maybe you're right. Maybe, I don't know what I'm doing." Crush shook his head, pointing behind us. "Back there we were dry. Dry! Our clothes weren't wet. We could have stayed in Hope for a couple of hours longer. It's not like we haven't been riding for weeks looking for Mahlee. What's the hurry? Why tonight? Why does it matter?"

I jumped up, spun around in a circle like a crazy hobo girl, tripping on the rocks in the mud, stomping in the brown water deeper than my ankles. "Stop bossing me. You are not in charge of me. You can go back to Jefferson anytime you want. I left by myself. I want to be by myself. I don't need you. Mahlee matters. She's my hope. She's my reason to keep going."

I slammed my satchel into Crush, right into his side, so fast, I stumbled like a toddler learning to walk, and fell to my rear. "I'm searching for Mahlee. She has to learn the truth. She didn't kill anyone. She's not a murderer."

"Mahlee is wanted by the police. The police chief believes she shot those two men. He doesn't know what you know. Remember, he didn't believe you, and all the witnesses are dead. It's not going to matter."

"It matters to me. I have to tell her. I have to." I spit water in Crush's already soaked face. "I have to let her know what happened to the bad men. She's family. She's my ... my could-be-would-be-mama. I have to find her. Without her, I can't go on. With her, I can." I rose to my feet and stomped ahead.

"Stop whining." Crush wiped the water from Tink's nose. "I'm not fond of walking in the rain, either. We should have stayed put for the night. We could have stayed dry."

"But, the longer it takes, the farther away Mahlee could get. Finding my Mahlee is important! It's life or death!" I pushed Crush's hand from my kitty. "The man at the train depot pointed this way. We're on the right road. I know it. We are."

The gray skies turned blacker, the sun hid behind the blanket of clouds, and my stomach growled, my legs hurt, and my eyes burned. Going without food for two days hasn't helped my mood much. Crush spent all of his money on our meals in the first three days. He's a big eater, hungry as an armadillo in a trash pile. A meal might give me nicer words to spew at Crush though. Or not!

Crush wrung out some water from his shirttail. "I hope you're right because this rain is running down my back, down my jeans, and into my boots. I'm soaked because of you." Crush pulled his cap down, clutching the handle on his suitcase. "Look! The wind is gusting as if a tornado is hiding over the ridge. Those trees are leaning sideways. This is not regular rain; the sky is heavy, and the force of the sideways rain is pelting my face. We need to find shelter."

Chug-a-lug. Shug-shug. Shug-shug. Chug.

I glanced behind us. "A truck. It's a truck. Maybe we could hitch a ride in the back. He's going our way. Hurry, stand in the middle of the road. His lights are on, and he'll see you."

"Or he'll run over me." Crush bellowed his tornado words at me, while I ran to the center of the road waving my arms. The truck slowed, honking at me.

Bleep!! Bleep!!

I dove to the side, as the truck bumped down the road, but then, like a lightning bolt, the truck stopped with a jerk, and a lanky man from the passenger side unfolded from the cab. A Negro in overalls spoke, "You kids lost?"

I mumbled under my breath. "We're not lost. We're taking a walk."

Crush slugged me. "Stop acting like a little kid. They're our ride."

The towering tree-man called again. "It's raining. Do you need a lift? We're headed to Washington. It's still four miles. The airport's over there. Need to catch a flight? Or need a ride? Make up your mind."

Crush pulled me along. "We'd be happy to ride with you, sir. Thanks!" He tossed his suitcase in the bed of the truck, but I held onto my satchel. He slugged my arm, whispering, "Did you see the coffin in the back?"

I twisted my head, "Yeah. Maybe we should walk."

The man waved us in, "Come on. The rain's getting the seat wet."

We slid inside the cab like puppies on a rope, and I sat closer to the door, even though the handle pushed deep into my ribs, when the door slammed closed. With the four of us inside, crowded we were, but at least we were out of the rain.

The hunched over driver at the steering wheel, a pale young man, slumped forward. "You kids shouldn't be out in this weather. A storm's coming in. Three days ago, Easter brought the Jonquils into bloom—but this spring is full of funnel clouds and flooding."

"Tornado? Are we safe?" I muttered, looking out the window.

Mr. Driver said, "I hope it's not a sign of worse weather to come. Last November, a tornado nearly destroyed our town. We had downed trees, twisted fences, and the roof from the Baptist Church landed on a cow, and the homes near the highway were torn apart."

Sighing, I wiped my face off. "I don't like tornadoes. Or Easter. People die on Easter."

The man next to Crush scratched his ear. "Since when do little girls not like Easter? Jesus rose for you, for all folks. He sets us free from the terrible sins, gives us hope."

"I like the word hope, but Easter reminds me of the Phantom Killer in Texarkana. I don't like a lot of days."

The Negro next to Crush countered my words. "I've heard of him. They never did catch the guy, but I tend to think each day is a gift. Make the most of it, or lose the best part of it. Before you know it you'll be pushing a cane or sitting in a rocker wishing for the good ole days." The man rubbed the stubble of gray on his chin, his deep wrinkles looked like tiny rivers.

I leaned forward. "Sorry. I don't mean no disrespect. We're hoping to stay in Washington. I'm … I'm fourteen. I can clean and cook. I can do chores." I mouthed, looking at Crush. "He's not a good worker. He's a good talker. But me, I'm good at everything."

Crush whispered in my ear. "Stop it. We might need them. You're eleven, so act like it. You're acting like a baby."

Before I could scream at Crush, the Negro man patted my wet knee, reaching over Crush. "Boney for fourteen. Small. But strong."

"I am strong. I am. Or I can be." I sucked in the damp air, and something under the hood of the truck smelled like oil scorching, and the odor swallowed up any good air.

The Negro introduced himself. "My name's Silas Jones. I work for Mr. Clifford Morning. He runs the Tavern Café. He's sadder tonight than some nights. Has to deliver some bad news to his wife."

Mr. Morning tipped his hat, holding the steering wheel with one hand. "Nice to meet you. Wish it were on a better day."

"A tavern? Like a bar? Where men gamble and drink away their life?"

The man with the yellow skin glanced at me, his eyes blue, his face soft and smooth. "It's our restaurant. We are known for home cooking and for our pies. It's the family business."

My stomach rumbled louder than the truck's engine. "Pie? I could go for some chocolate pie right now."

Crush rubbed his tummy. "Me too. We haven't eaten in a couple of days."

Mr. Morning smiled, "When we get into town, Silas will get you some supper. And help you dry your clothes. You didn't say why you're coming to Washington; do you have family here?"

I choked on my words. "I do. I might. Yeah, maybe. I have to see. It's possible."

Silas rocked in the seat like the trees bending in the storm, and his laugh swayed with the cab, adding a sweet sound like someone who loved life. Like someone who loved to see the good in people. His brown eyes pierced me like an arrow, like he favored someone from my past. I almost felt like I'd met Silas before, but tonight was the first time I'd ever set eyes on him.

Mr. Morning spoke up. "We're home. This is the old Sanders Farmstead. I bought it several years ago, and love this old place. Too bad I've got to break my wife's heart tonight." He looked over his shoulder at the coffin. "My wife's sister, Della, is in the coffin. She died in an accident at Union Station in Texarkana, and I arranged for her body to come to Hope by train, so we can bury her here. Daisy is due with our first child—any moment, and Della was coming to help with the baby. Now we're having a funeral!"

Spinning around in the seat, I looked at the coffin, watching the rain pelt the wood, and the memories of too many funerals rushed into my brain like ammunition going off—like a war zone of a new disaster waiting to implode and blow up. I slithered in the seat, holding Tink and wishing to find Mahlee before she was packed into a coffin or worse—never found!

The L-Shaped Life

Two yellow lights lit up the windows on either side of the porch, shooting beams across the puddles of water in the yard. The waterfall of rain turned into drips, more like dancing trickles, squeezing leftover water from the few clouds left in the sky.

Flickers of light danced through the windowpane from the room on the left, a sure sign of a fire burning. The white frame house reminded me of my grandma's manor in Texarkana. On a corner too. Opposite. But the same. Except this house has no second floor.

The storm floated east over the trees away from us, and Mr. Morning rolled the truck to a stop in front of the white picket fence. The pencil-like posts of wood wrapped around the whole block, land with livestock and a barn to the right. A family lives here, unlike the empty boarding house of Grandma Elsie's home—no one lives there anymore.

I miss the manor, more right now, more since my life was pretty much perfect for most of last year. Except for getting in trouble for sneaking out, and crossing paths with the Phantom Killer. I don't miss the school though, too much coloring and too many prissy girls.

Too much has happened since Thanksgiving of '45 until now, and for some reason, 1947 hasn't begun great, either. The love note Mahlee etched in the piano does tell me she loves me and Lizzy Beth. So why does she keep running away? And causing such havoc?

Grandma's in heaven with my mama and my daddy, and Mahlee's skedaddled out of my life—even after she's loved me best she could for the past six years.

Sniffle. Sniffle.

At the manor, I climbed the tree beside the balcony, played on the stairs, ate the best breakfasts ever. I did shoot a window out by accident, knocking books onto the spot where Skip played the piano at my daddy's pretend funeral. The funeral with no body. Texarkana was a town where chicken hawks dove at you and where the news was so important reporters from everywhere wrote stories.

Shaking, I held the silver handle on the pickup, and Silas reached across me. "Open her up. We're here. I'll take you two to the kitchen. Mr. Morning has to let Ms. Daisy know her sister is gone. We don't need to be there for her crying. She's due with a child and this won't be good on her."

The front door to the house opened wide between the white pillars, sending a ray of light through the blue-gray night, and a belly came out first wearing a long frilly dress. The lady's tummy was the size of two watermelons, and she waddled like a duck ready to topple. She held the pillar with one hand for support. "Honey. Where's my sister? You were picking her up? Right?"

Her muffled words dropped off, and Mr. Morning was on his way to the porch, wringing his hands together. "Darling. I bring you the saddest news. Della tripped over her suitcases, and tumbled backwards. She hit her head. Never woke up. The coroner said she cracked her skull."

"No! She's not dead."

Mr. Morning pointed to the coffin. "I'm sorry."

"No!! Not my sister Della. She was barely grown herself. She's not gone."

18

Ms. Daisy's high-pitched screams hurt my ears.
"No!! No!!" *Aheeee!!!!*
Mr. Morning reached for her, but she pushed him away,
and I froze on the walkway. Ms. Daisy wobbled a dizzy
swagger of lost hope and knelt on the porch. My heart broke
into pieces for her like a puzzle of scrambled sorrow. Her
horror became a reminder of having watched my own
grandma fall to her death on a train.

Now I'm here with Mr. Morning and Ms. Daisy, and my
Mahlee might be in town. I've got to figure out what to do. An
arm on my shoulder sent my hand slapping. "Crush. Stop
touching me. I don't like it when you treat me like a baby."

The deep soothing words of Silas assured me. "Sorry.
Missy. Tell me your name. Not sure we got either of your
names. Let me show you to the kitchen out back, past the
grapevines, next to the barn. Watch out for the rooster, the
black one. He's known to crow late into the night. Tends to
jump from the shadows too. He's got his days mixed up."

Crush wrinkled his lips, and stepped in front of me,
pointing his finger. "You thought I touched your shoulder."

"Get out of my face. I don't need you."

"So you two is brother and sister? You fight like it." Silas
grinned, like he was trying to distract us from the commotion
on the porch. From the hugging. The crying. The wailing of
arms. But no one could miss the display of pain.

I swung around, searching the ground. "Kitty? Where's
my kitty?"

Silas tapped my head. "There she is. On top of the fence
next to the corral." Silas spoke, his tone full of optimism.
"Come on. Let's get you something to eat."

Crush added his yapping. "We are hungry. By the way,
I'm fourteen. She's only eleven. She's always forgetting her
age. Her math skills are lacking."

"I'm great at math and at coloring trees with crayons."

Silas chuckled, "You color trees?"

"Once, when I didn't know what crayons were for, and the kids in school laughed at me. I climbed the tree and got so mad I painted a tree with every color in the box."

Crush wiped his nose on his sleeve. "She's been on the rail for too long. She's a wanderer."

I pursed my lips. The last thing I wanted was to let these strangers know we rode in boxcars. This is why getting rid of Crush is moving up the list faster than my stomach can growl for food. "You should keep your mouth shut, Crush."

"It's hard. I love to see you boil, and you get madder than I do—over the little things, like telling the truth."

"Whatever! I can tell the truth whenever I want to!"

Silas put a hand on my chin and his other under Crush's face. "You two need food. Grumpy hitchhikers, you are!"

I sighed. "Mr. Silas, I go by Shoelace on the rail. This is Crush. I gave him a hobo name. It's Ghost Boy."

Crush laughed. "I like my rail name. I may keep it."

Silas stopped to gaze at the engineer hat on Ghost Boy's head. "I've seen a hat like yours before. Remember it from somewhere. Not sure where though. Well, come on. We have some cheese and leftover cornbread. But it'll fill you up."

"Thank you. We won't be staying long. But the food does sound great." I smiled, but the noise from the front porch sailed over the roof of the house like a gust of wind.

"Missy, I figured you was a wee younger than you said. Too boney for fourteen." Silas moved with those long legs in giant steps to the right of the house. "Come on. I've got some chores to finish."

Crush snickered an evil boy laugh, sticking his tongue out at me, turning to Silas. "She's the baby girl in our family of

20

seven brothers. Our mama found her under a tree and felt sorry for her."

"Funny. A tree? I wasn't found under a tree. I … I was born and loved and cared for and …" The tears welled up in my eyes, and I wiped my face. "Never mind."

Mr. Morning rushed around the house to us. "Silas, take care of these two. Ms. Daisy is not well. Not well, at all. When you get these two some supper, come put this coffin in the front room. We'll have a funeral here tomorrow. With family."

"Yes, Boss. I'll get Molasses to help me. He's supposed to be getting them potatoes peeled while we were gone. I'll check on him."

I wiped a leftover raindrop from my brow, wondering how many funerals I would attend before life won, before happiness came, before Mahlee would love me.

Sticky New Friends

Standing on the steps to the kitchen house behind the big white mansion, I tapped Crush on the shoulder. "The main house is missing some walls. Look at the shape."

"It's an L-shaped home. Haven't you ever seen a Greek home with fancy porches?" Crush shook his head and bumped me with a thump to my noggin.

"Not in the shape of the letter L, and I haven't been in too many houses. Besides, how would you know this is a Greek home?" I mouthed my words again, without making any noise, and rolled my eyes.

"I've studied with my brothers. I pay attention."

Creak. Creak.

Silas pushed the door open, letting the warm smell of flour and sugar, and vanilla seep into my nose. I took a whiff. "This is the best smelling kitchen ever."

"I baked some sugar cookies this morning. Made some extra too." Silas placed my satchel on a wooden chair by the window, and showed Crush where to put his suitcase. "Sit at my humble table. Watch for crumbs. I leave them for my little friend."

I looked around. "You have a pet?"

"He's a little bit of a pet. He's a small spotted mouse who lives here with us. I named him Powder."

"What a great name. Oh no, my kitty might eat your mouse."

Crush wiped a loose strand of hair from his eyes. "Diseases. Mice are dirty. Stinky. They shouldn't eat from your table."

A high-pitch voice called out from the shadow of the doorway next to the hearth, holding a kettle of something. "Uncle Silas, stop with the stories. You have no mouse. Not one mouse."

A much younger version of Silas scooted into the kitchen, his black shoes sliding over the hardwood floor and his arms folded, as if he were going to continue correcting Silas. "Who are these kids?"

Crush tipped his hat. "We're passing through. Silas and Mr. Morning gave us a lift."

I spouted off. "Who are you?" I challenged the boy who had to be about the same age as Crush, except he towered as tall as Silas.

"I'm Molasses Jones. And who are you?" He pointed at my face, holding a potato in his palm.

"I'm Shoelace. I'm passing through town. This is … this is Crush. He's leaving before I do. I may stay in town for a while."

"I'm not going anywhere." Crush cracked his knuckles like stupid boys do.

Silas pulled two chairs out. "Sit. Soup's on the fire. Seems Molasses has your supper ready."

"Their supper? This pot of my special homemade soup is for Ms. Daisy. She's asked for vegetable soup with carrots, corn, okra, and yes," he held up a potato, "with potatoes."

Molasses' curly black hair and bronze eyes engulfed me, taking me to memories past, to somewhere on the tracks, to someone, and somewhere I've been before.

He grabbed a dish towel and held the spoon in the soup pan, stirring, "My uncle tends to stretch his stories to the sun, to the moon, and around the world. His storytelling is longer than a streak of lightning. But not deadly, fun mostly—but watch what he says. He does tell tall tales."

Silas danced a tap tap with his feet, twirling around like a youngster, bending like an old man. "Watch your mouth Son. I have a magic walking stick, and it gives out lashes."

"See, there he goes. He doesn't hit me. Don't let him fool you. He's the best uncle ever. He's raised me since my pa went off to play music. I'll be sixteen soon. I've almost stopped praying my pa would come back. But some days, I wish he would." Molasses poured soup into bowls, his words quieter than the crackling of the fire under the cast iron bowl.

Crush sat down, placing his face in his hands. "What town is this? We are in Washington, right?"

I knocked his hand from his cheek. "Stop being so rude. You know where we are. We're here, as guests. Act like one."

Crush made a fist. "You're one to talk. You don't have any manners yourself."

Molasses unwrapped cornbread from the wax paper on the shelf next to the wall and put it on the table. I glanced to the wall where jars of jam and canned goods laced the shelves with plenty to eat and plenty to borrow.

"Thank you." I sat down, my tummy rumbling for food.

Silas poured milk from the pitcher from the icebox for us, and then set a saucer on the steps outside for Tink. "I'm sure your kitty is hungry too."

Crush sighed, "I'm starving. Thank you."

Kablam. Kablam.

The door swung open, bouncing off the wall, sending a jar of red tomatoes to the floor, the glass splintering into pieces.

Silas jumped back. "What's wrong, Boss? What?"

Mr. Morning's tongue hung out, his nose ran, his eyes watered. "It's Daisy. She's having the baby tonight. Tonight! I phoned the doc, and he's not answering." He ran his fingers through his hair. "Silas, you've helped deliver babies for your people. I need you. You have to help Daisy. The news of her sister's passing, it's too much, and now ... now, she's having our child!"

Flames of Anger

"Why did Silas make us stay here in the kitchen house? I want to see a baby born. Don't you?" I swallowed the piece of cornbread stuck in the corner of my mouth, yanking up my dry pants.

Crush called to me from the kitchen table, since I was in the bedroom getting dressed. "After six brothers, I've watched enough babies yap."

I pulled on the dry jeans, the baggy legs dangling for miles below my knees, and I hollered around the wall to Crush. "I can't wear Molasses' pants. He's taller than you, and you're taller than me."

My shirt dripped like a leaky rag. Shuffling, I walked from Silas' back room where he and Molasses slept, showing Crush my problem. "Look at these pants. They are huge! How will I ever wear these? They're all legs. My other shirts in my satchel are wet too, and my other overalls." I stood in my bare feet, the Arkansas grit sticking to my toes.

Crush scowled. "I have extra clothes." Digging through his suitcase, he mumbled, "Here's some pants, they're almost too short for me."

"You'll let me wear them?"

"Sure, but only because you're all wet."

Grinning, I offered my thank you. "You have moments when you are nicer than you are."

"Here. Catch. I have plenty of clothes." He tossed me the jeans, a brown plaid shirt, and socks; they tumbled at my feet. Crush switched to his bossy self. "Get dressed. I need to change too. My clothes are glued to my skin, and the fire under the kettle makes this room feel like we're in a swamp. It's hot in here."

Bending down, I gathered up the clothes, hurrying to the room where two mattresses rested on top of crisscrossed ropes. "These are tiny beds. Have you seen how tall Silas and his nephew, Molasses are? Their feet must dangle over the end."

Screaming, Crush bellowed, "Get finished in there. And stop snooping."

"I'm not bothering Silas' bed, or touching his pillow, or rubbing my fingers over the blue and orange patched quilt. I'm not touching the soft pillow, either. I'm minding my own business." I sat down on the bed. "Did you know your socks are rough?"

I stood, slipping across the floor like I was mopping up the grit. I danced into the kitchen, bumping the chairs into each other, causing clacking sounds. Holding onto the rickety table like I was skating on ice, I glided, holding my shoes with one hand. "I'm dressed. I'm putting my PF Flyers by the fire. They're too wet to wear."

"Fine. I'm changing clothes. Don't open my suitcase or touch it." Crush vanished to the back room, the clunking and scuffling noises an indicator he was occupied with putting on dry clothes.

I placed my shoes closer to the ashes by the hearth, near the warmest part of the fire, the heat swooshing on my face, and I sniffed the soup, wishing for more to eat. Twiddling my fingers, my toes wiggled, my nose twitched, and I stretched my arms wide, leaning to the side, peeking toward the doorway and hoped I could catch a quick glance inside the secret suitcase.

Opening the top on the brown leather, I pursed my lips, bent down, and scooted on the smooth hardwood floor, tumbling to my knees. "Ouch!" Glancing at the bedroom door's entrance, I announced, "I hit my head on your suitcase."

Crush barreled into the room, slapping his hands together like a pa who scolds his children. "Get away from my suitcase! I didn't leave the lid open. I never leave it open."

I fumbled my right hand through the clothing, pretending to get my balance. "School paper? What's this? A teddy bear?" I hugged the cuddly ears. "Do you play with toys?"

"Get away! You are worse than Timmons and Tak when it comes to obeying me. The bear isn't mine. It belongs to Timmons; he must have left it in there. It's the only thing we have left of our ma." Crush shoved me and I became a boulder rolling across the room.

"Timmons and Tak are your little brothers. Who left you in charge?"

"I'm like their pa since we lost ours. We've talked about this. You love to repeat yourself. You love to annoy me."

"I simply remind you of your faults. Besides, I'm not related to you. I'm not your sister. I'm nothing to you."

Crush slammed the suitcase shut, almost snipping my finger. "You're right. You are an intruder in my life."

"Watch it. You followed me, remember?" I folded my arms, scowling at the unwanted sidekick who attached himself to me when I ran away from Jefferson. Toby Raike caught me with my satchel the day I snuck out the back door of Marion Kane's house and he told Mr. Marion, who sent Crush after me. I left on the train the very day Pastor Cody headed for me from Texarkana, but to stay would have meant I'd missed my chance to search for Tin Can Mahlee—my runaway mama.

Latching his fingers to the lid, Crush shoved his suitcase behind the table away from my side of the room, even though the kitchen was the size of a boxcar. He put the suitcase a few feet from my reach.

Sitting in a chair, I thumped the table with my fingers, mocking Crush. "What's the big deal? You have clothes. You have a toy. You have an engineer hat. Which is really mine."

"Leave me be. The way you hop trains, you're going to come up missing or squashed. You need to leave things alone."

"Whatever." I tested Crush with my words. "Do you sleep with the teddy bear at night? I bet you do."

He wrinkled his lips into a prune face pucker. "Stop it. You are bothering me."

"Am I? I'm proud of it." I placed my hand high like a salute to myself.

Crush shook his fist. "My things are none of your business. It's paper. Clothes. And a toy! I don't answer to you, either."

Jumping and standing in a chair, I towered over Crush. "I'm going to the big house. I'm going to see if the baby is here. I'm going without you. I'm putting my shoes on, and I'm headed out the door, down the walk, up to the back porch, across the back—I'm going. And I'm going to tell them you play with toys."

"Stop threatening me, and go."

I bounded to the floor, tore around the table, sat on the floor, and pulled my wet shoes over the dry socks. "I hope you're gone when I get back. I don't need you. And you don't need me."

Crush jumped to one of the chairs across from me, with his hands on his hips. "You're a silly girl with a mouth bigger than Texas. A silly girl who has no one, needs no one, but she's always looking for someone—looking for a mama she can never have and doesn't deserve. You cause more trouble by opening your flapping lips than anyone I know."

Springing at Crush with both fists, I dove at him, pounding his chest, knocking him to the floor. "Who are you to pick on me? You don't have a mama or a daddy, either. You're the meanest boy, and you make me feel horrible—so you don't feel so horrible."

"Horrible? You can't even use the word right in a sentence." Crush tossed me off like I was a piece of lettuce in a salad, and I floundered backwards like a fish who needed to be in the water.

Diving again, I pushed Crush toward the hearth, into the kettle hanging above the fire. The pot splashed, spilling potatoes to the floor, and he tumbled into the hot coals. Crush yelped like a hyena.

Ahheee!!!!

He wiped his shoulder. "Oh no! My... my shirt is on fire. My arm! I'm burning! Help me."

Running for the quilt on Silas' bed, I dragged the heavy fabric to the kitchen and blotted the flames devouring Crush's hair with crackling sounds. The smell of skin turning to ash sent a rotten egg stench up my nose. "Let me get the fire out. Roll in this quilt."

Pounding him, I smothered the flames with my arms, my hands red from hitting him, and together we coughed from the smoke. The suffocating sense of losing the battle with the fire was clear when I saw the burns on Crush, and my throat tightened. But the fire was smothered, and he lay crying on the floor.

"Let me get some ice." I opened the icebox, grabbing the pitcher instead with something cold and wet, tossing it over

Crush, over his right arm, which glowed red with bloody blisters.

Crush shrieked. "Get someone to help me. I need a doctor. I need …"

I scooted on my backside, sucking in smoke, and got to my knees. "I'll go to the big house. I'll be right back. I'm sorry. I never meant to do this. Never!"

Racing from the kitchen, I nearly stepped on the black rooster and he retaliated by flying at my face. I squealed like a little girl, like a baby. "Help us! Help us! I almost killed Crush! I almost burned down your kitchen!"

Tumbling to my face at the base of the stairs to the porch, a hand reached for me, tugging on my overalls, and the voice in the dark spoke. "Careful now. Before the night ends. You will tend to my little one. And keep watch, someone has my gun …"

The Angry Tree

The rooster flapped at my head, and my legs climbed the stairs. Yelling, I called for help, pulling myself free from the voice in the dark. "Help me! Crush is burned!"

Turning the doorknob to the room to my right, my ears listened, my heart thumped in my neck, and the fear of what I'd done to Crush swallowed me up. I heard no one talking, and looked at my raw hands, not burned, but sore.

My unafraid voice played with my afraid voice, the one shouting the screams like a crowing rooster. "I can't keep from hurting others," and my words sent a chill down my back, the humid air damp like a hot spring bubbling from the ground.

I tripped forward, landing inside the room, and my not-so-clear thoughts imagined a man behind me who begged for help, who lay collapsed on the stairs by the rail. His words were faint, a shallow cry—one drifting in the wind like a dandelion being blown from its stem.

Rising to my feet, I talked to myself. "Stop. You're hearing Crush call for help. You're not hearing a voice. Get help for him. Hurry." I gave myself orders so I would pay attention.

I pushed the door wide, and the light of the moon cast a blue beam, revealing a dining table. "What? This is the place where they eat? No hallway?"

Back on the porch, I sprinted to the double doors, and there were two sets. One to my right on the L-shaped house, and one set of doors right ahead. Choosing the door to my side, I dashed inside, standing beneath a chandelier of orange glowing light. The cry of a newborn made a declaration of life in the next room, and the sound of a baby's call spoke to my entire being like a resurrection of hope from the tomb of lost sunrises.

Silas peeked from the bedroom. "Come see the baby. Stand here. Ms. Daisy is sleeping; her body is exhausted from the news of her sister and now of giving life. She and Mr. Morning have a darling baby girl."

"Can I touch her?"

"Not tonight. Too fresh for touching." Silas washed his hands with soap in the washbowl on the dresser. I inched to the white-laced baby bed, and I glanced at Silas who grinned at me. "She's perfect. She's the pinkest white baby I've ever seen. Prettiest too. Look at her pitch black hair. And those dark eyes. She's got a button nose."

I smiled, "She looks like Ms. Daisy."

Molasses gathered up the towels and wiped Ms. Daisy's forehead like a gentleman with a kind touch, and he dabbed her chin too. "Daisy will sleep the night. Her breathing has turned restful. She'll love to hold her little girl in the morning."

I gazed at the tiny bundle, and Silas placed his strong life-giving hands on my shoulders as he towered behind me, and he whispered, "Babies come into this world ready to be loved, ready to be cradled, ready to live. The scars will come, and I pray she reaches for God. Her birth has trouble attached, much hardship ahead. She'll crawl, toddle, and walk—but her pa, Mr. Morning, will bring scars to her untarnished life."

"Mr. Morning?" I quizzed him, looking at Silas who quickly wiped his lips to remove the last part of his sentence.

"I said too much. Too much. I'm always telling the truth, but the truth isn't going to help tonight."

I jerked to my senses, not sure what he meant, but I didn't care too much, as I remembered why I came inside, and my arms waved. "Mr. Silas. There's been an accident … it's Crush. He's fallen into the hearth. His hair is sizzled, and the skin is gone from his arm. He needs … he needs a doctor!"

Molasses tossed the rags to the floor near the pile of other towels. "Where? What are you talking about?"

Silas echoed him. "When did this happen? We've been gone less than an hour. What have you done, child?"

"Nothing. I was changing clothes. We got mad at each other. It's what we do. He fell. I fell. The soup spilled. The flames jumped. The smoke tunneled up our noses."

Silas questioned me, "Where is your brother?"

I shouted, "He's not my brother!"

Then a quiver of noise came from the bundle in the bassinet, and I sucked in my words to a quieter tone. "Crush is on the floor in the kitchen."

Silas tossed a set of keys from the dresser to Molasses. "Here's Mr. Morning's keys. Get the truck. Pull it to the side by the garden. We'll drive Crush to Hope. Sounds like he's going to need a hospital."

Molasses nodded, and in a flash they left me tending to the new baby, but before I could stop holding my breath, Molasses stuck his curly head back into the bedroom. "Stay with the baby. She has no name, yet. Don't pick her up. Only watch her. Mr. Morning's in the parlor. He answered the front door. I'm sure he'll be in here in a minute."

I mouthed, but my words got clogged in my throat. "I promise not to touch her." I longed to tell Molasses and Silas not to trust me; but they raced to the back porch in a whirlwind.

Torn between following them and staying with this baby, and wondering how badly Crush was hurt, I found myself hearing the voice from the steps inside my head like an echo, and—the voice between my ears repeated the words, "...tending to my little one."

I put my hands to my ears, talking inside my head. Did I hear someone speak to me on the stairs? Am I hearing voices? I didn't imagine it, did I?

A bubbling sound like air escaped from the baby and she cooed a noise like a lullaby. "Hi, baby girl. Are you singing? Your mama's over there in her bed. She's asleep. Go back to sleep. You can see her in the morning."

Bending forward, I kissed her black hair, right above her ear, and I then planted a kiss right on her soft skin. "Pretty girl. You look like your mama. Did you know everyone told me I looked like my mama too?"

I glanced at the giant bed with Ms. Daisy. The bedpost rose to the ceiling and held a canopy of wavy maroon fabric over the top. The room engulfed me with sadness from my past, from losing my mama, from not seeing her smile, from not having her cradle me or sing to me, or be with me. Or sleep near me.

My birth took my mama's life. All her dreams. All her plans. And all of mine. She left me the night I gurgled and cooed. The night she saw me. It was the night her body gave in and her heart stopped. When life went dark. When the canopy of death swallowed her up.

Now when I cry, I wish for her—maybe a little more than I wish for my Mahlee, but only because I never met her. Folks keep telling me how God has her, like He has me, but wishing for things I can never have, rips my heart out.

Looking up, I screamed a whisper at God, "Why do some girls get mamas who live and I don't?" I backed away from the little baby, my eyes no longer wanted to see her.

Rubbing my face, I remembered how Tin Can Mahlee has acted like a mama on the rail ever since I was five, when my daddy saved her life. She rode with us in boxcars for months and months, but sometimes she came up missing. But she always came back.

She taught me to read. Taught me how to look sad at the missions to get extra food. Showed me how to roll up a blanket and sling it over my shoulder. How to search for discarded food in trash cans. She stayed with us under bridges, in the woods, in the lofts in them barns, she taught me to yell "Geronimo" when we hopped trains. She taught me how to be brave around spiders and snakes at abandoned houses. But I'm afraid of them worse than ever.

Swallowing the lump of sorrow, it felt like a bone lodged in my throat. "I want my mama! Or I want Tin Can Mahlee. God. let me have one of them!"

A whimper snuck out from the baby across the room, as I clutched my knees sitting on the hardwood floors. "Mahlee was the closest thing to having a mama, besides my grandma, but she's gone too. She's only been dead for a couple of months, after I re-met her a year ago when my daddy died."

Waaaa! Waaaa!

"Oh no! I am tending this baby. What do I do with her? She needs her pa." I ran from the bedroom in search of Mr. Morning, sliding into the parlor, to the front part of the L-shaped house. "Mr. Morning? Come watch your little baby."

I halted near a maroon velvet sofa and my hand felt of the soft fabric, and I plopped down next to one end where the wooden arm enveloped the cushions like a claw. Two reddish wood tables decorated the space at each end of the sofa, and a longer one graced the floor by my feet.

Across the room, the brick fireplace sat with orange embers burning inside the white bricks, brightening up the wall. On the mantle sat trinkets and glass bottles, and some photographs. "Mr. Morning? Where are you?"

My eyes were glued to the sketch above the mantle. Squinting, I moved closer and stood on my toes, glaring at the charcoal drawing. I whispered, "Look, it's Mr. Silas Jones on the right, and he's fishing at a creek. He's younger, and the other Negro, he's tossing fish behind him. I can't see his face. Why would Mr. Morning have a picture of Silas above his mantle? Maybe they're good friends."

The cry of the no-name baby brought me back to the present after disappearing into the sketch where fishing gave me peace. I listened, and the baby hushed, giving one little whimper, and I figured Mr. Morning joined his family, using one of the many doors on the back porch.

"I'm out of here. See ya!" I waved, excited my tending to the baby was over, and I darted from the house through the front door, hoping to catch Silas, but the truck was gone. I shimmied up the tree, and saw the tail lights disappearing in the darkness down the side road.

Leaning on the trunk, I hung onto the branches weaving in stretches toward the murky sky, as if this tree was angry—and yet, the limbs welcomed me to climb higher and higher. I moved up, to another branch, wishing to disappear to a place where I no longer cried for a mama or needed anyone.

The whoosh of the breeze brushed across my face, causing me to shudder, and I leaned back on the trunk, closing my eyes. The tears of my sad days burst from me, and I couldn't keep them in, because the memories of the last year swallowed me up. I was like a fish caught on a hook, the bleeding of my heart trapped by the fishing pole of suffocation and death.

"God, I'm eleven. Eleven. Do you hear me? You've let me see too many people die, and handed me nights with nightmares and days with hunger pains. I'm scared. I need my Mahlee. I've caught another kitchen on fire too. My Grandma Elsie would be so mad at me. Last year, her kitchen wreaked of charred cinnamon, rotten eggs, and stale smoke after the accident on the stove. I'll never forget that smell."

Tick. Tick. Tick.

My eyes popped opened, and an itsy critter sat on his hind legs gazing at me. "What are you staring at? You wouldn't be the mouse I've heard of?" I asked the mouse questions as if I expected him to answer, and I held out my hand. "Come here, fella. I won't hurt you. Your name wouldn't be Powder? Would it?"

The mouse scurried close to my fingers, wiggling his nose.

"I've never seen a black dotted mouse with a white body. So, you are a real mouse? Molasses doesn't believe Silas and his stories about you, but I have proof. You do exist."

For the next bit, I rested on the branch, talking to a mouse about riding in boxcars and wishing for a family. I told him how sorry I was for hurting Crush, and I pretended Powder was my pet, and pretended this was my house, and this was my tree—and those two horses over there belonged to me. And I closed my eyes to dream.

**

Kablam!

The front door bounced wide, hitting the wall. "What are you doing in the tree? Are you hiding?"

"I'm not hiding. You can see me, right?"

"We've taken Crush to Hope, left him there in good hands with the doctor. We parked on the side, and I've seen how you burned up the kitchen. What were you thinking? Your brother, Crush, will have to stay few days." Molasses scolded me like most people do. "And you! You were to watch the baby."

I sat up, holding onto a limb. "I did watch her. She went to sleep. And Crush isn't my brother!"

"You didn't watch her. Or you'd know."

"Know what? What are you talking about?"

"Mr. Morning is dead! We found him in the back yard by the porch steps. Silas phoned for the sheriff. Someone used a knife on him. As for you, you have some explaining to do!"

"Me? I didn't kill anyone! I didn't!"

Molasses shouted at me from the base of the tree. "I don't know why you're here, but you aren't welcome. You should leave."

"I'm after my Mahlee; then I'll leave." I folded my arms, listening to Molasses scream at me about the dead man, about Crush and the burns, and I disappeared into my hidden world of sitting in a tree, but I remembered hearing … *you'll tend to the little one.*

Shouting at Molasses, I defended myself. "Oh no! He spoke to me. He did! Mr. Morning touched my arm. It had to be him. Someone must have stabbed him right before I ran by, because he was alive, but low to the ground. He was. I swear!"

I lost my balance, and tumbled from the tree, crumbling like a rotten branch without life—like a baby who had lost her lullaby, like a mouse who wasn't real—and Molasses yanked on my arm, pulling me to my feet.

Funeral for Two

The wind tossed my loose hair in wild waves like a horse's tail, like my hair swatted away the flies. The puffy clouds hung low, but higher than the treetops on the side of a hill. The last few days made me sick—sick with being stuck with Molasses as my guard. Sick from all the questions of what I saw on the porch. Or didn't see.

So this day hasn't changed much, except now we're having two funerals. My tummy won't stop growling, and all I can think of are Sno Ball crème filled chocolate cakes like Crush bought for us in Texarkana when we jumped from the train to hide from the rail cops.

He used the rest of his nickels to buy a package for him and me. I stay hungry, am most of the time. I'm sure no one else is thinking of food right now at the double funeral, especially since Ms. Daisy is burying her husband and her sister at Pioneer Cemetery.

Molasses forced me to come to the cemetery to keep an eye on me. He doesn't trust me, and he's made me promise to work at the Sanders House until I pay for the damage from the fire. He's meaner than Crush, and has a secret—he slips off to the woods across the tracks east of town every afternoon.

In the morning before he leaves for school, Molasses is in charge of baking pies for the Tavern. He gets up early, and tosses sugar, eggs and cocoa together, and bakes them using his own original crust recipe. I can't sleep in because he bakes them in the oven built inside the bricks next to the hearth, close to where I sleep on the floor, on my pallet. Boy, do those pies make me hungry.

My nose always gets up first when I hear him slicing the apples for those pies. And when I see the chocolate cocoa on the table, I know he's making chocolate pies. He even stirs up some lemon ice box pies. He's made seven in three days. So far, I've not had one piece, though. He's stingy, and enjoys licking the spoon in front of me.

I get bologna sandwiches for lunch and bacon for breakfast with one egg. Maybe, a piece of bread. Supper is leftovers from the restaurant, so those meals are the best; chicken, green beans, and even roast beef.

As for where Molasses goes after school, I'm not sure. He goes somewhere to do something, and he tells no one. I've watched him leave after he puts his books up, and I'm going to follow him—secretly, without telling him and after my chores one of these days.

"Shoelace, get down. You should know better than to stand on top of a tombstone." Molasses, the self-appointed Watchman scolded me.

"I was trying to see where the other coffin went. Where are we putting Della?"

"Stop asking questions. You see everyone headed toward the fence in the shade. We'll do Mr. Morning's funeral first." Molasses wrinkled his nose at me. "Disrespecting the dead doesn't set well with God."

Jumping to the ground, leaping over the wilted flowers, I stood like a mouthy tombstone, mocking Molasses. "Are you telling me you can talk to God, and He's worried what a bunch of dead people think? I'm alive, and He doesn't care what I want or think."

"Stop your mouthing. Here comes Silas, he's driving Ms. Morning up to the gate."

"Don't tell me to hush. I may have burned up your kitchen, but you don't own me."

"Silas said Sheriff Tock asked you to stay close. You were the last one to hear Mr. Morning speak."

"I didn't plan it. I was getting help for Crush. He was on the stairs. How did I know someone would kill him?"

"Hush! Ms. Daisy is coming closer. She needs peace today. Not turmoil."

"Fine! I'll behave. I don't want to disrespect the dead. Or the living." I bit my bottom lip, changing the subject. "Hey, where's the baby?"

"My other auntie who lives near the Proving Grounds, Ms. Etta, she's looking after her, back at the house."

"Good. This is no place for a baby. Or even for us." Stepping in circles, I counted the markers as far as I could see, plus the rest of the tombstones on one end of the flat part of the cemetery, only to lose count and begin again.

I wondered how much paint it would take for me to finish the kitchen wall. As for the wood floor, I have to finish sanding the scorched spot, but I have to wait until Molasses is finished baking pies every morning. As for the quilt—I can't replace it, or take away the sadness I sensed from Silas, because his great-grandma handed it down to him.

The night of the fire, Silas smoked his pipe by the barn, after holding the ashes of the fabric to his chest, mumbling and talking to the two brown horses—for hours, way into the night, way after Molasses fell asleep. But I was up, and peering at Silas through the window, wishing for a new quilt or a way to pay him back.

**

Kicking the clump of dirt, I counted the townspeople circling Mr. Morning's coffin. An old geezer in a brown suit lit a cigarette. Two Negro men in overalls were situated by some trees. Four white men lingered off to the side, nodding and whispering. They laughed, as if they had a secret. Three ladies in long dresses positioned themselves next to the laughing men, and they had smiles on their faces too. And a small group of men and women sat in the folding chairs close to the coffin.

"Molasses, this is a funeral. These folks aren't crying; they're acting like we're at a party."

"Mr. Morning had plenty of enemies, most thought he was a con man, many were afraid of him, and now they've come today—to support Ms. Daisy. She's not trapped by him anymore."

"Trapped? He held her against her will?"

"Not at first. She fell in love with him when he moved here from Hope. Seems he goes after the things he wants, and gets them. Then he owns you." Molasses' words escaped faster than a train rushing down a mountain, and he put his hand to his mouth. "Shoelace, you bring sorrow with you, but don't leave your sadness in our town. We need relief. We need to make peace and live again."

For a second, Molasses let me see the sensitive and kind side of himself, the part he shows to Silas and the part he shows to Ms. Daisy, and to the little baby who has no name whom we're calling Baby.

"Molasses, I want peace too. We could smoke a peace pipe. I am part Indian, Choctaw."

"That explains everything. You're a wild thing."

"I'm not wild. I'm adventurous."

Shrugging me off, Molasses hushed me, something he does more than I can stand. *Shhh!!!* "Ms. Daisy is sitting down and Pastor Graves has his Bible."

"I'm not going to mess up a funeral. I'm minding my own business." Plunking myself onto a stump, I sat down.

"You better not interfere, because I see how you interfere without trying. Ms. Daisy's beside herself, with losing her sister, and now Mr. Morning, and not knowing where she'll live."

"What? She has the Sanders House."

"Not so. Not so."

"You talk in circles. She does. You live at her home too, well, in the kitchen house."

Using his quiet voice, Molasses knelt next to me, pulling up a piece of grass and biting on it. "Uncle Silas owns the house. He has the deed under his mattress. He paid for the house with his crop money and from when he sold his old place. We've lived there for several years, but Mr. Morning got what he wanted, or he did until now."

Molasses pressed his lips together, gnawing on the grass, and I tapped him on the shoulder. "Until now?"

"Yes. Ms. Daisy is free, and we're free. Lots of folks is free now."

"Silas won't make her move, will he?"

Molasses ignored me, and the pastor man held up his Bible. "Gather around. I'm sorry to say, we're having two funerals today. Let me pray."

I didn't close my eyes, nor did Molasses, and somehow I felt free lurking behind tombstones. And these people came to the funeral to mourn with Daisy, but somehow they were cheering Mr. Morning's death. Even the birds were singing twirl twerps of joy. And the squirrels chased each other up and down and around the trunks of the trees.

Aieee!

Ms. Daisy's burst of shrieking stopped the pastor's prayer. "Enough with the niceties. My husband is gone. Don't act like we're sad about it. We're not. Everyone's rejoicing." Ms. Daisy turned to the people, with her high-pitched scream. "He can't hurt you anymore. Or threaten you. You are set free. And so am I." She pointed at the suits and the dresses, and she sobbed.

The pastor placed his hand on Ms. Daisy's shoulder. "This is not the place for such an outburst. Let's proceed."

She pushed his hand off. "You have no business telling me how to react or what to say. I've been quiet for too long. I've hidden my bruises, and lost six years of my life. Most of my twenties have been in bondage to Clifford. He even ran Della off."

She pointed to Della's coffin across the cemetery and dashed to the wooden box, and a few of the ladies followed her, as did a couple of the men. She collapsed beside the coffin, and her screams were hollow like an empty tomb.

Silas was by her side, with his hands on her shoulders, giving her a soft embrace. His fingers were bent with age, but he had the touch of love which calmed her.

I couldn't hear him, but he consoled Ms. Daisy, soothing her with his kind way of speaking. No one could hear him, and everyone gawked. My heart calmed down with hers, but not my mouth, and I jumped to a stump, hollering, my arms directing. "You people should go home. Let Ms. Daisy bury her dead. Go live your lives. Live! You have been set free!"

Molasses grabbed me by the arm, and yanked me to the ground. "What are you doing? Can you not be quiet for one minute?"

I scowled, "They aren't here to pay her respect. They're here to gloat. They should go home."

"Stop it. Walk with me. We're going over to Della's coffin to show Ms. Daisy we're supporting her."

"I am here for her. Those other people need to leave."

He shook a fist at me. "Don't make me hit you."

"I'm not scared of you. You're all talk anyway. Silas would tan your hide for hitting a girl."

"Girl? Brat is more like it."

Shaking my head and rolling my eyes at Molasses, I scooted across the grass toward Ms. Daisy, who now balanced herself like a frail tombstone.

I sighed, my heart sad for her, as this was her sister, Della, and she did miss her. "Ms. Daisy." I inched to her side. "If it makes you feel any better, your sister is with God. She's with her Maker."

Daisy swirled around to me, wiping her nose with her hanky. "If you don't mind. I'm not thrilled about it. I would love to have her here with me. I need her more than God does."

"I meant no harm. It's how Pastor Cody taught me to get through these things. I've buried my daddy, but we didn't have his body. And well, someone buried my mama when I was born, and then we buried my grandma two months ago, and last year my friend who played the piano got shot, and he was put inside of a coffin too. Even my new Choctaw friend died last year …"

The tears burst from my eyelids and Ms. Daisy handed me her handkerchief, and Silas wrapped me up like a baby and held me, placing me onto my feet next to a tree, near two tombstones with the last name of—Shaw.

Blinking, I twitched my eyelids, trying to focus, and read the names: Sidney Shaw and Freda Shaw. I tried to remember why the name Shaw mattered to me, and I tiptoed closer, running my hand over each tombstone, while glancing into my memory where answers hide, where things blur.

"What are you doing now?" Molasses quizzed me like he cared, but more like he was nosey.

"I know this name. I know the name Shaw." Wiping my tears, I sighed. "I know someone named Shaw. I'm trying to remember."

"It's Daisy and Della's last name. This is their ma and pa. They died in the tornado last year. Ms. Daisy buried her parents here." Molasses patted my head. "Just stay out of the way. They've got Ms. Daisy calm now, and the pastor's using his preacher voice."

The dirt felt like sponge under my PF Flyers, and I glanced at the giant boot-like footprints in front of each tombstone by my feet. A newly picked Jonquil lay at the base of each marker, not wilted, and it was as if life bloomed to take away the death.

The chattering pastor continued to my left, and no one cared what I was doing and those who hadn't slipped off to their homes from the commotion—circled around Ms. Daisy to be—respectful. Silas held her under his arm, since he towered over her small frame, and Molasses chewed on a piece of grass across the way from us, lingering and listening, acting bored.

A glint of light shone in the sunlight atop Della's coffin, and a bouquet of Jonquils caught the ray of sunshine, making them deep yellow. Fresh and pretty. The flowers were yellow and perfect.

I picked up one of the flowers in the grass beside me, running my fingers over its petals, and sat down, crossing my legs, disappearing under the shade of the pine trees, while listening to birds chirping, and trying to block out the pastor's sad sermon.

I cast my gaze to the woods where the morning sun hung behind the trees—where a—where a—figure perched itself in the woods outside the cemetery. The silhouette almost shimmered with highlights between the thicket.

This person was close. But, far away. Listening. But, hiding. Attending. But, ready to disappear. "Who comes to a funeral and hides?"

I hopped to my feet, and shambled in the direction of the woods, and the shape of the figure became two silhouettes, and each stomped sideways, away from me, away from the cemetery. Dropping the flower from my fingers, I rose high, perching myself atop Sidney Shaw's tombstone for a better look, and there she was—the woman who taught me to read, to kill snakes, to hop trains. Who was with her? Was it two people or one? Or was it two men?

I blinked and a zinging noise caused me to jump, to drop my flower.

Pffft! Pffft!

The pops rang out like two fast claps, and one of the suitmen toppled backwards to the ground, one of the four men from earlier, the only one who remained—and he reached for his chest. "What in the world?"

I peeked around the tombstone, kneeling, and saw the blood oozing beneath his shirt as a red spot changed the white shirt to a death color.

The man folded in half, and curled up like a tree cut down by an axe. "My God! I've been shot! Mr. Morning shoots from his grave. And wins once more!"

Screaming, Ms. Daisy fainted, and Pastor Graves pulled a pistol from under his jacket. Unable to decide where to point the barrel, he wiggled the gun in the air. The Negro men bailed up the hill. A few ladies huddled together. And the rest of the town folk cowered and knelt to the ground behind tombstones and trees.

Silas held onto Daisy, cuddling her and protecting her from danger, while Molasses showed up behind the crowd, hurrying to the man on the ground. Molasses closed the man's eyes. "He's gone. Mr. Swisher is dead."

Pastor Graves crept to the side of the man on the ground, wiping the sweat from his brow and glancing with eyes twitching, he held his Bible close to his chest. Mumbling words no one could understand, he kept looking around as if he was afraid the shooter wasn't finished.

Molasses gave me a glare, his lips crooked. "Shoelace, I'm getting help. You stay there."

I reared up like a dead girl rising from a tomb, and offered my disrespect to everyone at the cemetery and to Molasses. "I'll stay put about as long as I need to, and what is wrong with you people? First, it's Della. Then, Mr. Morning. And now, the round man. I didn't bring this. I'm here to find my Mahlee, not to watch people die."

I paused with my tongue lashing, and gave a quick look toward the woods, because the two shadows required more 'vestigating. I was sure of nothing, and confident of something. Someone else is dead, and someone did the shooting. I prayed, "Don't let it be Mahlee shooting the gun."

I spun around, also wondering why anyone would blame Mr. Morning for a shooting when he is flat on his back inside a coffin.

The last bit of air went stale, and sorrow tumbled down from the clouds like invisible dust, choking me, and crushing hope from my day. Since arriving in this town, nothing makes sense and someone is taking lives, which makes me want to run, hop a train and get away. But what if Mahlee is in the woods? I need to know. I need to go—now.

Cupping my mouth with my fingers, I called to the branches. "Tin Can Mahlee? Is that you? Wait for me."

Barreling into the woods, and diving like a cannonball, I remembered why I knew the name Shaw when a vine whacked me in the neck. I rolled to a stop on a bunch of leaves, muttering to myself, and I announced to the bushes: "Shaw. Shaw is Mahlee's last name too. Well, it's Day now, since last Christmas, but before she changed it, her name was Shaw!" I jumped to my feet. "Wait for me! I'm coming for you!"

Make Me a Deer

I thrust myself between the thicket, stomping on the bushes and weeds, and running. But no sooner than I got my feet, both of them caught in a web of vines and weeds. My shoes were trapped in a tangle of creepers wrapping around in a web of green, as if the plants were attacking me.

I stomped and stepped, and ripped at the vines with my fingers, but each step sent me stumbling along in the maze. "Mahlee? Don't leave me. Wait! I have to tell you what happened. You're innocent. Your gun never shot anyone."

My overalls tore from the stickers, and I tumbled forward, landing on a cushion of leaves and spindly branches. Covering my mouth, whispering, I sucked in a bug. "Yuck! Oh no!" *Blah!* I paused to spit, and knew I best be quiet. The funeral is taking place, and I can't let anyone hear me.

Crawling, I hid behind a tree, peering through the trees to the cemetery toward the coffin. "Phew! They're all listening to the pastor. No one will miss me. Or care."

Using my quieter whispering voice, more like a hollow wisp of letters, I called to Mahlee, realizing I had no idea which way she darted, or if she was gone, or if she was hiding behind the next tree.

Crunch. Crunch.

"What's over there? Mahlee? Please, wait. Don't make me do this again. How long will you make me chase you? You're the only family I have left."

Crunch. Crunch.

The sound of sticks breaking sent my feet to high-jumping bushes and diving like a maniac set loose from the crazy house. My arms wagged, my eyes bugged, and I was going to catch up with Mahlee or else.

Huff-puff. Huff-puff.

The heavy breathing behind another set of bushes sent me climbing prickly plants and loops of vines. "What in the ..." My foot slipped, and I somersaulted down the slope, the ground giving way, the hill ending, and the ravine below calling me to its bottom. "Oh, my gosh! Help!"

Sliding face forward, I twisted in half, and unfolded like a broken toothpick, the jabs of sticks hit my arms and poked at my legs. I covered my eyes with my hands. "Why did I have to fall?"

Tumbling forward, I rolled like a ball collecting sticks in my pants, the fabric torn to shreds. My foot became tangled in a vine, which wrapped around my ankle like a knot from a rope.

Slap. Slump. Slug.

I flapped in a jerk, collapsing from the strain, and my left leg pulled tight, up in the air behind me, the vine holding me a few feet from the floor of the rift. My head inches from the dirt, upside down.

It felt like I'd fallen for hours, but my shimmy down the cliff took minutes, and my clothes were muddy, torn, and behind my ear, a throb with a heartbeat kept pace with my pulse.

Crunch. Crunch.

"Mahlee. Help me. I need you."

With the breaking of sticks, I glanced to the upside down trees, and a deer lowered his neck and placed his nose near mine. He gave me a long gaze, snorted, and then made a dash through the trees, dancing with precise steps, flying over the bushes and vines.

I peered ahead, with my leg in the air. "A trail. There's a trail. Mahlee, wait up." Untangling myself, and wiping the blood from my neck, I hobbled like a broken toy across the flat part of the woods. Barely able to see, I rubbed my eyes and twisted my head backwards, the sky hidden from the branches. The trail shaded. Everything seemed gray.

I felt like a shadow—alone, running, bleeding, and chasing the wind of *lost mamas*, again. Crunching to my left caused me to stop. Then, crunching to my right. Which way to go? Which way?

My leg ached, and a branch slapped me across the face. "Stop it! Darn ole woods! Why do I have to fight so hard to find a mama? I wish I could turn into a deer and live in the woods and prance around trees, hide, and never leave the forest."

Throwing a fit, I sank into a mushy part of dirt, like scrambled mud with mossy goo on top. Pushing through the swampy water, my shoes stuck to the bottom, and I yanked on my legs with my hands, huffing and puffing like a sick puppy. The water rose to my waist, and the smell burned my nose. "Get me out of this, it's too snaky for me. I'm covered in mud. Smelly, rotten mud. This is horrible."

Pushing myself up, I fell to the dry piece of dirt after nearly drowning in the two-foot water. "What's on my legs? What is crawling up my pants?" Shaking both legs, I rolled up my overalls to my knees, screaming. "What are these? They're eating me." I pulled on the wormy, swollen leeches attached to my calves and shins. "Get off. Get off. No!! No!! Get off me."

Swiping a hundred leeches from my legs, yelling at them, I couldn't stop shaking and crying, and then I felt it, a tug on my skin on my back from another leech. "It's on me. It's eating me. I can't reach the leech. It's … It's …" I twirled around and saw the fuzzy leaves poking at my face from the shrub, and fell to my knees, relieved to have been eaten by a vine.

I gulped, swallowing hard, and got up. "I don't know where Mahlee went. I don't even know where I am."

Chug-a-lug. Chug-a-lug.

The engine called to me from across the way, behind the next set of trees, and I swiped the bushes out of the way, careening over them, running hard, galloping like a horse, and imagined myself a deer, with strength, with keen sight, and with agility.

In minutes, I felt the sun on my face after not taking many breaths, and stumbled to the grass next to what looked like a cotton gin house, a giant building, made with slats of wood, many were faded gray, some were brown. The roof, rusty.

"There's the dirt road, and it leads to the tracks. Mahlee would go that way." The trail of dust left behind by a car or truck caused me to gag.

Cough. Cough.

I could see better if this dust would settle, but the breeze stopped somewhere back in the ravine, or by those nasty leeches.

Up ahead, the narrow road climbed a slope, and the dust landed in clumps waiting for the next vehicle. I paused, squinting, while focusing on a paper doll outline of someone at the top of the hill, a moving, disappearing paper doll rushing into the wooded area beside the road.

I raced with a gimp. "Mahlee. Stop. Talk to me. We need each other."

Limping, and dragging my cut ankle in the loose sand, I whined to myself, *I need you. I need you. Don't run away.*

At the top of the road, sitting sideways under a tree with a tire buried in the loose sand, a truck sat hidden by the bushes. I ran my hand over the hood. "Ouch! Still hot. This looks like Mr. Morning's jalopy. But ..."

I ducked between the barbed wire, my sideways glance taking in the dotted path of red, yellow and white rocks. Someone has created a hideaway trail under the canopy of these trees, and the trail disappeared through the woods. Glancing at my shoes, I stomped with my good leg, but no dust flew as the dirt was packed hard on this trail.

After about a mile, I gazed up and on a dome hill, a concrete bunker sat. A small section of undersized windows met the ground, like a lookout.

"Hello? Anyone there?" I paused, sucked in the damp air, my ankle throbbing. I circled the bunker until I came to a metal door and I reached for the handle. "Hello? Mahlee, are you in there?"

Crunch. Crunch.

I hobbled in a twisty motion, losing my balance. "Who's there? Mahlee?" I straightened up, ready to run, my heart locked in fear, crushing from the invisible concrete of terror sneaking up on me.

From the deep bend in the trail, Molasses yelled, "Don't touch the door. Or move. Watch where you step. I have this place booby-trapped. You could destroy us all!"

Bombs from the Past

Stomping on purpose with my left leg because the other one tingled with pain, I blurted grenade-like words at Molasses. "You? What are you doing? Did you drive Mr. Morning's truck over here? Why did you follow me?"

"I saw you go into the woods and someone did get shot. I knew you'd come out on the road by the gin. Silas put me in charge of you."

"Whatever. How did you know I'd come here?"

"I figured you might. I've seen how you watch me from the window when I leave the house."

"I didn't know this is where you went. I followed someone into the woods. I think it's my Mahlee and she's hiding out here."

"She's not in town. No one has seen her."

"What do you know? You sneak off in the afternoon to this place." I pointed at the concrete bunker.

Molasses snarled. "This is my bunker. Just for me. What I do here is none of your business."

I touched the door knob.

"Don't open the door. Or even think of going inside."

"Or what? What will a lanky Negro boy who, works like a slave, do to me? You aren't so tough. You bake pies! You can measure sugar. And roll pie crust with a rolling pin on a table. But you don't have any muscles. You may know how to drive a pickup, but you are a sissy, and you live in a kitchen-bedroom with your uncle. You have nothing."

Molasses towered above me, spewing his words. "You're the one who rode into my town. You have nowhere to live or sleep or eat or to sit. You are the one without anything."

"I have my Mahlee. She's going to take me with her. You'll see."

"How can she? She's not here."

I inched backwards, "Stop saying Mahlee isn't here. She is. And you're probably hiding her." My words gargled in my throat and Molasses tossed me to my knees. "Stop pushing me."

He growled, "You're a silly girl and if you stay out here, you'll get blown up. This is the Proving Grounds where the Army tested bombs, there's plenty still here, ready to go off, if you step on them. You have to be careful."

Peering at Molasses, I stared up his nose, and realized his voice turned grownup and serious. I rose, and backed up. "So I'm going to step on a bomb?"

"You could. See those rocks with the different colored paint marks. It's to keep you from hurting yourself."

"If I stay on the path, I'm safe?"

"Yes, safe. But you're trespassing. This is my bunker."

"I'd say it's not, and that you're trespassing."

Molasses snickered, "No one comes here. I needed my own place to … to think."

"Think? You have a brain?"

"Don't mock me."

I giggled. "Don't mock me."

"Stop it."

Laughing, I responded with, "Stop it." I turned to the door of the bunker, twisting the knob, and pulled hard on the heavy door, but Molasses grabbed me by the hair.

"Leave my bunker alone."

"Ouch!" I yanked free, and ducked. "Don't hit me. I'll leave. I've sprained my ankle, and them leeches ate my skin. If Mahlee's here and doesn't want me, I'll go. I'll go and never come back." I used words to get Molasses away from me, little girl words—deceiving words to distract him. I spun around when—

Bam!

"What? Oh no …" My head throbbed, my knees folded, and my eyes lost focus, blurring into a thousand shadows of my Mahlee. "Mahlee?"

She lingered above me like an angel, dancing in her boots on a cloud. Holding a log. And I collapsed into a ball, blinking, holding my head, along with my ankle. The world spun around me, the trees swayed, and then I was nowhere!

Lies. Lies. Lies

"Oh, my goodness! Oh! My head is killing me, and my skin—it itches! Where am I?" I sighed, my body cringed, and it felt like leeches were crawling under my clothes. "Get them off. Get them off. Someone. Anyone." I screamed, sitting up, noticing the room, seeing the two small beds, and sniffing the fragrance of an apple pie baking—which sent the warm Grandma memories to my heart.

Silas stepped into the room. "Missy, you have a concussion. Doc says you're gonna make it, but your headache might linger."

"Are you real? Mr. Silas?" I scratched my arms, the stinging and itch like a sunburn with an achy ripple under my skin.

"You've been in and out for a couple of days. You were dazed. Molasses said you ran smack dab into a dead tree with your noggin. The doc stitched up your head too, and your right ankle is swollen. It's not broken though."

Shaking my head, I cleared my throat. "What are all of these red marks. They hurt!"

"Oh, that's poison ivy. Seems you might need to watch for the three leaves and keep away from them. If you see five, those can thrive."

"You have it all wrong. Molasses knows what happened. A dead tree didn't happen to land on my head in the woods."

Silas patted my tangled hair with his strong hand. "My nephew was there, this is for sure. He's known for being honest with me. He found you by the cotton gin, in the lower ravine where the mud and water mix with the snakes and the leeches. He figured you got tangled in the vines."

Wrinkling my nose, and choking on my anger, I swung my feet to the edge of the bed. "I'm getting up. I have to look for Mahlee. She's here. I've seen her." My ankle shot a pain up my leg, and I held onto my leg. "Molasses didn't find me—"

Silas reached for me. "You're gonna rest right here in Molasses' bed. He's taken to the porch with a pallet to give you a place to heal, to get rid of this poison ivy." Silas spun his shoes on the grit on the wood floor, sliding with ease like a young man dancing in an old body.

I argued. "He's taken to the porch to spy on me. He's afraid I'll go to his ..." My words burned with hate, and I bit my lip, clearing my throat, changing my words softer, not wanting to share everything with Silas until I figured out what to do next. "Oh, how nice of him. He's the sweetest. Isn't he?"

"We both know you two struggle to see eye to eye. But Molasses is a good boy, tends to wander since his pa left, he's not been the same."

"He does wander. I do too." Saying words to not upset Mr. Silas, I curled up on the pillow. "Whose pajamas are these?"

"Ms. Daisy picked them up for you in Hope when she and Molasses rode into town, and they checked on Crush. She thought you'd like a yellow gown to go with our Jonquils."

"Tell her thank you. I do like it." I touched the fabric, soft and warm. "How is Crush? Is he getting better?"

"Yes, he's on the mend. The burns aren't as bad as we thought, and you'll be well soon too. Crush is coming to the big house in the morning, and Ms. Etta's helping with the baby until Ms. Daisy gets over her mourning. She's offered Crush the front bedroom to recover too."

"Thank you, Mr. Silas. You have been good to me, even after I caused the fire and all. Have they got any idea what happened to Mr. Morning?"

"The police have no leads. But I have a few. I'm doing my own investigation."

"I'm a good 'vestigator. I could help you."

"You best get well first." Silas left the room, and the clanking of wooden spoons in bowls, or in a pot made my stomach growl.

Mumbling to myself, I slipped from the bed, limping, and saw the lantern on the table. The light lit up the black cover of the worn Bible, and a pair of spectacles sat on it. The sunset of the day shut off the light coming in the windows, and darkness fell like a fog.

I hobbled to the side door next to Silas' bed, and peeked out the window, gazing out to the porch where Molasses sat chewing on a piece of straw, his legs crossed Indian style.

Tapping the window, I waved him inside.

He turned his back to me, and hung his legs over the edge of the porch. I tapped again, and he twisted his neck, and crawled to the window, pressing his nose on the glass, mouthing words I could not hear, and he stuck his tongue out at me like a kid.

"Stop it. You are annoying for a boy, and worse than any I've ever met."

He smiled like he knew what I said, and I didn't care one bit. Molasses was anything but a kid—he was my enemy. He knew who knocked me out with the log, and I was going to do my own 'vestigation. For right now, Molasses wasn't talking, at least, not to me. But he made faces at me through the window, which sent my mind to angry, and my hands made fists.

I twisted the side door knob and staggered, pushing the screen open, and tumbling with a hobble to the porch.

Molasses moved to the edge of the porch, swinging his feet. "You better get in bed. You're sick."

"I wouldn't be sick if you hadn't let someone hit me." I yelled a whispered growl of bitterness. "I think it was Mahlee. I saw her in the cloud."

"You saw a dead tree! It was right in your way. And I saved you."

"Saved me? You saved yourself by telling Silas where you found me, which isn't where we were, and now you're taking credit for saving me?"

He patted his chest. "I'm a hero." Molasses mocked my words with his.

I shouted with a chicken hawk scream, like a bird that was ready to dig her beak into a boy. "Stop making fun of me. I didn't mean for any of this to happen. I just want a mama."

"Go on. You have nothing to say to me that matters. You owe my uncle for the disaster in the kitchen. And once your friend Crush gets well, and once you finish painting and polishing, you can be on your way."

"I may stay here. I can live wherever I want." I swung my yellow pajamas with a swirl, and danced on one foot, while scratching my poison ivy. I moved inside, climbed into the cot, covered up with the blanket and drifted off to the in between place of sleeping and waking, to a place where I could see clearly. To a place where my Mahlee waved at me from the clouds. To a path with painted rocks. To a bunker in the woods. To a dead tree with the roughest bark!

Shaking my head, I whispered in my dream. "No! It wasn't a tree. But who did I follow into the woods?" I popped up. "Where is my Mahlee?"

"Missy, rest now. I'll pray them nightmares leave your bedside and slip on down the tracks." Silas bent in half with his torso, leaning into the room.

"Thank you, Silas. Thank you for sleeping in the kitchen on my pallet while I'm contagious."

"Them scratches will heal, it's your heart I'm worried about. You have some deep cuts inside, and they bleed when you go to sleep. I know them nightmares, because Molasses has them ever so often, since he lost his pappy."

I wrapped my fingers around the pillow, trying to figure out why Silas felt like family, even though we met only days before on the highway—days which brought flames, and death, and bunker bombs—and way too many chores.

In Search of the Past

Sitting at the table near the hearth, I patted myself on the back with my own praises. "Silas, all my polishing is done. The floor shines better than before the fire. I did all my work in between my scratching, and the headaches."

Silas turned away from the cornbread cooking in the skillet. "You did a fine job for a little girl."

"I'm no little girl."

Molasses smarted off across from me. "You are a little girl who has invaded our town."

"It's not your town. You don't own anything."

"I own more than you think."

Ahem!! Silas cleared his throat, something he does whenever Molasses and me argue.

I hushed, but stared at Molasses with cutting glares, with evil eyes.

Silas broke the screaming silence. "It does appear you have shined up my whole kitchen, Shoelace. The walls look great, and those extra streaks of paint do add character to the walls. Now, as for the white specks on the hardwood floor by the door, it does make this kitchen the first polka-dotted one in these parts."

I rubbed my elbow where the poison ivy itched. "This kitchen matches your mouse. I saw him in the tree the night, when Mr. Morning … the night when Crush caught fire … the night the prettiest little baby with black hair was born."

"So you saw my mouse? Powder only shows himself to those who can see him."

64

"What? To those who can see him?" I wrinkled my nose, trying to figure out this wrinkled man's words.

Silas bent down like a seesaw, flipping the cornbread from the skillet onto a plate, setting the hot warm bread right in front of my nose on the table. He smiled, "If you can't see Powder, then he's not showing himself."

"You talk in circles. So if I see him, he's showing himself?"

Molasses, who was flipping a spoon in a cadence of annoyance, slapped the table in front of me. "Silas has too many stories. He's an old man with an old mind."

Silas thumped Molasses on the head. "For a boy wanting to be treated like a man, you've got a disrespectful mouth. Your pa would take you out behind the barn and settle it, if he were here."

I rolled my eyes at Molasses, cheering on the inside, and thankful the discipline landed on a teen boy who has more secrets and smart words than me. Who also wears overalls like me. And bosses me when Silas is working at the big house, up front. Or when Silas goes to the café across the big highway.

Silas has folks helping in the kitchen over there, cousins who love to cook like him, and they're waiting on tables too. He said business has picked up since Mr. Morning died, and was proud folks wanted to help Ms. Daisy, to give her pennies in her pocket for her baby girl.

He said Ms. Daisy's caught between two worlds, the one with scary nights, the one without hope. Says she's stuck. Like a wagon wheel in the mud.

I feel stuck too. Stuck in a town where breaking and burning and blasted chores keep me from tracking down my Mahlee. And I haven't seen my kitten in days.

Molasses caught my glare, my way of disappearing with my eyes open. "Where is Shoelace?" He waved his hand in front of my nose.

"Stop it." I slapped his hand away.

Molasses teased, "Where do you go? Do you write stories in your head too?"

"Leave me be. I don't write stories. I write poems. I'm thinking hard on my next move. Crush will be better, and we'll be on our way, to looking for Mahlee. I told the policeman I know nothing about how Mr. Morning ended up on the steps. Other than ..."

"Other than what?"

"Other than hearing someone mumbling, which I told you about. But I'm not sure it was real, probably was one of my poems in my head. They get stuck on rewind when I cause trouble."

Silas touched my shoulder. "You heard a mumbling noise?"

I shook my head, "No." I regretted saying anything about the mumbling sound, because now Molasses was peering at me with his big brown eyes.

Silas stepped closer to me. "Did you hear something, or not?"

I gulped, "I didn't hear a thing. Sorry, I got mixed up."

Silas added his comments to mine. "We all get mixed up from time to time."

Molasses mouthed. "Whatever. She's caused more trouble in two weeks than we've known in years."

Silas corrected Molasses. "Disrespecting others is causing me trouble. Best we get ready to go."

I grinned at Molasses who shouted at me. "What are you laughing about? You're the one who disrespects this place.

You've left your burn marks on the floor, and left the black
soot on the walls, and now you're working off a broken
window."

"I should have opened the window before I threw my PF
Flyers at you the other night. You act as if you're the
watchman over me. But I don't answer to you." I stood in my
chair, my arms waving like a monkey set loose from its cage.

Silas stomped to the end of the table, his right arm
extending straight out, like a fence placed in between us, and
he was putting a halt to our mouthing at each other. "You two.
Stop this arguing, now. Accidents happen and happening right
now is disrespect from the two of you—and I'm calling a
ceasefire."

Molasses nodded, and I put my hands to my side,
swallowing my last hate-filled words. Molasses choked on his
and his eyes bugged. It's like we withdrew our invisible guns,
and raised the white flag.

Sitting down, I sighed, not happy Silas raised his voice at
me, for he's the kindest grandpa-like man, and he's treated me
with respect, even though I've torn up the place. He's like
sweet milk on a sour stomach. And Molasses is like a mule
without a heart.

Somehow, I'm going to figure out a way to get myself on
down the road to the bunker again. I have to search for
Mahlee. The nightmares have snuck into my sleep the last four
nights and they include Mahlee, and the dead tree, and more
shadows than light. I also wanted to know what made the
bunker so special for Molasses too.

Silas placed the kettle over the charcoal, and peeked under
the lid. "This will simmer. Potato soup for tonight will be
great for Crush and for Ms. Daisy. She loves my soup."

Molasses scooted his chair, moving next to the door facing
the garden, cracking the door open. The door faces east, and

the back porch door where Molasses has slept faces south. I need to go east to find the bunker. I kept reminding myself, so I wouldn't get lost or turned around when I do slip off from the Sanders House.

Silas grabbed the keys from the shelf by the jars. "Shoelace, you get yourself on up to the house and help Ms. Etta. She's changing sheets on the beds, and could use your help with the baby. Ms. Daisy's not into her nurturing self yet, so help her. Her heart's having trouble at night, during the day too. Losing her sister, Della, and also after losing her sister … Mahlee … the loss has been hard on her."

"What did you say? Her sister Mahlee? She has a sister named Mahlee? I knew it. I knew it. I knew it, but I forgot it. I figured it out, then I forgot. The tombstones at the funeral had the last name of Shaw, which is Daisy's before-getting-married name, and it's Mahlee's real last name too. When I got whacked in the head, the sorting-out got knocked out of me, and all my remembering drained from me. Ms. Daisy had two sisters. Two!! Della! And Mahlee!"

Molasses spun around from leaning on the screen. "She did have two sisters. And they're both gone. Della is dead. Mahlee disappeared from here years ago, but she has come and gone. Silas said so."

Silas finished the story, "Mahlee was the oldest, then Della, then Daisy. Some folks say they see Mahlee now and again, but she's a ghost story like my polka dotted mouse. But she shows herself to those who can see her."

I jumped next to Silas. "Have you seen her? She's my mama from the rail."

"I know you hope to find her. Molasses told me. You told me about her the other day. You told Ms. Etta too. And you told Pastor Graves at the funeral before the shooting." Silas scratched his ear. "Back when my eyes were good, Mahlee ran off, but her name is still etched on the oldest Magnolia tree in the state. The tree is next to her family's old spot. Well, there's a new house there now, because a tornado roared through town when she was barely a teen herself."

Molasses lingered close to Silas, and reached his arm around his waist, listening in.

"The Shaws were good folks. They never got over Mahlee running away. Seems Mahlee thought she hurt this boy when he collapsed on the road. They had raced home when the twister came, but a limb hit him from behind, snapping his head sideways, breaking his neck. I saw the whole thing, but she kept on running and screaming and mumbling."

Silas went on explaining, "Mahlee ran for help at her house, but the porch was all that was left in the storm. Everything was a wreck. She figured her parents and sisters had died when she rushed by me, when I hung onto a tree by the courthouse. No one ever saw her much after that, until Ms. Daisy told us of Mahlee's secret visits a few months ago."

I wiped tears from my face with my hand. My sobs grew to a shrill, and Molasses handed me a rag to wipe them off.

Silas finished his story. "Then just last year, a tornado ripped the roof from their house, and Della and Daisy's ma and pa were caught under the rubble as the house folded in on itself. I guess Mahlee was right after all. Her parents died in a tornado, it just happened years later."

"So you have seen her?" I quizzed Silas who now stood sideways in the doorway with Molasses, and I hovered behind them. I had more questions than they were willing or ready to answer. "Silas, have you seen my Mahlee?"

"Sometimes, I see her when she shows herself."

"Then she's here."

Molasses cocked his head back, "She's not here. No one has seen your Mahlee."

I yelled at Molasses, "What do you know? You haven't ever seen the mouse, either. And I have." I stomped off to the bedroom, putting my shoes on, and planning my escape—to go search for Mahlee—after I help Ms. Etta.

Silas called to me. "Let it go, Missy. Mahlee doesn't want to be found, or she'd show herself. Get going, Ms. Etta needs you in the house. We're headed to Hope. Going to pick up your buddy."

"He's not my buddy." I called from the bedroom.

"Go on, now. Go help Ms. Etta."

I assured Silas with the words he expected to hear. "I'll help her. I will."

The screen slammed, "We'll be back with Crush in a couple of hours. Got a few things to take care of with a lawyer for Ms. Daisy."

"I'll be fine."

"I'm not worried about you. I'm worried about everyone else." A chuckle from Silas filled the room, but when I stepped into the kitchen, Molasses and Silas were gone. The soup was simmering, and my head too.

I grabbed my neck, the pain shooting down my shoulder like needles stabbing me. "Darn ole head. How many times will I get smacked before I lose myself?" The stitches felt bubbly like they oozed, like they were gonna leak with pus.

I peeked through the screen, glancing to the front house, pondering what to do, where to go. This would be the perfect time to check out the bunker while Molasses was in town, and look for clues to see if Mahlee left any trace of herself.

She might show herself, I might show myself. Then we could be together.

Dead in the Ground

A swoosh of red flew above me in the back yard near the water pump. "A redbird. Hi, little fella. You remind me of my grandma. She loved redbirds." I glanced at my red PF Flyers and remembered how I had borrowed my first pair when Mahlee and me slept in a barn on our way to Texarkana, which was the same time Daddy spent the night in jail, again.

But the jail burned, and we found him along with the rest of the prisoners at a mission. I ran with my daddy out the back door of the mission, and we hopped a train. I worried about running from cops. It made me sad for my daddy—that he was caught between the rail and the law.

At night, the bad memories do come—because Daddy fell from the train over a bridge in Memphis, seconds after giving me my hobo name. No one calls me Annie Grace Kree. Now I'm simply Shoelace.

Flutter. Swoosh.

The redbird flew into the loft of the barn, disappearing from my sight, but on the rope dangling in front of the opening I saw movement, and jogged to the fence, hopping onto the first slat, holding onto the top board. "No way. It's you again?"

The mouse froze in place on the rope—as if he figured his spots became invisible by not moving.

"I see you. You're my little beady-eyed friend, Powder. You're showing yourself to me, again. You're real." I climbed over the slats, tumbling to the packed dirt, and held my head, the pounding behind my ears rising with each heartbeat in my chest. "I'm ... dizzy. This head of mine doesn't like falling

71

and jumping and climbing and running." Standing at the base of the rope, Powder scuttled upward, changing directions, as if I had gotten too close, or maybe, I'd gotten too loud. I lowered my voice. "Come to me, Powder. I want to be your friend. I need a friend. I need someone, and a mouse will do right now."

Holding out my palm, I grabbed the rope with my free hand and begged Powder to join me, but he scampered to the top, to the slanted roof, into the branches hovering over the barn—to an out-of-sight place. He had his own bunker place like Molasses.

"Darn it. I wanted to show Molasses how this mouse existed, to help him see that even Mahlee's real."

I moved to the highway behind the barn, standing once again on the fence, gazing outward, over the top, and staring at the café across the dirt highway where Mr. Morning's family restaurant, The Tavern, sat on the corner. A twisty tree spindled to the sky, and two sidewalks led to the front porch where folks gathered for lunch. "There's Tink. My kitty has moved closer to the food, probably hoping for some scraps."

I sighed, thinking of the other kitten from the same litter living in Jefferson with my half-sister, Lizzy Beth, Mahlee's other daughter. The one she gave up long before me.

Pinching myself to reality, I hollered, "What am I thinking? Silas and Molasses will return before I even get to the bunker."

I jumped over the fence and landed on both feet this time. "Oh, my head. The pain is getting worse."

Turning to my right, I counted the street signs I could see ahead, remembering to pass one, then turn, or pass two, then turn. How many roads do I pass before sprinting down the hill? I struggled to make sense of my thoughts, they were

muddled, murky and mixed up. I stopped at the second road,
sure I needed to go left. But decided to walk to the next road
first, only to go back to the second.

Wrinkling my nose, I rubbed my eyes. "There's the
Sanders House. The Tavern. And … a big courthouse? A giant
two-story courthouse bigger than four houses. I didn't even
see it the first time I went by. Oh my, I'm sure I need to go the
other way."

Wheet. Wheet. Whoo. Wheet. Wheet. Whoo.

I shuffled in the dusty road toward the whistles coming
from the side of the courthouse. "A church? How many
churches does this town have? There's a Presbyterian Church
catty-corner to the Sanders House, across from the post office.
And a Baptist one on the hill. Now a Methodist Church." I
moved to see who was whistling and saw someone watering
the grass next to the church. "Pastor Graves?"

Glancing at him, I paused, gazing at the steeple on the
church. I found myself perched in front of the green church
laced with a white picket fence. A front porch led to the
sanctuary, and yet another dangling rope. "I bet that rope goes
high to a church bell."

Wiping the sweat on my forehead, I was distracted and
muddled, and for a few minutes, I twirled in confusion at what
I was doing, or where I was going. I twirled in the grass,
causing my brain to jumble with pain. Do I go back to the road
between this one and the next, or the next one over there? Do I
go right, or left? Which way?

Back at the cemetery, I had fallen down the ravine so I
went the way the land took me, the way of the shadows. The
way of the deer. The way of the trail. Then the road. But now,
I may be on the wrong road and mixed up. I clutched both
sides of my face, cupping my ears. I can't think, because the
hammering inside my head is making my thinking, not think.

Closing my eyes, I realized the whistling stopped, and the slushing sound of dirt puffing beneath shoes made me jump, and my eyes bugged open. "Pastor Graves? You're the pastor from the cemetery."

"I'm right here in plain sight. Are you lost? It's a small community. I can get you to where you need to go, and back."

Sighing, I stretched the truth. "I'm getting fresh air. Mr. Silas told me I needed a walk. So I'm walking. He said a stroll to the cotton gin would be a good piece of steps for me, and to turn around and then return."

"A stroll?"

"Yes, he wants me to get well and pay him back for my burning and breaking his stuff." I showed him my rash. "I have poison ivy, and I cut my head."

"I don't need your rash."

"Can you tell me how to find the cotton gin? Which road do I want? The sign over there says I'm on Franklin." I rambled, my head leaning one way and then the next, the twirling of the ground and the sky made me woozy. I straightened my chin to a right-side-up fashion so I could see straight.

"You're on the right road. We call it the Southwest Trail, and by the way, you need to go east. You made a wrong turn."

I peeked over my shoulder. "Thank you. I'll be on my way." I moved to the right, but the pastor's hand touched my shoulder with a grasp of you-better-listen-to-me. I pushed his hand off. "Did you need me for something, Pastor?"

"Not today. Not tomorrow. Best be in church in two days if you know what's good for you. A girl alone. On the run. On the rail. Might not be safe. You need God to direct your path. To keep you from harm." He cleared his throat. "So where is your family?"

74

Shuffling ahead a few feet, I called to the pastor. "I'm here to find my family because my Mahlee is here. I've told everyone, so everyone can tell her—I'm here! She's my mama!" I shouted with sharp words, with a tone of ugly ready to jump from within. "Sorry, I've got to go."

"But, wait. You're mixed up with a stabbing and a murder, and things are not what they seem. Some are who they say. Others are not. Beware. You were at both crime scenes."

I bolted with a harsh response. "And you were at one of them. And I saw your gun."

"I carry it for protection. My gun wasn't fired that day."

"Oh, how do we know?"

"What? You better watch yourself. This is not a game, little girl." Pastor Graves let water stream from the hose, and he doused the loose dirt next to the church.

I moved away. "Don't be telling me nothing. Or anything." I corrected my own grammar. "I'm not alone. I'm not afraid. I'm not involved in anything. Not this time. I was simply walking by Mr. Morning when he spoke to me. And I was at the funeral, like you."

"What did Mr. Morning say to you?"

"He told me I'd be tending his baby."

"He didn't mention anything else?"

"Why would he? We didn't know each other." Stomping in the mud, I realized I had circled the pastor, arguing with him. "I'll leave your town as soon as I find my Mahlee. She will go with me. I'm sure of it."

"She's not known for doing what others say. She's a misfit. A runner like you. She's been gone for a long time, only some say she rode into town a few weeks ago like shadow in the woods."

"See, you think she's here too. But Mahlee's not showing herself. I don't know why she's hiding." I lied to Pastor

Graves, because since Mahlee's wanted for murder in Texas, two murders—I did know why she was hiding.

Pastor Graves pushed me, his hand once again on my shoulder, and his wrinkles flopped under his glaring eyes. His skin looked older than Silas' hand, but his face younger. "Move from where you're standing. I'm watering my late wife's grave."

Leaping backwards, I yelled, "What? You're watering a dead person?"

"No, I'm watering her burial site. See, the marker on the ground, she's buried here next to her home church. This is her family's land, or used to be for a hundred years. I planted Jonquil bulbs here. They're her favorite flower."

I touched my chest, shaking my head at hearing about another dead person. "Has she been dead long?"

"Six months. Her bones were brittle. Fell down the steps inside the church as she left her Sunday School class. Died in church. I was right behind her, and couldn't do a thing. Her spirit went to heaven in church. But her body is here."

"So you've been the pastor at this—" I glanced at the sign, "at this Methodist Church, for a long time?"

"No. Just for six months. I used to work for the city of Hope. But times change."

"What? So you're an in-training pastor. You got a late start."

"I consider it a new assignment. One keeping me from going to … well, from going to jail …"

"Jail?"

"Silly girl. I said, hell."

"You said, jail. I heard you."

"No, it's a new assignment keeping me from going to hell. Saved by grace. Has saved my face." Pastor Graves smiled, his belly jiggled under his shirt, and the same firm grasp from before landed on the bib of my overalls. His clenched fist causing me to stand on my tiptoes.

"I don't think grace saved your face. Besides, Jesus doesn't save faces, He saves souls." I scowled at him, my preaching words harsh, not so full of grace.

He nodded, "This is true. For some, I suppose."

"I wouldn't like your preaching."

"Girl, you need to learn your place."

Gulping, I let out a squeal. "Can you let go?"

He yanked on the bib, shoving me backwards. "I know what I said, and you heard me wrong. Understand?"

"Yes sir. Didn't mean to argue with a pastor." I yanked free, and ran away. "Sorry. I'm gone. I have an assignment from God, and it's to find my Mahlee and get out of this town."

I raced past the main highway, jogging past a candle shop to my left, and a general store to my right with a bicycle out front, and on down the road. I found myself barely able to breathe, skirting to a stop at the top of the hill, and then I saw how the dirt sloped away like a roller coaster dropping downward.

"I'm close. So close, I can taste the trail." Licking my lips, I realized the sour thick goo was blood. My stitches were bleeding and the blood dripped down my face. "I don't have time for blood, or scary pastors, or people dead in the ground."

I pulled out a cloth and blotted my head with a handkerchief given to me by my boxcar friend, Archie. I stared at the white cloth with red bloody spots, and turned toward the Methodist Church, although I was blocks away, shouting at Pastor Graves. "Archie would make a better pastor than you. He has wise words, knows Bible verses, and has hope in his eyes—and he would never hold onto me like you did."

I twisted around and moved down the hill. "I hope to see Archie again sometime. He always made me feel better, even if he made me tell the truth. He's out there somewhere on the rail, or maybe he's still working with the circus, taking care of the elephants. Maybe he'll find me. Or I could find him. He would make a good daddy. But for now, I need my Mahlee."

Rushing past the cotton gin, over the tracks, and swooping, I charged up the slope like a deer running from a hunter. At the next rise in the land, I saw the opening to the painted trail, knowing I was close, and I watched for signs of movement behind the trees.

I'm not sure if there's old army bombs outside of the trail, but blowing myself up might keep me from my rail-mama. "Mahlee, are you there? Mahlee? I'm outside the bunker. If you're in there. It's me. You can show yourself." I clutched the handkerchief, wishing and praying and worrying. Putting my hand to my heart, I felt the booming inside my chest, like a bomb of hope and despair—all at the same time.

Creak! Creak!

The bunker door swung open.

I swallowed, "Mahlee?"

No answer.

Skip Straight to Molasses

"I command you to come out. Mahlee, I know you're in there. You can't keep hiding from me. There's a killer in this town." I shouted, and the echo of my command stirred nothing.

"Mahlee?" I pushed the door wide open, the dim light slipping into the bunker from the window slits. The light caused a blinding glare in front of me, and I marched ahead, staggering and determined to find out who was inside. I wasn't sure where the bravery came from, or if I was too stupid to know when to stop, or too stubborn to give up.

A rustling in the leaves sent birds flying, and the silence falling over the hill lingered with no breeze, no movement, and no one answering me.

Eeek! I jumped back, the shadow in front of me taller than anyone in real life; and shifting my head sideways and then forward, the shadow mocked my moves. With my hand on my neck, I knew who it was. "Oh my! I'm afraid of my own shadow."

Moving closer, my eyes focused on the items inside the bunker. "What is this? A tomb? Or maybe a sanctuary?"

I held my breath, the musky smell clogged my nose. *Cough. Cough.*

"Mahlee, if you're hiding. Show yourself."

Nothing. Not one sign of a person hiding. Not one sign of anyone.

Tick. Tick. Tick.

"What? Powder?" My gaze landed on a rectangle box against the wall in front of me. "A chest? Sketches on the wall? And a mouse who keeps showing himself to me?"

Powder zipped to the side of the trunk, and darted out of sight. "Silly mouse." I ran my fingers over the top, shifting myself to the side to let the light shine in from the outside, and I knocked something with my hand.

Thud-tink!

Bending down, I picked up a smoker's pipe. "Molasses, smokes a pipe?" I placed it on the trunk, and saw the shiny glare of an item leaning on the trunk's end. "What is this?" I ran my fingers over a saxophone. "So, Molasses smokes and plays music?"

I spun around. The too-quiet, dead air, felt eerie with the noise of danger. Trespassing, sneaking around, and wondering if my chasing this shadow was my Mahlee, made me weary. I worried I was following a killer and not her too—which made me nervous and afraid.

"I need to go. I need to get back to the Sanders House." I put both my hands to my sweaty neck. Shaking my head, I argued with myself. "I need to stay. I need to find out what to do, where to go, and find out who ran from me at the funeral."

Tramping to the other side of the trunk, my shoe clunked a large piece of wood, sending it dinging and clanging. "A guitar? What is this place? Molasses must have his belongings out here." I stood the guitar up, and ran my fingers on the strings.

Strum-a-strum-cling.

"This is a music sanctuary for Molasses. It's like a fort, a special spot. Climbing trees is my special spot, where I fly high to pretend-land, to where kids are happy, and they have mamas and papas."

The shifting of the sun moved the ray of light to another wall, and lit up the area above the brown trunk. Stepping closer, my knees knocked a stack of paper to the concrete floor. "I better not mess his stuff up. I can't let him know I was here."

Gathering up the paper, I placed it next to the pipe, and saw the sticks of charcoal, the kind used for sketching. I raised my hand, and felt of my head where the heartbeat throbbing pounded, and I gawked at the four sketches tacked to the wall.

I touched the corner of the first paper. "Look at this. A boy fishing. He favors Molasses. Younger though. He's sitting on a log by the bank fishing, and next to him is a tall Negro who is fishing too."

Wrinkling my nose, I realized it was almost like the sketch in the Sanders House. Except … except this one had something different. They hadn't caught any fish yet.

I glanced at the second sketch and the third almost at the same time, my eyes crossing. "That's Molasses in the wash tub, and Silas pouring water over his head. The others must be workers in the cotton field, dozens and dozens of them. All Negro." They were holding sacks and sacks of cotton, and were peering at me as if they could see me from the wall.

Shivering, I stared at the left part of the cotton field in the drawing. A white man on a horse held a rifle. His grin ugly. The eyes of the cotton workers were bigger than normal like they longed to see freedom. Or they were afraid of the gun.

The last sketch made me shudder and my knees wobbled, my hands tingling. "I know who he is. It can't be!" I leaned in. "But that man wearing the overalls, and standing on a rickety porch is wearing an engineer's cap like the one Skip gave me. The same one Skip wears, like the one in Crush's suitcase. It's my friend Skip."

I glared at the drawing of my alphabet-game friend who rode the rail. Who died in Texarkana. Who knew my daddy. And Mahlee. And knew my grandma. And played the piano for my daddy's funeral. Who got shot by the officer in Texarkana.

Hovering, I stood on top of the trunk, knocking the pipe, the paper, and the charcoal to the floor; I shook my head until the pain rattled through every vein in my body. "Those sketches all have Skip in them too!! It must be him! My Skip!"

I tumbled to the floor like a girl figuring out life, not understanding any of it, and I opened the unlocked trunk. Rolled up sketches were stacked inside, many were smeared like an eraser had gotten them, but the one I glared at now— had a small Negro boy playing the piano. I wondered if the boy might have been Skip when he was small.

I rolled over to my side, sobbing at having no one, and wanting everyone, and crying for anyone to want me.

I tried to put the pieces of the puzzle together. "How is Molasses related to Skip? Or is that even Molasses in the drawings? Does he play instruments too?" I clasped my knees with my arms, noticing the scattered paper around me, the littered floor. I sat up and piled the papers back onto the trunk.

Grabbing the last piece of paper, I noticed something in the corner. "Are those bedrolls? I'm probably being watched from the woods. What am I thinking?"

Giving the bedrolls a shake, looking for clues to the 'who' they belonged to, a tiny piece of a paper floated to the floor, shifting in the air like a butterfly without wings. A beam of light shot between the trees outside shining a spotlight onto the paper, and I crawled over to it. "What? A bunch of names?"

Wadding up the paper, I rose to my feet, sensing the eyes of the woods watching, and knew I needed to get going. But I was caught between the memories of Skip when I first met him on the tracks outside of Memphis, to worrying who might be killing off people in this town. To wishing Mahlee would show herself.

Goodness, I have discovered Molasses is an artist though, and it looks like he knew Skip. I'm asking him when I get back to the house, because if they were friends—I might need to cut Molasses some slack.

Crickety. Crunch. Crunch.

"Who's out there?" I stepped from the bunker as I held an invisible sword and shield, but cowered backwards shaking from my toes to my ears.

No one answered. I heard the rustling leaves, and the crunching stopped. Inhaling the last bit of courage, I backed myself against the door, and it slammed shut, making a slapping sound. It felt like a hammer cracking over my head, and I grabbed my aching ears.

I charged up the trail, hurrying from the woods, running faster and faster, limping like a horse afraid to jump a fence. I bolted to a halt in my tracks. "Wait? What were those names on the paper?"

Rushing back to the crumpled paper, I unfolded it, and saw the scribbled names. "Clifford Morning. Pax Shaw. Phillip Shaw. Buck Graves. And Samuel Swisher. Morning's name had a line through it. Swisher too. They're dead. Who's marking off people?"

Arrgh!!!

A deep growl surfaced, and the garbled voice shouted. "Get out of these woods. You are better off not knowing, and what you already know is too much—and the list is mine. Drop it! Run! Or die!"

Tumbling over my rubber band legs stretching sideways without my body, I held my head as my arms slammed me face first to the ground. I looked back over my shoulder, sure a hand would choke me, sure the eerie-creepy-crawly feeling up my back meant the voice was hovering over me, but … I was alone.

I sat up, glancing behind me, then over by the bushes, and back to the other side, and again behind me. Calling to the trees, I announced with a crack in my voice. "I'm leaving. I'm not staying. I don't know why you let me go through the bunker only to scare me now. You're not a good scary person." I mouthed to the wanna-be bad person, not sure if I was talking to a man, although the voice was deep like a well, but high like a woman.

"You saw what you saw because you needed to, but now you must go."

I lost my footing and tripped over a rock on the path, falling to the land beneath the trail—to the area where Molasses buried his booby-traps. "Yikes! I'm out of here. I can't blow myself up. I have to get back before everyone misses me, before my name gets marked from a list."

Stumbling, running, and yelling under my breath, I called to God, to let me live, to let me get away.

I had to talk with Molasses too, even if he tied me up with rope and beat me. He has secrets and I need his help. I galloped like a wild horse toward the road, ready to figure out my next step, and remembering I was supposed to be helping Ms. Etta.

Sticking the names into my overalls pocket, I held my aching head, rushed past the cotton gin, and hurried to the Sanders House.

Cutting between the street where the post office sat and the Presbyterian Church faced it, I paused under the glow of the moon. I faced the steeple and the front of the sanctuary. "God, I had nothing to do with these killings. I mean the fire was my fault. And hurting Crush, but not the stabbing or the shooting in the cemetery." I put my hand to my heart. "But you've sent me here to learn about my Skip. So help me learn more about Mahlee too. And please, if you're listening, don't let her shoot anyone or stab them. Or be a bad crazy woman like I remember when Daddy and I first met her six years ago. Amen."

I shuffled across the street to the picket fence, and the house was lit up like a bunch of sunrooms. In front of the house sat a pickup, which meant Crush was out of the hospital.

But ... whose truck was parked next to Mr. Morning's? Could it be? I screamed under my throat, nearly choking. "No!"

I turned back to the church building, muttering at God. "I'm not leaving. You sent them to get me, didn't you? How dare you? I don't belong to them. I belong to Mahlee."

I sat with my back to the fence, thinking what to do next, deciding whether to hide, to run, to go, or to stay.

The voice from the yard made my decision for me. "Shoelace, you better show yourself. Mr. Marion has come all the way from Jefferson, Texas, for Crush, and there's a pastor from Texarkana, he's here to see you. You best come inside."

I rose up, facing Silas who was on the porch—who looked exactly like Skip!! And had all along!

From Carroll Street to Crush

Standing in the breezeway with the front door closed behind me, Silas towered over me with his hand on his hips, a stance my grandma used when punishment came my way. "Child, I have no idea why you wander, and why you disrespect, and disobey; but at this house we listen to our elders and we all do our part."

"Yes sir." I found my sad voice, the one I use to get my way, and hung my head.

"Molasses went searching for you, and I've driven around town. Pastor Graves told me you stomped on his wife's grave, and you went running down the old Indian trail by the gin. Can you tell me why? Why hasn't Ms. Etta seen you today?"

I sighed, "I had to find Mahlee. I'm sure she's here. This is her hometown. Daisy is her sister."

Silas coughed, pulling a wrinkled handkerchief from his pocket and wiping his nose. "Sweet girl, we all know you're searching for Mahlee. She's hiding if she's here, and if she's not here, you're seeing her with eyes of hope. Hope sees things others don't sometimes."

I raised my eyebrows, ready to get my question in, waiting for Silas to pause with his correcting.

"And after I'm finished with you, please, use your manners and answer Officer Tock's questions. He's in the parlor waiting with Ms. Daisy and Ms. Etta."

I bumped into the skinny wall table, and peeked around the doorway. I backed up to the corner. "I already told him. I didn't see a thing on the steps. Not a thing."

"Then it won't take long." Silas ran his fingers through his hair. "Time for answers. Any piece you have is a part of the puzzle of what happened to Mr. Morning. It's been two weeks."

Gulping, I figured talking to Officer Tock would end faster if I got in there, but I couldn't help but stare at Silas. "I need to ask you something. Are you ... do you have a brother? Is his name Skip?"

"What? How would you know of Skip?"

"I met him in Tennessee on the tracks. He played the Alphabet Game with me, like spelling words but more fun."

"You have seen him?"

"No. Not anymore."

"Why? Where did he go?"

I rattled on with more explanation than Silas asked for. "Well, me and Mahlee and my daddy were riding in a boxcar to Texarkana, and Daddy fell into the river and died, and Mahlee took me to my grandma's boarding house. She left me then too. But came back. For my daddy's funeral, Skip came and played the piano."

"He was in Texarkana?"

"Yes, he was playing at night where people drink their whiskey, and Pastor Cody invited him to play for Daddy's funeral. Turns out he knew my grandma when he was a little boy and she was a girl."

"Who is your grandma?"

"My grandma was Elsie Kree. She's dead too."

Silas sat on the fancy wooden chair with the cream colored fabric. "Sit here." He patted his knees.

Jumping into his lap, his bony knees poked my legs. "So you're not mad at me for running off today?"

"No, I do wish you listened better, and I do wish I'd known more about my brother. He ran like many, lost in the past whippings from our pa, the leather strap never kept him in line. He broke the rules, hit others when angry, stole food, and got lost in the river of dreaming for fair pay and fewer beatings."

Shaking my head, I told of another side to Skip. "But, he was kind and funny. Smart too. His fingers played the piano, he loved hymns, and he was full of choruses and verses. He was my friend." I leaned into Silas, my hair falling into my face, and I felt his heartbeat and rested for the first time in weeks.

"My brother is gone? Dead?"

"Yes, he's buried there."

"Shoelace, what is your given name?"

"Why?" I looked into his chocolate face.

"Tell me. Aren't we friends?"

My headache left, and my feet dangled. "We are, I suppose."

"What's your given name again?"

"It's Annie Grace Kree."

"Kree? I knew an Elsie way back when. I don't remember her last name. We was just kids. Her pa bought root beer candy sticks for Skip. And sometimes, he shared them with me."

I sat up tall. "You knew my grandma. I'm sure of it."

Silas smiled a giant grin, and hugged with his long arms. "You come from good stock. You might want to go home."

"I don't have a home. Mahlee's my family. Grandma died earlier this year, so I have to find Mahlee."

Creeeaaaak.

The door across the breezeway opened, and a jolly man who loves syrup came into the breezeway. "Well, what do I see here? If it isn't our girl, Shoelace."

Running to Marion Kane, I wrapped my arms around the fat part of his stomach. "Why are you here? How did you find me? So you know Crush is here, and I'm here? Is Crush in there?" I pointed to the room in front of me.

"Too many questions from a girl who needs to answer a few herself. Yes, Crush sent me a letter writing how he was burned, how you did it, how you were working to pay for the damage. Then he called me, letting me know someone was stabbed, and another shot. Pastor Cody and I decided it was time to pick you both up."

Almost gagging on my snot, I poured out the questions. "Pastor Cody? He's here too?" I pushed the door wide and my pastor who preaches to hobos smiled and rose from the chair next to the bed.

"Shoelace, you were gone when I came for you, which made it hard to drive you back to Texarkana. Marion sent Crush with you to keep track of your running and your hopping trains, until you gave up this search for Mahlee. I'm glad we found you." He cleared his throat. "Mahlee's gone. Remember, she's wanted for murder. She's not coming back."

I glanced at the boy in the bed wrapped in gauze, the same boy who gave me a kitten, who shared my food in a boxcar, and who now looked more like a spy than a friend.

Slugging the edge of the mattress, I spouted hate at Crush. "You ratted me out. You were never my friend. You were on the train to follow me, and I never want to see you again. I'm not going with anyone. I'm on my own. I can make it without any of you." I stomped my shoes on the hardwood floor, shaking my head at how deceived I felt, the tears rolling down my cheeks like leftover sorrow and new sadness.

Marion circled to the other side of the bed. "Crush is asleep. The doctor gave him something to rest. I'm thankful he didn't hear you shouting, and you didn't wake him up. He followed, you by the way, to protect you."

"To protect me? I don't need protecting."

"Apparently. Look at Crush. He's got a few scars from this trip, but he'll live and be stronger from it, I'm sure."

"The fire was an accident. I didn't mean to hurt him. Honest." My tears leaked in drops, big enough to douse a flame. "I'm sorry. I am."

"I know you are. We'll leave tomorrow or the next day. My truck's outside and I'll run you and Pastor Cody to Texarkana on our way to Jefferson."

"No, I have to find Mahlee."

"She's not here, child."

Pastor Cody slid up next to Marion. "Shoelace, you can stay at my house. I've got some new roommates. Sisters Sally and Nora lost their house to the bank, and Wingnut lost his job. I could use your help passing out the hymnals at the creek service this weekend."

I sighed, letting out the hope I'd ridden into town with, and it escaped, hiding under the bed. "But ... but ... I don't need a regular home. I need my Mahlee."

"But Shoelace, no one has seen her since she left Texas."

"I saw her at the funeral in the woods in the bushes. She's hiding from us." I countered Pastor Cody with my words.

"You might be seeing things. You could be wrong."

"I'm not. She's out there."

Marion sat on the edge of the bed, glancing over at Silas. "Sir, we do appreciate the hospitality. Any damages we need to pay for, I'll write a check for it."

"No need, sir. All is fixed. A little paint helped. And the floor never looked better." Silas held onto the iron frame at the bottom of the bed. "Shoelace does liven up a place. It's nice to have her around. She's a good worker, when she works."

I grinned at the man who now had a part of my heart. "But I don't like working. I do like eating and climbing trees though."

Pastor Cody laughed, "She does like to eat."

Marion ran his fingers across the forehead of Crush. "I can't wait for the boys to see Crush. The triplets are fighting as usual, and Thomas is making good grades in school with those new glasses, and Theodore is putting music to your poems. Timmons and Tak are sleeping with Toby, seems they miss their big brother."

Silas held up his fingers as if counting. "How many boys you got, sir?"

"Toby's my grandson, and the rest are adopted. We're family."

Pastor Cody added his thoughts, "Shoelace is like family for me."

"I'm not family. I'm trouble."

Silas winked at me, Marion nodded, and a uniform came into the room. "How long will I have to wait. There's a killer loose in town." The police officer glared at me. "Shoelace, may we talk?"

"I don't want to."

Silas stepped between us. "Shoelace, maybe you could visit with Officer Tock in the parlor. Ms. Daisy is in there, and Ms. Etta is with the baby, and Molasses is probably back by now. He went looking for you, more than once today."

"I bet he did. He's so nosey. Why does everyone need to look for me? I'm not lost. I always know where I am. Unless I don't."

Pastor Cody walked over to me. "Come along. I'll go with you. I haven't met Molasses yet."

Silas spoke, "He's my nephew, and he's lost in the past of saying goodbye to his own pa. He's like Shoelace—looking for things he might not see, and seeing things others might not."

I whispered to Silas, "I saw your polka dotted mouse today. He was at the bunker." The word bunker slipped out before I could retrieve it.

Molasses stepped into view, hovering in the doorway like a spy—and he slapped his fist into his hand. "Did you say bunker? Were you at the Proving Grounds? You better not have gone out there. I've warned you."

Suspect the Suspect

Swallowing my ugly words, I sighed, as I was thrilled Silas squashed Molasses with "Leave her alone. Whatever you have to say to Shoelace can wait," so I didn't have to tell him where my adventures had taken me. Now he's frowning like a pouty kid who didn't get his way, his arms folded, his eyes glued to my every step.

I gave him a grin, and he scowled, and Officer Tock caught our evil-eye glances. "You two having a fight?"

I snarled, "Fight? He's not worth fighting. Taller boys fall hard and slow like timber in a forest. They snap at the littlest push."

Molasses shook his head, and knelt down on one knee, close to the breezeway, probably in case he had to run from me.

Officer Tock pulled on his uniform slacks at the knees, and sat on the sofa. "Shoelace, come sit over here, between Ms. Daisy and me. We need to talk. I've got a few more questions."

Before I moved toward him, Pastor Cody stepped into the room, holding out his hand to shake the officer's claws. "Anything you say to my friend here, I'll sit in on—she's like a little sister to me."

"I have to clear up a few things from the funeral shooting, and from Mr. Morning's death."

Pastor Cody and the officer exchanged sentences of how Cody met me, to how I left on the rail, and rode in boxcars, to why he was looking for me now. "We had a misunderstanding on when I was picking her up in Jefferson. She got scared and left."

I squinted my eyes at the glaring chandelier, gazing at it, trying to digest Pastor Cody's almost true statements, and glad he used his version and not mine with the officer. I'm sure he'll get forgiveness from God for stretching the truth.

Officer Tock scratched his chin. "So she's not a runaway?"

"No sir. She's coming with me. We were planning to meet up. This happened to be the spot." Pastor Cody cut his eyes at me, and the silence in the room shrieked the loudest orders to obey him or else, his firm words clear, his not-taking-any-nonsense from me obvious.

The two men discussed the murders, and Officer Tock caught Pastor Cody up on the investigation. Silas swayed in front of the fireplace, his stance wobbly, his hand wiping his cheek, and I slipped next to him, happy for any delay in talking with the officer.

Silas squeezed my hand. "See the sketch up there?"

"Yes sir. The younger man on the right is you, right?"

"Yes, I was out for the summer after finishing my learning. No more school for me. I was fishing at Spring Lake Park for my supper."

"Spring Lake Park? In Texarkana?"

"Yes, we lived there for a time working on farms."

"So who is the other man? I can't see him."

"It's Skip. We're ten years apart. He's the younger one, but not always the wiser brother." Silas chuckled. "Maybe he was wiser, he did see the world, had friends in every state, and did what he liked to do, from how he'd tell it."

"He was wise. He played words games with me. Laughed a lot, and could play the piano."

Molasses marched up to me, blocking my view of the sketch above the mantle. "How did you know my pa?"

"I met him on the rail. He knew my pa too. He knew my grandma too."

"Great! He never did anything with me."

"I'm sorry. I knew Skip on the rail. I didn't know he had family." I pointed toward the sketch. "But he did come home sometimes, didn't he?"

Silas nodded. "Yes, he popped in long enough to stir up trouble, or to work a job to get some money, and he did finally marry Nannie, to make her respectable. That was Molasses' ma who was with us for his first ten years. As for Skip, having a child so late in life, it didn't sit well with him. He didn't know what to do with a son."

I glanced at Pastor Cody who was still talking, and I asked the frowning Molasses. "What happened to your mama?"

"She's gone too. All them years picking cotton in the heat from sunup until after dark didn't help, and then when my pa would come home and then up and leave for months at a time, all she did was cry. She died of a broken heart." Molasses put his hand to his throat, and gulped. "Not me, though. My heart works great. I'm leaving this place in two years, and going to become an artist."

Silas smiled, "But you'll have your cooking to fall back on, since all my pie recipes are inside your head. You'll need them if your drawings don't pay."

"They'll pay. I'm going to be free of this town." Molasses leaned against the wall, his eyes on the floor. "I have to take care of a few things first."

Silas agreed. "Yes, like finishing high school."

Molasses choked on his words. "I will finish. I need to graduate. I'll be the first in the family. Not like my pa. He didn't, but he found the tracks gave him the freedom we all wished for. Seems he would forget about me though, but I'm thankful for Uncle Silas. He took me in like I was his."

Silas responded with a crack in his voice. "You're my boy. You've been with me more than you haven't. We take care of each other."

"Yes, we have. You taught me how to live."

Silas put his hand on Molasses' shoulder. "Come with me outside. Let's talk on the back porch. I need to tell you about your pa."

Like a snail not in a hurry to leave the parlor, Molasses left the room, glaring at me as if our chat would come later—the one about the bunker.

**

I ignored Officer Tock who waved a hand in the air, explaining something to Pastor Cody, and I hoped he'd forget why he came to the Sanders House, so I made my way to the rocker where Ms. Etta sang a whispering tune to Baby.

"I'm sorry, Ms. Etta. I never got around to helping you today. I'll do better." Trying to make amends for my behavior, to find someone who was on my side.

"Child, we have plenty of chores to do tomorrow."

Hearing the deep breaths of Ms. Daisy, I tiptoed over and stared at her. Her head was nestled against the cushion, and I wondered why she never held her baby much, and also wondered why she acted like she wasn't a mama.

"Well, it's getting late. I need to visit with you, Shoelace." Officer Tock interrupted my quiet judgment of Ms. Daisy.

"What do you want to know? I told you I fell on the stairs. That Mr. Morning was there. And I don't know why. I don't."

"Well, it appears the knife came from Silas' kitchen. He's confirmed the knife was one of his."

"The door wasn't locked to the kitchen house. Anyone could have gotten it."

"This is true. Just wanted to see if you saw anyone in the shadows by the house. Or remember anything?"

"No. I don't know anything!" I shouted, which caused Ms. Etta to leave the room with Baby, and my mouthing woke up Ms. Daisy, who wiped her sleepy eyes.

"What? Where am I?"

Officer Tock patted her arm, since he was sitting on the sofa near her. "Ma'am, I'm asking this little girl some more questions."

Ms. Daisy straightened her skirt, and her green eyes pierced the officer as if she might scream, but instead she took a deep breath. "Make it quick. It's time for bed. I'm exhausted."

Officer Tock turned back to me, "In interviewing the people who attended the funeral for Della and Mr. Morning, more than one person mentioned your running into the woods when Mr. Swisher was shot. Tell me why you left."

Stuttering, I made up a story. "I ... I ... I was picking wild flowers."

"Sure you were. We have Jonquils all over the cemetery. Try again. Could it be you were looking for someone? I've heard you're after Mahlee Shaw, you're searching for her, right?"

"Yes, I'm here to find her. She's my almost-mama. We need each other."

"She isn't a woman you need to contend with. She's volatile and unpredictable, and we haven't seen her in years in these parts."

"Well, I've seen her." I spouted off, letting my secret out, the one of seeing her in the shadows, of thinking it was her, and wishing it was. I'm almost sure it was, but now I've gone and told the officer. Back pedaling, I rephrased my sentence. "I've seen her with me and my daddy on the rail. She rode with us. She did."

"I see. Well, this is an open investigation and I'll ask you not to leave town. We might need to talk to you again." Officer Tock turned to Pastor Cody. "I could use your help with this. Will you see to it she stays a few more days?"

Pastor Cody nodded. "Absolutely. We can stay, if Ms. Daisy doesn't mind. Or we could stay in Hope."

She sat up, giving an alert gaze. "You're welcome to use the room Crush is in, and the girl, Shoelace can sleep with me in my feather bed."

I couldn't believe they were making plans for me without asking me how I felt. "I might want to leave. I don't answer to all of you. I answer to me."

Pastor Cody sneered, "Your late grandma might disagree."

I sighed, "Using guilt on me isn't nice, Pastor."

"I know. But when dealing with you, I use measures of trickery before you trick me."

"But I'm not a killer. I didn't stab anyone. I have no idea who shot the other man, either. I'm innocent, except for the fire in the kitchen-house, and hurting Crush."

Officer Tock clicked his finger on my earlobe. "Respect for authority is what you need. We need to figure this out before anyone else is killed."

Ms. Daisy jumped to her feet. "What? Officer Tock, you're acting like this precious little girl is a suspect. She's not. If you want to find the killer maybe you should check with your other officers. My husband paid many of them off to keep quiet about his illegal dealings, and you might also check with Graves. He's no pastor. His record with the illegal ballots in the election last year in Hope only got tucked away because of my husband and his money." With the screaming, Ms. Daisy's face strobed a red glow, and her blood vessels in her temples were showing themselves in strips of blue.

I froze in the middle of the room with Pastor Cody on one side, with Officer Tock in front of me, and with Ms. Daisy who extended her arms out as if calling me to her side.

"Me? You want me?"

"Yes, sweet girl. Come here. I hate you're going through this. You have no idea what's happening in our town. You hitched a ride on a dark night and got caught in our sorrow."

I inched over to Ms. Daisy, who stroked my hair like a mama waking up from a nightmare of her lost days, and Pastor Cody offered his insight. "Shoelace is a messenger of hope. Her grandma knew it, and I know it. Seems Ms. Daisy might know it too."

I grinned, and for the first time in a while, I realized Pastor Cody cared for me, and Ms. Daisy was starting to care too. It's like she was sleepwalking before, and now she's waking up to her own feelings—and to mine.

Silas showed up across the room, and checked the temperature of our talk by asking questions. "Everything going good in here? Anyone need a glass of sweet tea?"

"I'm thirsty. I haven't had supper either, in case you have leftovers from earlier. I didn't mean to be gone for so long. I get to walking to places …" I didn't finish my sentence because Officer Tock's ears appeared to twitch like he figured he was learning a clue about my whereabouts today.

Pastor Cody answered Silas. "We're all better, since Shoelace is here. No tea for me, but I'm staying a few days because Officer Tock may need to talk to her again, and this will give me time to sort through 'what's next' for Shoelace. She's lost her family."

I spouted off with a pretend confidence. "I have a family. It's Mahlee. I need to see her and she'll remember how much she loves me." I blinked hard, holding back tears. "And for the record, Officer Tock, I'm not a killer. Just so you know. I happened along when bad things happened, but it's not my fault."

Silas chuckled at my disrespect, putting his hand to his lips. "Shoelace, if I had a daughter, you would be the girl I'd ask God for."

My heart felt an extra hope-beat. "Thank you. At least someone wants me."

Silas excused himself, "I'll run Ms. Etta home. Then I'm headed to my room unless you need something, Ms. Daisy."

"No thank you, Silas. Your voice is weak. Are you all right?"

"Will be. I learned my brother Skip's dead. He died last year in Texarkana. I told Molasses, and he's taking it pretty hard. He showed no tears, but he's mad. Mad at his pa for not being a pa."

"I've not been a ma myself to my new baby girl. I have no feelings, they're all stuck in the past. I can't break free. Skip's absence must have hurt him; I hope I'm not doing the same." Ms. Daisy cast a glance toward the other breezeway leading to her bedroom, and she pulled me closer, hugging me around the neck. "And you're wanted. You can stay with us as long as you need to."

Pastor Cody followed Silas to the back porch, his words assuring Silas he'd pray for him, and he told him how he knew Skip too.

I glanced up at Ms. Daisy. "Thank you. I'm just visiting though. Once I find my Mahlee, we'll be leaving."

"You do know she's my sister?"

"Yes ma'am. I know. Della was your sister too. Huh?"

"Yes. I was so looking forward to her coming to help me with the baby. But ..." Ms. Daisy stumbled backwards and crumbled to the sofa. "She was my best friend. We were so close. I can't believe she's dead."

Officer Tock jolted to a salute stance like an officer who was going to burst. "I almost forgot. I should have said something already. Today, a call came into the station. A man in Texarkana believes Ms. Della was arguing with someone at the train station, and thinks she was shoved, and left for dead. The call came from an Officer Teacup. He's coming to see you tomorrow, Ms. Daisy."

"No! I have nothing to say. Nothing! I'm tired of police officers and tired of my husband's men calling me about wrapping up his business affairs. Tired! Do you hear me?"

I nodded, although she wasn't looking at me, she was glaring at Officer Tock, turning her scream to the ceiling. "Lord, why have I lost my family?"

Baby Bliss and Shoelace Kiss

I found myself in the bedroom with Ms. Daisy, and her sleeping baby girl. Ms. Etta's home now. Crush, Pastor Cody and Marion Kane are sleeping in the front bedroom of the house. One of them gets the cot. Silas went to his kitchen-house bedroom, and I could care less where Molasses slept.

Officer Tock left right after Ms. Daisy's fit, and she ushered me to her room. She had me get my pajama clothes, and I also grabbed my satchel to keep it close. She poured water in the ceramic bowl on the dresser. "Shoelace, the grime of the day is on your face and on those hands, along with the mustard from the fried bologna sandwich Silas made for you."

Holding out my palms, I licked the mustard from my fingers, "Yes ma'am. I'll wash up. Why are you being so nice to me? I've come with death around my steps."

"You are not death. You are life. You are a girl trying to figure out why her family is gone, as I am. You are me. I am you. We are the same."

"We are the same?" Questioning her, I rinsed my hands in the water, wiping my face with the cloth, on the white, now brown, rag.

"We are. You have lost your parents."

"Did I tell you that I did?"

"Not exactly, but Pastor Cody caught me up on your story, and how your father kidnapped you from your grandmother when you were five, how you rode the rail with him, how you knew my sister Mahlee and how she cared for you, and how your daddy even saved her life. And how she's wanted for murder in Jefferson, Texas."

"But she's innocent. She didn't shoot those two men. The man who did the shooting confessed to me, but he's dead now. So the cops don't believe I'm telling the truth. If Mahlee acted like a regular person, someone might have listened to her, but she ran away."

"She never has fit into regular shoes."

Not sure what Ms. Daisy meant, I agreed. "She likes to wear work boots."

Ha! Ha! "She does?"

"Yes, those ugly boots. Flat ladies' shoes make her walk like her hips are out of joint."

Ms. Daisy held her tummy. "You're the funniest little girl. You say what you think and we know where you stand. I wish I could be so honest and brave and open with others." She unpinned her bun, her long hair unraveling to her waist like a horse's mane, shiny and silky.

"Your hair is so pretty."

She picked up a brush and stroked her hair, counting, "One brush. Two. Three brushes. Four. Five brushes. Six. Pickup up sticks."

"Sticks?"

"Yes, I was the sister who picked up the teeny branches after storms. I was dainty, not them. Mahlee was allowed to use an axe, and Della too. They were the tomboys when we were growing up, and I was the fragile sister. The one everyone said the boys liked better. And the one my parents made sure got courted by Clifford, who was mean and controlling when we were alone, but cunning and sly when others were watching."

I sat on the cushioned chair with no back, in front of the mirrored dresser, gazing at my tangled hair. Touching my cheekbones, they appeared bigger than I remembered. "So will I be like Mahlee or like you?"

"You, my dear girl. You are like your mama. I'm sure of it. Not too dainty. A little braver than most. Sure of your words. Stronger than everyone who has gone before you." Ms. Daisy ran her white bristled brush through my hair. "You might need to brush this mane once in a while."

"I forget to brush my hair, so I keep it pulled up, mostly."

"I wear mine up too. You, my sweet one, you should wear your hair however you wish. It's your hair."

Waa! Waa!

Ms. Daisy spun around facing the bassinet, and her reflection in the mirror showed fear. "Oh my, when she cries at night, we cry together. I can't seem to make her stop. She gets worse. Can you hold her?"

"I'm not sure she wants me." Getting up, I took Ms. Daisy by the hand, and we shambled to the baby. "Hold her like you held me earlier, and you'll do fine."

"She's such a reminder of who hit me, of the hand on my neck, of being locked in the house for speaking out of turn. She's Clifford's baby. His! And he was evil!"

Waa! Waa! Waa!

My heart broke at her sadness. "But Ms. Daisy." I patted the little bundle. "She is you. I see your black hair, and I see your face. She's fragile like you."

Ms. Daisy let go of my hand and reached for her baby, running her fingers through the angel-like hair of her little girl. "I struggle to forgive, and I hold grudges. My life was planned for me before I had a say."

I nodded. "My life isn't letting me have a say either, but Pastor Cody and my grandma said we're all messengers of hope, if we'll follow God. I'm trying, but my following myself gets in the way of obeying God sometimes."

"I've argued with God and even said horrible things to Him."

"He'll forgive you. He's like that. Besides, you're a mama now, and you can show your little baby good things. Show her how to be brave. Give her you."

Weeping, Ms. Daisy's hands covered her face, and her muttering became a duet of crying, hers and the baby. She couldn't bring herself to pick up the tiny thing.

So I cradled Baby in my arms, and moved across the breezeway into the twilight of the parlor, and sat in the rocker. "Jesus loves you, this I know, for the Bible tells me so. Little ones to Him belong, Baby, you are weak, but He is strong." Singing my revised version of this song, one I learned in the short time I was with Grandma Elsie, I stopped mid-rock, startled by the shadow in the room. "Ms. Daisy?"

"Yes, did you notice? She likes your singing."

"No, it's not me. It's the music. It calms her. Here you take her, and sit in the rocker with her." I passed Baby to her mama. "Hold her close. Never let go. She's you. Only smaller."

Ms. Daisy cuddled her little girl, singing the same song, "Jesus loves you, sweetheart. This I know," and the creaking rocker sang its own tune as a calmness settled in the house, and the moon's glow shone through the window.

"Twinkle, twinkle, little star …" Ms. Daisy broke into a new song, almost as if she sang to herself, for the baby's eyes were closed sound asleep.

I gazed upon the beauty in front of me, lost in the love exchange taking place. This picture was an artist's dream for sure. Molasses would love to sketch this for a good memory.

Sitting on the floor, I pretended this is how my mama would have held me and how she would have looked at me, as she gazed into my face. That is, if she had lived.

Daisy slowed the rocker, and motioned to me to come to her.

"Me?"

"Yes, Shoelace."

I rose and shuffled over to her, and Ms. Daisy kissed me on the forehead. "Thank you for being you, for reminding me to be me. I see my little girl with new eyes, and my heart is hers." She kissed my cheek. "And I have you to thank for this."

"Me?"

"Yes, you. You, my sweet little blessing."

"Me, a blessing?"

"Well, I'm sure it depends on who you ask. But for me, you have given me hope."

"That's it."

"What?"

"That's her name."

"What?" Ms. Daisy kissed her little girl on the head.

"Her name ... her name is ... Hope!"

"And so she will be from this day forward. Her name is Hope Morning." Ms. Daisy scratched her head. "But I can't stand the name Morning. It's not who I am, either. I am tired of Morning and mourning."

"Then change it back to Shaw. She could be Hope Shaw, and Daisy Shaw, and I'll pretend you have another daughter, and her name could be ... Annie Grace Shaw."

Ms. Daisy reached for my chin, "Your name is Annie Grace?"

"Yes ma'am. My birth name. My hobo name is Shoelace."

"Then my little girl will be called Hope Grace Shaw after you."

Thud-a-thump. Thud-a-thump.

Ms. Daisy carried Hope in her arms, and walked through the breezeway, opening the door to the L-shaped back porch. "Goodness. It's the rooster. No one put him in the coop."

"I'll take care of it." Although, I had no idea how I was putting a rooster up, as I'd never done so before, I volunteered. I couldn't ruin this moment for Ms. Daisy.

"Thank you. I'll put Hope to bed."

"I'll be right back." I charged to the porch, and down the stairs on the other end of the L-shaped house, to where no one has died, and bounced off … a shadow.

It hovered in front of me, holding a gun!

Rooster with a Gun

"Mahlee! It's me! It's me! Shoelace!" I stumbled over the first step, going down, and rolled like a ball to the boots of the person backing up in the yard. I called to the face showing itself. "Mahlee?"

"Get up. No need to cry." The voice was heavy with fog and dampness, and I crouched on my knees.

I called from the ground. "Mahlee! I've searched for you everywhere. Followed you through the woods. To the bunker. Everywhere. Why do you do this? Why?" I skirted backwards on my hands, my fingers clinched the grass, and I crawled like a tarantula—reaching for the huff-puff person.

The voice responded, "I should have known you'd come out here."

"Come out here? I shouldn't even be in this town. I shouldn't be anywhere except on a boxcar with you. We could ride to the mountains and watch the waterfalls. We could go where I have you. And you have me."

"You're not right in the mind. You're confused. You should be in school. You need a real family. Riding the rail isn't something little girls do. And did you say something about a bunker?"

"No! No! I am not confused. I'm in my right mind."

The low growl moved closer to me. "You need help. We can get you help."

Standing up, I raced up the porch steps, and remembered my strength comes from God, and I used my brave voice, the one tucked deep inside. "I don't need help. I need you. My feet slip when I'm not with you. I need you to watch over me. To protect me. I see death in this town. You're the shade over me. Mahlee, please stop running from me."

"Running? You're the one running."

Shaking my head, I heard a garbled voice, not the one my Mahlee would use. I took a step closer. "Come from the shadows. Come out where I can see you." I wiped my eyes, "I can't see your face. I need to see your face."

Huff-puff. Huff-puff.

Mahlee moved away from me as I hopped back down the steps, my loose hair whipping against my shoulders. "Don't you know your own daughter? It's me. Your Shoelace."

Darting to her, I pushed the gun from her hand, and she grabbed my arm with the other. "Come to your senses child. What are you doing?"

"My senses? I've looked for you for weeks, and every time you have left me, You're the one who needs to come to her senses."

"Me? I'm not the one standing on the back porch of a family who doesn't belong to me. I'm not the one who has moved in with Ms. Daisy."

"I haven't moved in. I met her husband when he picked me and Crush up. We were soaked from the rain, and hungry. Then Crush and me got into a fight, and he got burned in the hearth. I had no plan to stay, the plan kind of happened."

"So you're not here with them?"

"Here with them?" Straining, I gazed up and Mahlee stepped to the side where the moon's light lit her face. "You're not my Mahlee. Why did you act like her? Why?" I pounded my hands on the chest of a uniform, the one belonging to Officer Tock.

"I never said I was your Mahlee. But apparently she's here, or you wouldn't have had a conversation with her in the dark. Child, you should be in school, not running from life."

Squirming free from his grasp, I hollered, "I shouldn't even be here. I shouldn't!"

"But tell me. What are you and Mahlee up to? Why did she come home?"

"So you think she's here too?"

Sighing, Officer Tock grumbled. "You're a mixed up child. I'm sorry you're involved, but the unraveling of the sins of others has trapped you too."

"I'm not trapped. I'm free. I can go where I want. Do what I want. I don't belong to you. I'm free."

"Then why? Why search for Mahlee, or pretend to be searching for Mahlee? Why go after someone who doesn't appear to want you?" Officer Tock placed his gun back into his holster.

"I'm not pretending anything. You're the one pretending to be a cop in the shadows, but you're up to something yourself. Who lurks in someone's yard in the dark?"

"I'm an officer. I'm keeping you all safe."

Rolling my eyes, I folded my arms. "Sure you are."

"Mahlee's got you planted here in the house with her sister, doesn't she? She's wants you to be her eyes. Seems everyone wants the money. Everyone."

"Money? I don't know what you're talking about. I came outside to get the rooster, and then you tricked me. You pretended to be Mahlee. And you think I want money?"

"I didn't pretend anything. I was patrolling the area and making sure the Sanders House is secure. I heard a noise, and came around the house to check on everyone."

"Sure, you did."

110

"And you're a hobo girl who sees things in the dark."

I stomped the ground in my bare feet, my toes gritty, and they glued to the grass like sadness stuck on a heart. "I don't see things. I see ... I see ... possible."

"Possible?"

"Yeah! Possible. It's like Pastor Cody tells his people at the creek, he tells them ..." I fumbled for my defense, sure I had one, sure it was inside, sure I could talk my way out of this one. I paused, leaning on the rail and saw a twitching nose, and there he was, Powder. The polka dotted mouse ticked his little feet on the rail, and his beady eyes watched me.

"What are you looking at?" Officer Tock's tone grew intense, his patience with me long gone.

"I saw the rooster over there by the water pump." Lying about seeing Powder—I knew what I saw—and I saw a mouse with dots. No one can tell me different, so telling Officer Tock isn't going to change a thing.

**

Creak!

"Shoelace? What's taking you so long?" Ms. Daisy's kind voice bounced from the doorway to the side breezeway, and her silhouette brought beauty to the dark night. "Who is there with you?"

Officer Tock used his firm in-charge voice. "It's me, Ms. Daisy. Just making some rounds. Heard a noise."

"Go home, Harold. It's too late for you to be on my property. People get stabbed on this porch. You and I are not friends. Never will be."

"Sorry, Ms. Daisy. Meant no harm."

Gulping, I found myself standing between the officer with a gun on his belt, and Ms. Daisy, who wore a brave face and a nighttime 'I'm-gonna-stand-up-for-things' stance. I moved toward her, smiling, and something inside told me, she's made like Mahlee on the inside. She's braver than she knows.

"Come on, Shoelace. It's late. Too many things wander in the night hour. Some are what they seem. Others are not worth seeing."

Ha! Ha!

Grabbing my belly, the sorrow of the last two weeks turned to uncontrollable hysteria, and I fell on the porch, holding onto a rail, while putting my hand to my mouth. "Officer Tock isn't worth seeing even in the daylight."

Officer Tock made a fist, but put his hand in his pocket before Ms. Daisy saw him. "I'll be watching you, child. You are not who you seem, either." He disappeared around the corner of the house, grumbling words not worth repeating.

Ha! Ha! Ha!

The tears poured from my eyes as if a dam of sadness had burst from the rising water of lost boxcar rides. I was tired from being alone, exhausted from wishing for hugs, and lonely from watching other families. I sucked in the tears landing on my lips, and tried to stop laughing, but I couldn't keep the giggles inside.

The salty taste of laughing tears became a reminder of all I prayed for and wished for, a reminder if I played my deck of cards right, I might get more than food and a place to sleep. I might get a family. I might get Ms. Daisy, who is like Mahlee, but prettier and daintier, and a whole lot cleaner.

My daddy taught me how to act sad for food at the missions these last few years, and how to act hungry by slumping over, and looking downcast. Folks would give me a potato or some apples, and yes, good cheese too.

I glanced up at Ms. Daisy, making a second plan in case the first plan never shows itself. In case I never find my Mahlee, and wondering if I was seeing things in the night, real or unreal—or having a nightmare without hope.

I whispered to the wind. "I dream of places where nothing is left unseen. Where the river washes away the hurts, and where little girls without a home get one."

Ms. Daisy tiptoed in her long gown to me. "Come child. Come to me." Her arms were reaching for me.

"Me? You want me?" I found myself asking this for the second time tonight, and hoping to believe Ms. Daisy's words were real.

"Yes, child. You need someone to love you tonight." Ms. Daisy's confidence rose up from her toes, a sign of the Shaw strength. I had it too. I had strength. Mine comes from God. Pastor Cody said so.

Running to her side, she corrected me for my attitude, "Shoelace, laughing at Officer Tock isn't needed this late hour. Come to bed." She giggled under her breath. "Sorry, he is the funniest little man, much like a cartoon character. Just not sure which one."

Together we laughed, hugging each other like a good laugh might solve everything.

Ha! Ha! Ha! Ha!

We walked hand in hand, sauntering together through the door like a mama and her daughter. I paused, glancing at the yard, seeing Silas kneeling beside his cot in the dim light through the bedroom window of the kitchen house. "Do you smell smoke?"

"No, it's fog, my dear."

Gaaalampt! Gaaalampt!

I spun around with Ms. Daisy and we jumped like two rabbits, and she called to the thump. "Who's there? What in the world?"

Officer Tock screamed. "Get Silas and Molasses. The Methodist Church is on fire. We need buckets of water. And we need them now!"

Ashes to Ashes

Smoke billowed from the rear of the church, and swirled upward like dark angels ballooning to the sky, disappearing above the trees. More flutters of smoke puffed up, spitting ash from within the flames. The orange glow hung low, flickering for a second, only to shoot a burst of embers like a volcano ready to explode.

Staying at the Sanders House was the order I received from Pastor Cody when he hurried to the church, but obeying the command fizzled as soon as Silas drove away with Marion Kane, as soon as Molasses and Pastor Cody went with them.

I remember saying, "I'll stay here. I promise," but remembering and doing what someone asks me isn't easy when I feel my toes buzzing to run—especially when there's a fire. So I ran behind Silas' truck like a puppy chasing its master.

The crackling of the church wall sent Officer Tock and Silas scrambling too. Tock yelled, "Someone set this church on fire. I can smell the gasoline." He ran for another bucket of water from the line of men bending and pushing buckets into each other's hands. The well in the yard next to the church held enough water to put the fire out, but getting the water to the church was like pouring a single glass of water onto roaring flames.

Cough. Cough.

Choking, I bounded through the chaos, my ears burning, and a man in the smoke yelled. "This is my old home church. It's been here as long as I can remember."

Another woman wearing her nightclothes and with rollers in her hair, held her hand to her chest, and wept. "This is where I married my husband. We raised our children in this church."

On the dirt road on the other side, pickups lined end to end, and they were covered in ashes. I tried to see what was happening, to see the fire. To get a good look. Why a fire draws me in, I don't know. It's deadly. It burns. It causes pain to Crush because of me. But I couldn't leave.

Folding my arms, I talked to myself. "You should go back. You bring trouble. They don't need your help."

A slug on my arm came with those exact words. "You should go back. Your bring trouble. We don't need you." Molasses' words echoed mine, but when he said them, they ripped my heart out.

"You don't have the say over me."

"And you ... you stay away from my bunker. Stay away from my uncle Silas too. Leave town with your Pastor Cody as soon as you can. This town doesn't need a little white girl stepping on toes."

"I'm not a little girl. It's not my fault I'm white."

"It's not your fault you run everyone off, either."

"You have a chip on your shoulder. I'm not your problem. Something happened to you before I got here. You're taking it out on me." I stomped. "When I do leave, you'll still have your issues. And the color of our skin isn't the problem. It's what's in our hearts that matters."

"Who told you such a thing?"

"Pastor Cody. He's full of words that help me. He's got verses in his head, and he shares them with me."

Shaking his head, Molasses turned away when Silas called to him. "Boy, help us here. The grass is burning. We need to

116

keep it from crossing behind the church to the old jail. History lives inside those walls. Can't let it go up in flames."

Crackle. Crackle.

The night air turned to a blaze of flames, and I could feel the heat like a knife blade cutting the air into pieces. A scream behind the church hollered, "The trees are on fire!"

A silhouette of a person appeared on the church porch, emerging from the sanctuary, and he carried a body, a limp person who must have been inside when the building burst into flames. He called for help. "It's Pastor Graves. He was on the floor in his office in the back."

Two men rushed to the porch, and a *Kaboom* forced them backwards. The silhouette, along with the men tumbled to the ground, and the pastor rolled to my feet like a long ball being tossed on the playground.

I backed up from the pastor, who groaned. "Get the box. It's buried near my wife."

I knelt down. "What box?"

"The one buried by the church where I watered her grave. It holds the ... and they are trying to kill me."

He collapsed with a whoosh of air, and I bent over to see if he was breathing. "Help! Someone help, Pastor Graves!"

The same men got to their feet and two of them carried the pastor to a truck, and I parked myself on the ashy ground wondering what he'd told me and why. "The grave. It's on the side of the church." I rushed to the place where Pastor Graves had watered the ground, but the crackling wood on the side of the church sent me running.

Stumbling over something, I tumbled forward and stared at an empty metal box covered in soot. "What? What does this mean?"

Someone shoved me out of the way, and the night engulfed me, the screaming, the men shouting at each other, it felt like I too was falling into a black box. Like suffocating. Like an alone feeling. Like death in a grave.

A sorrow grabbed ahold of me, and the night, which ended with hair brushing was now a place I could barely stand to be—and I took in deep breaths, my lungs burning with the pain of this place. Why did I ever come to Washington?

I felt like I was slipping through the cracks of life. I needed strength, and needed to go home. But I have no home. I paused, thinking out loud. "But I do have Pastor Cody. He is my best friend when others desert me. He keeps coming for me. But I'm in the black hole inside this night, and no dreaming of living with Ms. Daisy, or getting my Mahlee back, is working. I need to go with Pastor Cody. I'm tired of chasing the wind."

Blinking, I stumbled around, unsure why I chase Mahlee, why I care, and I found myself unsure of everything. I weaved my steps between the townspeople, bumping into some, bouncing off others—holding a small box with no answers.

A hand on my shoulder made me jump. "Shoelace, you were to stay at the house with Ms. Daisy."

"I know. I had to see." I gazed up and into Pastor Cody's eyes, and he pointed toward the house.

"I'm going. I'll go."

"You'll get hurt here. The fire's taken out a whole side of the church." He pointed again to the place where Ms. Graves was buried. "They're taking a man to Julia Chester Hospital. Not sure who they found, but he was found unconscious near the pews."

"It was Pastor Graves. He's not a pastor though. He talks with hard words, not words like you use. He told me someone did this to him, how someone took his stuff." I held out the box for Pastor Cody to see.

Pastor Cody threw the box to the ground. "We'll talk about this later. Get yourself back to Ms. Daisy. Promise me?"

"Yes sir. I'll go." I kicked a weed, and stomped toward the road, and spun around as a crackling kaboom sent the back part of the church into a pile of embers and splintered wood, and the boom enveloped the church in flames.

Squinting, I moved to the left, then to the right, and then back to the left, trying to see around the shirts and pants, the buckets and arms. "Tink? You can't be here. Not on the porch. Not at the church. Not near in this fire. Not my Tink."

Barreling to the steps, I stood in the furnace of heat scorching my face. "Kitty? Kitty?" I peeked into the smoke-filled church foyer, not able to see one thing, not sure if Tink went inside. But I was sure of this, I couldn't leave without checking. "Tink? Are you in there?"

A man shrieked from the yard, "Girl, get away from here. This is no game. She's gonna blow. These sparks are flying." The man tugged on my overalls, pulling me away, knocking me to the grass.

Kaplunk.

He dropped something on the porch, and it rolled to my PF Flyers. "It's a flashlight." Fumbling for it, I shot a beam of light into the foyer door. "Tink? You have to come to me. I'm sorry I haven't petted you. Here, kitty, kitty."

Cough. Cough.

Gagging, my free hand went to my mouth, my throat burned, and my eyes stung. "I can't breathe. Tink. Come here."

A few feet to my left, I saw a door leading into the church, but the orange glow near the other end sent me to my knees. "Tink! I can't get you. Come here."

Meow. Meow.

I pointed the light toward her cry, and on the back of the pew sat my kitty who jumped into my arms. Dropping the flashlight, I hurried from the building, racing to the side road, and up the hill, where I landed in a bunch of Jonquils, wilted, no longer yellow—mostly black.

"Kitty. You are safe now."

**

"Pastor Cody, she's not inside the church." Marion Kane's voice landed like syrup on my ears. "She's not there. She should be back at the house."

Molasses hollered, "I saw her. She was here, but she left."

A man rushing by cried out. "I saw a little girl on the porch by the front door of the church. I pulled her from the flames."

Listening to the chatter about me as if I didn't exist made me feel invisible, and my kitten jumped to a branch over the fence.

Pastor Cody ran to the man carrying water. "Did you see where she went?"

I stood to run to him, and tripped on my shoelace. "Darn it." Getting up, I fumbled my way to my feet.

The man answered Pastor Cody. "No. She was calling to a kitten. I pulled her back."

"But did she leave?"

"Buddy, I have no idea." The man dropped his bucket, the water splashing, and he scowled at Pastor Cody. "Do you mind?"

"Sorry. I have to know where she is. To know if she's safe. To get her. She's like my child." Pastor Cody charged to the porch where crackling noises caused him to look up, and I jumped in giant steps, racing to him. "Pastor Cody. I'm here. I'm right here. I'm …"

A crackling and booming sound rumbled like thunder, and I shouted to Pastor Cody. "The steeple is falling and the church bell … is coming down."

Pastor Cody lost his footing when the wall crumpled, when the slats to the porch shifted. The steeple twisted and shook and lurched downward—crushing—crushing—him beneath the debris.

I staggered like a little girl who lost her soul and I got stuck in a cloud of smoke blinding my eyes. "Pastor Cody?"

Men yelled. Women shouted. Water buckets stopped moving. And no one moved. Everyone gawked as the ashes and flames turned into a bonfire of death.

My Cody lay beneath the rubble somewhere, and shoots of fire shot from the church like pages in a hymnal—where life was losing its chorus, and the glass windows blew from the backside, as the roof folded in on itself.

I wept and screamed, kicking my legs like a riled up mule, and wiping my eyes, I waved my arms in despair. My tears were spent, and I had none left to give. "No!!! No!!! Not Pastor Cody!"

Falling to the grass and rocking in place, I mumbled, my hope evaporating faster than I could blink. I watched the fire consume my joy—and I wanted to die too.

Marion Kane cradled me in his arms, and he wept for the both of us. Some cried for the building. Others knew a man died. Silas knelt and prayed, and Molasses stood next him, holding my kitten in his arms.

Pam Kumpe

Crazy Girl Crazy Boy

With my eyes closed, I block the morning sunlight. I wanted to hide. To disappear. To stay in the bed. To rot like a dead tree. My sadness takes over when I get up, and it fades when I'm asleep. I'm a dead bloom and my petals are dropping to the grass like lost beauty. Pain is all I feel. Pain is all I bring.

The days are passing slowly and I'm in a place so dark, praying for the day when Pastor Cody wakes me from this nightmare. But it's a real nightmare and I'm reaching through the fire, the one, which snatched his life. I keep asking why I came here. Why Pastor Cody had to die. Why Mahlee isn't showing herself to me. I haven't seen her in the shadows or in the woods, or even in my heart. And my heart is broken.

But I see Pastor Cody in my head. His smile. His lanky walk like a tower of strength. I can hear the way he talked about God. I wonder if he's happier in heaven. Wonder if I took his life by running from mine.

I'm shattered like the windows in the church. I'm a pile of ashes, blowing away, unable to move on. Unable to look at tomorrow, as yesterday haunts me.

Scuffle-tap. Scuffle-tap.

I know those footsteps for they come every morning through the door. Ms. Daisy crosses the breezeway by the parlor to wake me, and I'm awake, but I'm not talking. Looking but not reacting. I have no good morning. Only a wishing for goodbye. I feel nothing.

122

Ms. Daisy peeked into the room. "Shoelace, you're a candle in this house. You are light for me. You gave me my smile. I pray I can give you yours back." She petted my arm, rustling my hair. "Please, get dressed. I've got your overalls cleaned, and a shirt for you too."

Sighing, I glanced at her. "I don't want to get up. I want to stay in bed."

She sat on the edge of the green and white quilt. "You've been in here a week. It's time to leave this bedroom. I've placed your plate at the table for every meal, and every time your chair is empty. Please come to breakfast. Silas made pancakes."

Sitting up, I rocked in the bed, mumbling under my breath. "I'm not gonna eat. If I don't eat, I can die."

"What did you say?"

"Nothing." I rocked faster.

"Stop that."

"Why?"

"It's not you. You're hiding in this room." She put her hands on my shoulders causing my rock to get off kilter.

"I am me. I am me. I am me."

"Enough with the mumbling and muttering. Mahlee lost her way when life crumpled around her. You have to try. Try to live. Try to push through."

"I don't want to live. I have nothing."

"You have me. I'm here for you."

"You are only babysitting me, until Marion Kane sends my cousins, the O'Malleys. They are coming, aren't they?"

"They are. He sent for them once he got Crush home in Jefferson. He phoned me yesterday saying Crush had his bandages removed from his shoulder and arm, and his hair is growing back."

"Good for Crush. He's with his brothers. They need him."

"You're needed too. You are."

"No one would miss me if I'd burned up in the fire. Not one person." I paused, biting my lip. "Except for Pastor Cody."

"I know. He did care for you. His eyes sparkled when he talked about you."

I swallowed hard. "He looked at everyone with loving eyes. He wanted to save folks." I sighed. "But I couldn't save him."

"He's perfectly safe in heaven. He's with God. Seems you told me of this when we buried my sister, Della."

"It figures you'd use my words against me."

Ms. Daisy tossed my clothes to me. "I'm headed to the dining room. It's the last room before the steps."

"I know where it is. I might come. I might not."

"One day you'll come eat with me. I hope it's today." She strolled into the front room, her skirt waving like a breeze of hope, but my clothes were lifeless, ragged and torn, worn and thin.

Dealing with my demons and with my past, I slid to the hardwood floor, crossing my legs, and sat in the chair, unable to move, to get dressed, to rise up, or to find strength.

I never dreamed home would be where I don't belong. The O'Malleys are nice cousins, but they aren't my family. They don't want me. They might take me, but it's only because of pity. I'm the girl without a home, the leftover girl who doesn't belong.

I closed my eyes, disappearing into the land where no one cares, where folks might stare—and I am too tired to fight, and I don't even care anymore.

Tick. Tick. Tick.

My eyes popped open. "It's you. Powder, it's been a week since you came to me. Since you showed yourself." I reached for him, but he scooted across the floor. "You have no idea what's going on. I've lost my way. I've killed my Cody. And I can't remember if seeing shadows in the woods or in the night, if they might be Mahlee or not. I see her. I want her. I need her. She's the one I need, but I don't think she needs me. This pain is worse than it ever was before."

Rattling my words to the mouse, his ears twitched and his dots danced with a wiggle, and he scampered away beneath the box springs under the post holding Crush's engineer cap.

Knock. Knock.

"Who's there?" I asked, knowing Ms. Daisy never knocked, knowing no one comes to see me.

"It's me, Molasses." He spoke from behind the door. "You dressed?"

"No. I'm in my gown. Just a second." I pulled on my overalls and my shirt, and took a moment to peek under the bed. "Powder? You there?"

"I'm here." Molasses answered, "But my name isn't Powder. Are you talking to the imaginary mouse again?"

"He's not imaginary. He's real. He shows himself to those who believe in him." I plopped on the top of the bed. "You can come in now."

"I've got your tray. Ms. Daisy figured it was time for you to have company. She thought you're staying alone is making you lonely."

"Lonely? What do you know about such things?"

Molasses placed the silver tray with pancakes and syrup, and a glass of orange juice on the foot of the bed. "You forget. I lost my pa a while ago. I always figured he'd show up one more time before we lost him for good. I used to get so mad at him. He never was a real pa, anyhow. Silas was, though. He's been good to me."

"I liked Skip. He was kind to me. His smile was like Silas' smile, crooked and big."

"I'm glad he was nice to someone."

"You bring anger with your words. You don't like me, do you?"

"I can't say I do. Your hitching a ride the night you did, well, you and Crush got in the way ..."

"The way of what?"

"Oh, never mind ..."

Reaching for a pancake, I threw one at him. "In the way of what?"

"Are you crazy? You stay in this house like you're the queen. You've burned the kitchen. Burned your friend. You were on the stairs when Mr. Morning got stabbed. You were at the funeral when Mr. Swisher got shot. Then, you were at the church when Pastor Graves was left for dead. And your own friend ... now, your Pastor Cody friend is dead."

I yelled, standing on the bed, knocking the glass of orange juice to the floor. *Kasplat!* "I never planned any of those things, and I didn't stab or shoot anyone. I wish I'd never come here."

"Me too. You've gone to the bunker and gone through my sketches. You meddled. You're not welcome here."

I threw my pancakes at him, one landed on the wall, sliding down. The other hit Molasses in the face. "I didn't invite you in here. You brought me breakfast, and not because you wanted to be nice. I know you're just following orders. Don't worry. I will be leaving. Don't you worry yourself one little bit, you big, selfish ... selfish ... spoiled boy ... who spends too much time wishing you were not who you are!"

"You're one to talk. You're the one chasing after a crazy lady who is the talk of the town. She's mentally ill, lost in her world. Just like you."

"I don't mind being crazy if it's like her. She's the best mama a girl could have." Those words stung the second I shouted them, for the best mama a girl could ever want was someone like Ms. Daisy. She dotes on her baby girl, Hope Grace. She sings to her. Loves on her. Takes her for walks. Holds her. Rocks her. I would love to have a mama sing to me.

"You need help. Your Pastor Cody didn't deserve you. You aren't worth anything to anyone. You're an orphan. I heard Ms. Daisy talking on the phone to Mr. Kane, and he had to beg your cousins to take you. Seems they think you're too much trouble too."

"Get out. Get out. Don't ever talk to me again. You're evil. Your pa was better than you. Better! Do you hear me?"

Molasses stormed to the door, as Silas slid into the bedroom. "Now, what in the world has gotten you two all riled up?"

I plopped on the bed, turned my back to him, and didn't answer.

"Who made this mess? Pancakes on the wall, on the floor, and orange juice on the bed and floor. Shoelace, you've lost your friend in the fire, but you're alive. You are alive, child. Go live your life. Get it back—do what it takes to find your joy."

I wiped a lone tear from my face. "But I'm all alone. I don't want to live with the O'Malleys. I like them. But they don't want me. I'm a lot of work."

Silas knelt in front of me. "You're a part of a grand plan. It's leading you to where you are. It's so you can continue being light in the dark, hope for the lost, and you can carry the

127

message Pastor Cody lived for to the broken people you meet in life."

"I don't know how. I'm pretty broken myself."

"Maybe you should take a walk to the ashes of the church, and let the resurrection of a new day speak to you there, child. Try saying goodbye to your Pastor Cody there."

When Silas mentioned the church, I remembered the metal box, and the words of Pastor Graves, and I stood, walking to the front window facing the angry tree. "Mr. Silas, do you know if they've caught the person murdering folks in your town?"

"Not yet. They have some leads, but that's all."

"Is Pastor Graves going to live?"

"He will make it. He's not much of a pastor. He was one of Mr. Morning's men, crooked like a twisty tree."

I stuck my hand into my overalls pocket, remembering I once had a list of names. "Oh no! It's gone."

"What, child? What's gone?"

"I had this paper in my pocket, and an acorn, and a dime. They're gone."

"No, honey. I cleaned out your pockets last week when you were covered in ash, when Ms. Daisy poured water in the tub for you. I put them in your satchel, over there by the dresser."

Running to my satchel, I clutched it to my chest. "Thank you."

"I best be checking on Ms. Daisy, and calming down Molasses. His anger is worse these days."

"Why's he so mad?"

"He's not happy with the deck of cards life handed him. He would like to get even instead of letting the cards fall and playing the hand he has in front of him."

Nodding, I sighed. "I'm not so good at liking my hand, either."

"You will find a way. You have Ms. Daisy on your side, and she has a good amount of kindness for you to draw from."

"She is nice. I do like her." I found myself smiling for the first time in a week.

Silas shuffled to the door, "Be careful. Seems there's talk of Ms. Daisy's brothers being loose in the woods. But, we're not sure anyone knows what's happening, except Officer Teacup came while you slept last week. They believe Ms. Della was killed by Mr. Morning in Texarkana. A witness identified him as the one who pushed her, and who hovered over her."

"Mr. Morning killed her?"

"I expect she's not the first he's taken out. He was a lost soul, a man with power and too much control. And now, Ms. Daisy is getting phone calls and threats. She's fearful, but she's being strong for you and for her baby."

"What do they want?"

"The money. The money. It's always about the money with them men."

Shade from the Sun

Curls of gray puffed around my shoes as I muddled through the ashes on the lawn. Empty water buckets littered the grounds. The destruction had folded the church into a heap of charred wood and ashes. All the townspeople tried to put the flames out, but the church burned anyway, killing my Cody.

The not-a-pastor man, Mr. Graves went to the hospital with a knot on his head. He was rescued from the fire, but again—not my Cody. The nightmares of his lifeless body are vivid at night, and real in the daytime. I put my hand to my heart. "My heart's barely letting me breathe."

Kneeling on the ground, my eyes glued to the spot—the porch—the place where the church bell lay on its side, where the smash of death crushed my hope. Pastor Cody believed in me. He saw me. And I loved him. He would have made a good daddy.

"God, why? Why do I have this life? Why do people die and leave me behind? Is this my fault?" I squinted at the silent blue sky, watching the clouds float away with the answers to my questions.

Sighing, I replayed the past three weeks in my mind, days of death, nights of longing, sunrises with hope and sunsets ending with horror. Of chasing shadows. Of finding bunkers. Of seeing bodies. Of watching them fall.

I rose, kicked a bucket, and inched closer to the blackened steps, glancing over the debris, to where I could now see the old jail behind the ruins. Broken glass and pages from hymnals plagued the lawn too, and the breeze sliding over the land sent ashes in twirls and paper to the road, as if the songs were searching for new pews.

Gathering up pieces of broken glass, I created a flat cross on the grass, longer than me. The top of it pointed right at the church bell. Beads of sweat poured down my temples, and my ponytail hung in my face as I stacked the glass in memory of Pastor Cody.

Stepping back to admire my masterpiece, the sparkles coming from the ground bounced a rainbow of color into the morning, like hope trying to rise up from the ashes. "Look, Pastor Cody. A rainbow. A rainbow. Can you see it? I see it. Do you? Oh wait. You're in heaven. Can you even see me?"

I waved to the sky, wondering if people in heaven see people on earth, wondering, wondering … twirling, dancing, holding my arms straight to the side like a windmill spinning in the new day. "Pastor Cody, the colors of the rainbow are so pretty after a storm, but look at this one. I've made a rainbow for you. It's a rainbow for me too. I hate saying goodbye, it's like following darkness into a cave. I will miss you so much."

I stopped twirling, put my hand to my ear, and pretended I heard talking. Falling to the grass beside the cross, I talked to the glass rainbow. "What did you say? Pastor Cody? Are you calling to me from heaven?"

"It's me. It's me, child. Stop crying. Keep trying. Get your life. Go live. Be a messenger of hope for God. Be you. Tell others about Jesus."

"I can't be me. I don't even know how. I can't live with the O'Malleys, either. I can't be the girl without a family whom they feel sorry for. I can't go with them. I can't. And I do love Jesus, it's just that He has you, and I want you."

I screamed, kicking the glass, breaking up the design, and shouting at the wind, at the trees, at the bell, at the clouds. As the rainbow faded, I cupped my ears with both hands, and talked to myself. I stared at the sky, lying on my back in the grass. "I'm not in my right mind. I hear voices. I talk to dead people. I see shadows. I chase them. And they all disappear. I'm acting like Mahlee."

"Child, how can I help you?"

From behind me a calm and soft voice spoke, causing me to roll over, and I jumped to my feet. "Who? Who are you?"

"I'm the shade for your day."

"Great. A man wearing a silver suit, with a gray hat, and who has a smile as wide as the Red River, you are my shade?"

"You seem like a girl who is lost. Who needs advice. How can I help?" His extended arm felt inviting, but the eyes of the chocolate gaze went deep to my soul.

Backing up, I shook my head. "I have no idea who you are. How will you help me?"

"I can give you a place where hope starts, where little girls make money, where you can pay your way."

"I don't think you have what I want." I moved to the road, to the side of the church and picked up my gait. "I've got to go now. See ya!"

The shiny shoes of the suit-man joined me. "Where are you headed?"

"None of your business."

"I can help you. You need money? I have money. You need a home? I can give you a home. You need a family? I can give you one."

Running around to the other side of the fence in front of the old jail, I put the wooden slats between us, with me on one side and the suit on the other side. Stomping on the green shoots of Jonquils whose blooms had died, I inched along, ready to run out the gate on the other end, when his hand reached across the fence like a snare.

"Get away from me. I don't need a home, and I've got money." I remembered how Grandma must have had some of her money left in the bank when she died last year. Maybe the O'Malleys have it put up for me.

"Sure you do. I can help you. Our business isn't for all girls, but for little girls like you—it's perfect. You need us. And we need you."

Shouting, I charged to the jail's door, hoping it opened, to get away, but the latch was locked. "I don't need you. Get away from me."

The suit-man jumped the fence, and his face flushed with each word he spoke like sin swallowed him up. His ugly proposal made him sound younger but he was old enough to be my pa. He grabbed my arm, peering into my eyes, smiling.

"Let go of me. You have no idea who I am."

"Oh, yes I do. You're the girl who witnessed the stabbing, who saw a shooting, who knows more than she knows, and who came to our town and stepped into our plan. Now you're a part of something you can't get away from."

Creak. Creak.

The metal door to the jail swung open, and another man wearing a matching silver suit came into view. His face held wrinkles, like a man lost in the crevices of bad choices—of sins greater than mine. "Pax, let her go. Stop scaring the poor child. She's going to help us."

"I was only playing with her." Pax backed up, his eyes stuck on me.

The curly haired man who stepped outside lifted my chin, and stared through me like a streak of lightning. "Seems we might can help each other. You help us. And we'll help you."

Pax ran his fingers down my arm. "Awe shucks, Phillip. She's young. Pretty. We could make some money on this one."

Phillip pushed Pax away from my side. "She's a girl. You know what happens when you act like this, and we don't need more—problems like we faced in Shreveport last year. We're only after money right now."

Pax raised his voice. "Shreveport was an accident. She didn't have to die."

"Stop talking, Pax. These little ears don't need to hear of your sins."

Phillip stroked my hair. "But she needs to help me."

Pax fidgeted his fingers together. "Well, if Skip hadn't seen us. How did I know Skip would be there of all places in the woods with us that night? Thank goodness, he's dead now. He can't talk, either."

Phillip put his hand up, like a stop sign. "Stop talking. Stop."

Pax shouted, "Skip always was afraid of us. Throwing rocks at him when he worked in the fields never stopped him from chasing us, but after we locked him into the outhouse with a snake—he never wanted to get near us again."

The two suits snickered as they laughed at their crimes.

Phillip laughed. "It was only a king snake, but it taught Skip to leave us be."

I blurted out, "You knew Skip?"

Pax licked his lips. "We grew up together. He was older, but everyone knows everybody here. He got married and had a family here."

Phillip shook his head. "He didn't raise his son. Or stay home with his wife. He wasn't with them much, but Silas did raise Molasses. That Skip was a wanderer, always on the lookout for something better than being a farm hand."

"So who are you?" I put my hand to my pocket, remembering my list of names found in the bunker last week.

Phillip placed his hands on my shoulders. "I'm the oldest Shaw brother, and this is Paxton, he's second, then we have Mahlee who is our sister. We know she's been on the rail with you—matter of fact. And Della is our sister. Was our sister. And Daisy."

My throat tightened with fear, and I wished to disappear. Wishing to be back in the bed under the covers, I yelled. "God, if you're watching me. I need you. This is worse than I figured." I turned to the ugly brothers. "So you're Mahlee's kin?"

Pax slapped my face.

Ouch!

"Isn't that obvious?" Pax rubbed his hands together, and I rubbed my cheek.

I screamed, "Your both uglier than I figured."

Phillip smirked, "Why? How do you know us? What do you know, girl?"

"Nothing! Not one blasted thing!"

Standing on the porch, the brothers debated about letting me go or about keeping me at the jail to interrogate me, to see if I knew where Mr. Morning's money is hidden.

"I don't know anything about any money. I met Mr. Morning the night he died. So what could I know?"

Pax circled me. "Let's keep her. Let's keep her. She's fresh and young."

"No! We need the money to leave town. If she knows, we'll see her again. If she doesn't, she can find out for us. Daisy must know. She must have hidden the money. It's a small town. This girl is staying at our sister's house."

"So you don't think I'm going to tell them how I met you today? Don't you think I'll tell them about what you have said? I'm not afraid of you." I talked big, but my heart was stuck in my throat, along with a million tears.

Pax wrapped his fingers on my neck. "Talk, and you'll see what happened to the girl in Shreveport. You talk. You die. You hear? We've been watching you. We're everywhere."

Tuck-a- thuck. Tuck-a-thuck.

Hoping to wake up from this nightmare, another page in the Shaw family history revealed more broken pieces. The brothers were criminals and my Mahlee must be hiding out. No wonder she's not always in her right mind. Gosh, and Della is dead, and Daisy is being threatened. Now I am in bigger trouble than before.

I grabbed my neck, trying to push Pax away. "Let me go. I don't know anything. I followed Mahlee here to get her back. She's my mama."

Pax backed away, staring down the road, and the brothers laughed like wild men who dressed in suits to disguise themselves. They shook just like me and their shoulders bounced in sync with the shriek of laughter coming from their faces.

Ha! Ha! Ha!

Pax slapped his brother. "Mahlee! A mama? Never!"

Tuck-a-thuck. Tuck-a-thuck. Honk! Honk!

Waving, I charged to the twisty tree next to the fence. "Silas, I'm right here. I'm here. Silas. Here I am."

Time stopped, and I caught a glimpse of the metal box behind the church on the ground—knowing it was the same box I'd found in front of the church near Ms. Graves' burial site. I ran to the gate, and the silver suits dashed inside the jail.

Screaming, I ran to the passenger door, the window open.
"Silas! I've seen the Shaw brothers. And they are going to kill
me. They're inside the jail."

Silas grinned, "They're not in that jail. Them boys hate
jails. You're seeing shadows again. That old jail has ghosts.
Come on now. A ride over the hill is fitting for this Sunday
afternoon. I brought you a sack lunch. Let's take a ride to
where birds fly free."

Cotton Gin of Hope

Sitting in the seat next to Silas, I bit into the bologna sandwich, and the bread melted in my mouth. "So am I going to be like Mahlee? Am I really seeing things?" I glanced down the road behind us, making sure the silver suits were gone, trying hard to remember if they were real or if my fear wrapped me up with shadows again.

I swallowed the bologna. "Do I act crazy?"

He patted my leg. "Not you. You're more sound than many I know. You aren't like Mahlee when it comes to struggling. She gave up. You won't."

"How do you know?"

"It's the sparkle in your eyes. I see hope. You won't give up as long as those eyes see hope in tomorrow. The way you keep searching for Mahlee is how I should have searched for Skip. But he gave up too. His eyes wandered. His thoughts drifted. He didn't see the precious son he had at home as a gift, or the wife who longed for his smile." Silas wiped his nose on the back of his sleeve.

Touching his shoulder, my tears formed, and blinking, I poured them out like a glass of sweet tea. The river of sadness leaked from my face, as the memory of those I've loved flashed in front of my eyes. Mahlee. Lizzy Beth, my sister. Taddy, my first best friend. Priscilla, his mama. Grandma Elsie. Pastor Cody. Now Silas. And Ms. Daisy.

"Why are you so nice to me?"

"I see what a gift you are. You need someone who sees you as a prize. The O'Malleys will love your eyes."

"I do like their daughter, Sally. But, they love her. Not me. I'm an extra sack of flour to lug around. They want me only because I'm a leftover."

"Being leftover is better than spoiled food, child." Silas smiled, cutting a glance at me. "I love leftovers."

Giggling, I smacked my lips on the last bite of bread. "You act like I'm food on a table."

"And you, my little one, you act like you're dead. But you are a priceless gem, a treasure created by the good Lord. He gave you this life. Soon enough, you'll be old and bent like me."

Holding out my hands, my tan skin glowed with a copper color. "I have big fingers, and skinny legs."

"You have all you need to touch lives and to walk the life God has given you."

Sitting back in the seat, I felt cherished next to Silas— which is the same way my heart rested when Skip was near me—or when Mahlee is with me. "Do you think I'll find my Mahlee?"

"She'll let you find her when she's ready for finding."

"You talk in riddles like a Choctaw friend of mine. Chula used to get me so mixed up. She would have my head going in circles, and I couldn't unravel them."

"Chula?"

"Yes, she's an angel. A real one." My words filled the cab of the dusty pickup before I could stop them. "Well, to me, she's a real angel. She was someone I saw, but others didn't see her."

"She's like my mouse, Powder. A friend to our heart when friends are absent."

"I've seen him. I've seen your mouse, you know."

"He shows himself to the weary, to the heavy-hearted soul."

"But you're not so weary."

Silas sighed, "I've watched my family work hard and struggle to feed everyone. Times have been tough, but the deepest ocean of my wealth was with my family—where I could rest and be loved and where I could love them."

I touched my eyelids, wondering if they were like stars of hope.

Silas rattled on, "Life is beautiful when families hold each other. When they treasure each other."

"I want Mahlee to treasure me."

"But, child. The truth is, she may not be able to be in your dream—she's lost in her own nightmare of lost trails and endless railroad tracks."

"I know." I laid my head up against the side of Silas; his overalls were ironed with creases in the legs. He looked as if he was going to a Sunday meeting, and I closed my eyes, letting the bumps in the road soothe my wounded heart.

Silas hummed a tune with low tones coming from deep inside his chest, hollow and round. The day filled up with music like a piano being tuned for new songs, for new choruses.

His voice changed to words. "Shoelace, the way you fight to live, you have buckets of love inside you. You're driven to shine in the shadows. You bring hope to me. I've missed the spark of youth you bring, and the drive you have. I'm encouraged."

I glanced up, opening one eye, and Silas gazed at his hands, holding them up, letting go of the steering wheel. "These old hands won't be here much longer. I'm an old man now. You remind me of how bright life looks through eyes with a future."

"Bright? I come with a lot of problems." I raised up.

"Silas, put your hands back on the steering wheel."

"You can take the wheel. You should learn to drive."

"Not right now. I'm only eleven, and I'm not even sitting behind the wheel. We're gonna bounce into a ditch." Looking to the side. "When did we leave the main road?"

Laughing, Silas slid his fingers around the wheel. "Child, we're on the same highway. I hope you don't get lost in these parts, your sense of direction is mixed up. Not to worry, I'm going slow. We are the only truck going to Ozan."

"Ozan? Why there?"

"It's a place where good friends live, so I thought you'd like to meet them. They stay in the shade and draw strength from each other. They're like my kin. I expect if you stayed in the shade of the O'Malley's kindness by living with them, you could rest and see what tomorrow holds."

Pondering his words, I thought of the tree house behind Sally's house in New Boston, a memory from my only visit to her home before the doors got taken by the police—after the Phantom Killer came to the country. Shivering, I responded, "They are kind. Not too picky, either."

I rubbed my neck thinking back to the killer who never got caught in Texarkana, and to the silver suits from earlier. Shouting, I called to Silas. "Look at my neck. Is it red? Is there a bruise?"

"No bruise. You do have some scars on your forehead and on those arms. But they're still attached to the prettiest blonde in Arkansas."

"Pretty? Me? Are you sure you can see?"

"I see beauty everywhere, and you are a flower of beauty." Silas nodded as if to agree with himself as he glanced in the rearview mirror.

I crawled onto my knees peering backwards too, taking in the load in the bed of the truck and the railroad tracks running to the side of us. "Benches? What's with all these benches in the truck?"

"I'm taking you to a spiritual meeting tucked away beneath the trees. We need some gospel take-me-to-the-river time with Jesus."

Spinning around, I plopped on the seat, smashing the air from my paper sack. *Swoosh!*

Tapping me on the knees, Silas continued his lecturing. "Now as for Mahlee, her life took her down the crooked road, and she's in them troubled waters." He shook his head. "And she has a hard time grasping the steady walk."

Looking at my PF Flyers, I wiggled my toes inside my socks. "I wobble too."

"Her wobbles turn into crimes, though. Your wobbles are mischief steps, at least—for now. You can make better choices and change your walk, by trusting the Lord for His guidance."

"I could use His help. He might have given up on me. I need new steps. Mine get broken."

"Mahlee's considered by some as crazy, but you're not. She may come to her senses, but she needs a mighty help beyond our means. We need to pray for her."

"Will you pray for her?"

"Why don't you, my child. I'm driving."

"You might not like how I talk to God."

"What matters is, you do talk to Him."

Putting my hands over my eyes, covering my nose, I whispered. "Dear God, I'm back. Silas is making me pray. So pretend this is Him, and I know you'll listen. Find my Mahlee. Keep her from herself. Send her to me. Amen."

Silas added a bit more. "And Lord, guide the heart of this precious young'un beside me. She's searching for hope. She needs you. Amen."

We sat in silence for the next umpteen bumps, and then a swerve to the right sent me tumbling sideways. "Where are we going?"

"We're here. We're meeting behind there. It's the Goodlett Cotton Gin. Our building burned, so we meet here twice a month on Sunday afternoons." Silas clamped his fingers tighter, and the last bumps sent us bouncing up and down like kids jumping on a bed mattress. "Hold on. The last hole in the road is the worst."

Sitting up to the dash, we rounded the gin, skidded to a stop, and dozens of Negros hurried from the shade trees to unload the stacked benches from the truck. I stood out like a polka dotted mouse with blonde hair in this group.

Silas held my hand as I slid from the seat. "This is Shoelace. She knew my brother, Skip. Make her welcome." Silas embraced some other grownups wearing suits, some in overalls, others in slacks. The women wore hats bigger than their heads, and others had scarves wrapped around their hair.

Molasses appeared clasping a guitar, and he pushed between the little kids who were touching my hair. He mouthed, "What are you doing here?"

"I should ask you the same thing. Is that Skip's old guitar?"

"It's mine now. Don't you get in the way; we're having a meeting. And we're going to be thankful." He whipped in a circle, facing me for one last scolding. "You're going to hurt Silas if you get too close. He hates goodbyes. The sooner you leave, the better."

Before I could slug Molasses, Silas called to me. "Shoelace, come here. Sit with me. I feel some foot stomping coming on."

Sliding next to him on the bench, Silas clapped, and everyone's hands clapped with him. The stomping of boots and the swaying of bodies flapped with the breeze blowing beneath the branches of the giant oak trees. Their voices singing *wading in the water with Jesus.*

A group of big-hats joined Molasses up front, and he strummed the guitar strings, closing his eyes. His smile emerged. I didn't know he owned one. And the chorus of voices singing sprouted up in the air like cotton growing in a field. But behind the trees—behind the thicket—a shadow floated across the edge of the fence line—as if hiding—as if the shadow looked at us, but not showing itself.

I wondered if anyone noticed, or if I was the only one seeing the shadow. Was it real? Or was it in my head?

Standing on the bench, I joined the other kids who sang and danced on the benches, who clapped their hands. I squinted, trying to focus on the movement behind the trees, but the swaying turned into a spiritual meeting.

Then I saw two silver streaks—but then again, were they real—or imaginary? Was I even in a town called Ozan? Could I be asleep? Was this a dream? Shaking my head, I sang out, "Wait, Molasses is here—this has to be a nightmare."

Train of Death

The rustling of leaves swayed by the fence, and the music engulfed me. Silas tapped his shoe with a cadence about three beats behind the clapping, but his smile and singing drew me in. Everyone chanted in a singsong tempo. "Wade in the water, wade in the water, children, wade in the water, God's a-going to trouble the water."

Sitting with Silas meant I was safe, and I ran my fingers through my tangled hair, whispering to myself while both my shoes tapped with the song. "I've got to start combing my hair. Pretty hair needs brushing. Maybe I'll be pretty like Ms. Daisy when I grow up. Her black hair shines even in the dark. Mahlee's brown hair is like murky water. No shine even in the sun."

The songs ended, the big-hat women sat down, and Molasses leaned his guitar up against the tree. Stretching to see over the fuzzy hair of the boy in front of me, I examined the man in the big black suit. His jacket hung off his shoulders. His slacks bunched up over his shiny black shoes, and the Bible in his hand—small, not much larger than my foot. He looked older than Silas, and had gray hair at his temples.

"Brothers. Sisters. The train's a-coming into the station." The pastor man spoke with a dancing twitch, leaning from one foot to the other like a seesaw.

In unison, everyone shouted. "Amen," and Molasses stepped over the bench next to Silas from behind us. Sitting next to him, Molasses glanced at me with a hard stare.

Ignoring him, but sensing his gaze, I whispered to Silas, pointing, "Is he your pastor?"

"He's our Chief Apostle, JC Golitely. His sermons are being compiled into a book."

JC Golitely shouted, "The train's a-pulling into the station. It's called the Black Car of Death. Don't get in. Don't step inside. This train is for liars." He pointed to the other side of the benches. "The train is for murderers. Gamblers. Sinners."

He had my attention, and I crawled into Silas' lap, shaking.

"If you want to live, stay off the tracks that take you to death. Stay on the path with God. He's your strength."

The crowd egged him on. "Amen. Amen. God is our strength."

The pastor stepped on his own shoe, almost tripping, and the people must have thought he was getting spiritual because more than half of them jumped to their feet, hollering, "Preach it. Preach. Amen. We are on the path with God."

The apostle raised his Bible. "Follow the Devil, and you will run off the tracks. You will run to death. You will go to Hell." He pointed to Molasses, and I smiled.

Silas let me down, setting me on the bench as he joined the uproar of amens. He rose to his feet, lifting both arms to heaven. "The Lord is with us. The Lord is with us."

I couldn't help but stare at everyone, and found myself whispering an amen to fit in. Molasses leaned over behind Silas. "Your amens don't go with ours. Go find you a train. There's bound to be one coming through. You can ride it away from here. Stop pretending to like our songs. Stop it."

Molasses' words ripped the joy from my heart in one blast of his ugly words. I pursed my lips, laying into him. "Shut up. I'm leaving. You don't have to worry."

"You come into my town, ready to take my Silas from me. He's all I have. He's mine."

Slamming my fist into his shoulder, behind Silas, and without letting Silas see me, I went on a tirade. "You lost your pa. And I saw him last. He was kind to me. Maybe there's a reason he left you. You aren't exactly the nicest person in this part of Arkansas."

Molasses sucked in all the praising and amens floating in the air, and they mixed with his anger, boiling over, and he dove at me, shoving me to the ground behind the bench.

"Get off me," I screamed. No one could hear me as I was pinned down.

The biggest feet showed up next to head, and I cringed, but the giant of a Negro, who was probably another apostle, grabbed Molasses by the neck of his shirt and hung him in the air like laundry on a clothesline. His feet dangled in the air. "Now boy, your uncle needs to get ahold of you before you grow up to be like your pa. We're in church. Leave the little girl alone."

Molasses swung at the man whose muscles bulged from his jacket, whose feet were larger any I've ever seen, and the mighty arms of the man sailed Molasses to the side like a sack of potatoes.

Jumping to my feet, and running to Silas, I climbed over the bench and raised my hands. "Amen. God is our strength."

Silas copied me, "Amen. He is our strength."

Smirking, I peeked behind Silas to see Molasses glaring at the trees behind the pickup, and he motioned to something or someone—like a 'get out of here' swing with both hands.

Once again, a blur beyond the fence post, to the same area where Molasses was gazing, zipped by—and my feet leapt to the bench. I held onto Silas, my neck stretched high, my eyes hoping to see—

Zing. Zing.

Silas tumbled forward to his knees, holding onto his arm, and a red splat of color soaked through his sleeve—and all the amens turned to screams and hollers, and Molasses shoved me aside like a leftover. "Uncle Silas. No!"

Unlikely Friends

Holding onto the branch, I balanced myself in the angry tree in the front yard at the Sanders House. I hoped to see the polka dotted mouse—to tell Powder about Silas. He would want to know, so he could scamper to the kitchen house to Silas' cot for a visit.

The evening sun hung in the sky, and it peeked from beneath the bottom of the trees across the main highway, next to the Tavern. And the hazy shadow of night took over the day and made my eyes water, since the summer temperature mixed with the spring breeze, making it sticky.

Leaning on the trunk, with my legs draped on either side of the limb, I wrapped my feet together.

Earlier, when the gunshots sent two bullets into the no-walls, no-church sanctuary—I crumpled to the ground, afraid. I rocked on the grass next to the pickup too, not sure how I got in the truck, or how I rode home, or if Silas was dead in the back. I was scared he was gone. Scared another person who liked me was dead.

Seeing Silas collapse, and hearing the giant-man bellow out, "I've been shot," rattled me, and I didn't want any more people to die. I'm sure my heart stopped for a few minutes during all the craziness, as men raced to the woods, and women held their children. No one found the shooter, but someone had said they saw footprints in the dirt behind the fence.

Now, I'm sitting in a tree again, and looking at the sun, as the shadow of another dark night is pushing on my head, falling faster than a tick-tock on a clock. "God, why? Why do people get hurt and die? Why can't my life be normal?"

Standing, I grabbed the trunk of the tree, and wrapped my arms around the bark. I talked to the tree, "My world includes too much death, and I bring pain to others."

Pretending the angry tree was a person, I asked the arms of the tree. "When someone loves me, everything feels beautiful. Then beautiful ends with blood, sorrow, and crying."

The tree caught the breeze slipping from beneath the grapevines, and the skinny branches clapped in the wind as if they were saying, "Someone will dry your tears. You will see."

"Who? Who will dry them?" I shouted to the happy branches trying to take over the angry tree.

"You will see. You're not alone."

"I am alone. Do you see anyone else in this tree?"

The other happy branches danced in the gust of wind, and they all clapped, and then a short new branch bent itself closer to me, "You should be happy. Silas is alive. He's not dead. The bullet grazed his skin, and lodged in a bench. The giant-man has a deeper wound, but his muscles are strong. He's going to live too."

"But it's my fault."

Little Branch said, "How can shooting two men be your fault? This place had trouble in the water before you rode into town."

I swung around, and sat back down on the long arm of the tree, the one reaching toward the street, the one pointing for me to leave. "I should go tonight. I've added to their trouble. No one will miss me. No one will care." I rubbed my clean hair, and felt of the long braid in the back where Ms. Daisy fixed my hair after my bath. "She might miss me, but she has Hope. She'll forget me."

A growl came from the front porch. "Who are you talking to up there? Are you taking to the mouse? Silas wants you. He's resting. But he's calling for you." Molasses scowled at me, and I wrinkled my nose at him. "Come talk to him. He is worried about you. But I could care less."

"Of course you aren't worried about me. If a bullet had shot me dead then you would be happy, wouldn't you?"

"I only want you gone. Not dead. I'm tangled in something worse than you know. So come on down, and go see Silas."

For a half of a second, I felt sorry for Molasses. "I'm coming. Let me get my foot on this one spot." For another half of a second, I remembered how my best friend, Taddy, tumbled from a tree when we first met, and how he pretended to fall, and pretended to be knocked out.

Molasses ordered, "Hurry up. These mosquitoes are in my face."

I became a circus performer and released my grasp, and tumbled into a somersault like a trapeze artist, splatting to the ground like a broken girl in a broken world.

"No! Not you too. You can't be injured." Molasses bellowed, his words sounded soft, like he might be human. Rolling me over, he whispered, "Shoelace, can you hear me?"

Ha! Ha! Kasplat!

I burst into laughter. "Sorry. I didn't mean to spit, but you acted like you were worried about me."

He wiped the *ka-splat* from his cheek. "I don't care about you. I care about Silas."

Rounding the side of the house, I headed to the backyard, wishing I hadn't tried to play with a teenage boy who has no happy branches. "I'm gonna see Silas. He needs me."

Molasses bounded next to me. "He needs me. You remind him of things we don't have."

"Like what?"

"Fun. And family. We used to fish together. We used to laugh."

"You can still fish. There's a creek down past the gin, and you can laugh." I searched his face with my eyes. "Maybe you could borrow a laugh from someone. Yours is broken."

Ha! Ha! Ha!

Molasses squeaked out a chuckle from deep within, and his hand went to his mouth. "I have a laugh. It's tucked away."

"It needs work. You're out of practice."

"I agree. I haven't had many reasons to laugh."

We strolled through the grass, in silence going by the water pump and the black rooster charged us. Shouting, I ran. "Oh no! He's gonna get us."

Molasses pulled me along. "Hurry. He's on a terror, those clucks mean he's not stopping until he flies at our heads."

We dove into the kitchen house, tumbling to the floor beside the kitchen table, and the screen slammed tap-tap-tap shut.

Molasses held his stomach. "He hasn't chased me like that in years."

Laughing, I responded. "I'm sure it's my fault. Or you'll say it is. Maybe he wants to see you laugh."

Sitting up, crossing his legs, Molasses sighed, "I have been hard on you. I've not been me since my pa left. I've been angry at him." He stopped talking, and put his hand to his chest. "I wanted a regular family. With a pa and my ma. But my plans went down the tracks."

I crossed my legs, wiping a tear. "I wanted a regular family too. Your uncle makes me feel like he could be my pa."

152

"He's good at caring for folks. He's built for it."

Glancing at the door leading to Silas' bed, I froze. "He's not mad at me, is he?"

"Mad at you? He's upset with me for how I've treated you. He's mad at me." Molasses unfolded from the floor, and reached for my hand. "Let me help you up. I'm not all bad. I'm trying to figure things out, and my temper is like boiling water."

I let him help me up. "You do boil over."

"And so do you."

"I can get hot fast. I get it from my daddy. He could fly off when losing at a card game. He hated to lose."

A mumbled voiced called, "Shoelace, are you there?"

Running into the dim light which shadowed part of the room with an orange glow, I answered Silas. "I'm here. How's your arm?"

"Sore. Seems I'm going to have a scar on my arm. I guess I'll match you."

I touched the scars on my own skin. "I have plenty. You want one of them?"

"No thanks. But I wanted to ask, did you see anyone in the woods?"

Sucking in air, I sat on the edge of the bed. "I saw … I saw … nothing. Just heard the pops."

Molasses moved to his cot, sitting down. "No one saw a thing, Uncle Silas."

Silas coughed, "But those bullets went too close to this little one, right here. You did ride in with only Crush, right?"

"Yes sir. It was me, and Crush. We are looking for Mahlee. I promise. I don't know who could be mad at me, unless it's Pax and Phillip, but earlier you made it sound like I imagined them."

"You did, imagine them, right?"

"If I did, how would I know their names?"

Molasses cut me off, "I'm sure she heard Ms. Daisy talking about them and how she didn't want her brothers coming to Della's funeral."

Puzzled by the silver-suit talk, the tingling sensation of choking earlier made my throat tickle, reminding how someone had touched my neck in a not-happy-way over behind the church. "I did meet two men by the jail today. They talked big, seemed proud of talking about murder and doing ugly things to girls. I'm sure it was them. They told me their names. I'm not imagining."

Molasses wiped his brow. "You sure?"

"I wouldn't lie. I'm sure."

Silas rubbed his brow with his hand. "The Shaw brothers would be crazy to come here. They're wanted in Arkansas and Texas for crimes involving Mr. Morning's men. Our folks have read it in the paper."

Frowning, I turned my head, wrinkling my face. "I may need to get out of here, before you all get hurt."

Molasses agreed. "The O'Malleys will keep you safe."

Silas touched my chin, twisting my head toward him. "You will find your life. And you will give everyone a reason to love you."

"To love me?"

Molasses mocked Silas. "Love her?"

"She can be loveable, like you can be—if you want to."

I mocked Molasses this time. "There's not much loveable on him."

Ha! Ha! Ha!

I got to cackling when Molasses pretended to hug himself, and we giggled like brother and sister, like friends. Molasses slapped his leg, pausing. "Shoelace, I need to ask you to forgive me. We began wrong a few weeks back."

"We did have extra bumps."

Silas interrupted, "I'm as happy as an old tree. It's nice to see you getting along."

We nodded, and I hugged Silas around the neck, knowing my pretending to fit in, was only pretending. My plan to run away was in place. Too much is going on here, I've got to go. Giving Silas my goodbye gaze brought tears to my eyes. "I'm going in the house to sit with Ms. Daisy, and to see baby Hope."

Silas raised his voice, "Let Molasses walk you across the yard. We've got Officer Tock adding us to the rounds. He's going to make sure we're safe."

"Yes sir." I used my obedient, good-girl, not-misbehaving voice, and Molasses escorted me out the door.

I paused on the steps. "Where's the blasted rooster?"

"He's by the barn. Hurry, and you'll make it. I'll watch you."

"Thanks." Charging to the steps, I barreled up the stairs, and across the porch, turning to yell one last thing to Molasses. "Hey, if you see my kitty, kiss her head, and let her know I love her."

"I'm not kissing your cat. You can kiss her yourself."

I answered him under my breath, but Molasses couldn't hear me. "I won't be here to kiss her, it's time for me to go and find my life. And let you have your life back."

Pam Kumpe

When Shadows Talk

The moon cast its sleepiness on the town, except for me.
I'm up. I'm awake. And I'm out of here. Pulling the front door
closed, a gentle wind brushed my bangs from my face, and the
angry tree waved its branches at me, as did the happy branch.
Glancing at the house while twirling around, I walked
backwards toward the highway on the other side of the barn
and corral, staring at the house.

Keeping my eyes on the picket fence, I then glanced at the
barn where the two horses stood in the open corral. I wished
I'd gotten to ride them and wondered if Powder was watching
me. I focused on the fence posts and limbs of the trees, hoping
to see movement, but he wasn't showing himself tonight.

Waving, I whispered, "Bye little fellow. Take care of
Silas. And Molasses. Show yourself to Molasses. He could use
a friend."

I wiped the wet from my face, and stumbled over a crusty
tire rut in the road. "Darn ole road."

Bending down to tie my shoe, the headlights from a car by
the post office shot two beams of light into the night. The
engine idled, and like a snail, the car came into view. "Oh no!
It's Officer Tock's police car. He'll see me. He'll stop me. He
won't like finding me out this late. But I had to wait until after
midnight for Ms. Daisy to turn her lights off for good. Little
baby Hope was fussy tonight."

The car crept forward, stopped in front of the angry tree,
and the driver's side door swung open. Officer Tock uncurled
from the car, pointed a flashlight on the porch, up the tree

156

trunk, then to the grapevines, and then he shot a beam toward the corral.

Ducking between the fence and hiding inside the corral, I squatted, and my satchel pulled on my shoulder. "This thing is heavy." Pulling on my engineer's hat, I made sure it was in place, in case I had to run.

I ran my fingers over the striped cap, the one Crush claimed as his, but left behind. I gave it to Lizzy Beth in Millerton, Oklahoma, and she traded the cap for a ghost tour in Jefferson, Texas. Now it's a traveling hat, and I've gotten it back.

Watching the officer, I noticed his waddle was like a tired man who should be asleep. He moved to the corner by the side street, and flashed the light along the house, only to hurry to his car, folding himself back into the seat.

"He's coming this way. Be still." I scolded myself, and lay flat on the dirt like a snake ready to coil, ready to slither away.

At the highway, Officer Tock drove ahead, and the red lights on the rear bumper became dots in the night. Sitting up, I sighed, letting the fear escape, hoping for the bravery to come so I could make my escape.

Slinging my satchel around in front of me, I unbuckled the flap, digging inside, moving clothes around. "Why is this so heavy? What in the world?" My hand felt of something sleek like a skinny cylinder. "What is in my bag?"

Wrapping my fingers around the metal-like tube, I jerked the—the pistol from my satchel. "No! I don't have a gun. Why? Why do I have this?"

My head twisted in every direction, wondering who put the gun in my satchel, wondering if the person was watching me, wondering how it got inside the bag. Pouring the rest of the contents of the satchel on the ground, I dug through my things. "Bullets. I have bullets?!"

My chest pounded from all the blood in my body rushing to my heart, and I couldn't catch my breath. Digging in the small pockets, I found my last two pennies, and the list of names from the bunker. Standing up and losing my ability to move, I stared over the fence toward the kitchen house. "Silas put my bag in the bedroom at the house. He also put this wadded note inside, he told me so." Shaking my head, "Not Silas. He didn't put a gun in my bag."

Falling back to the ground on my knees, the throbbing heartbeat rose to my throat, and sucking in the dusty air, I gagged. My hands went tingly and damp, and I felt inside the other pocket. "Ouch!" Something sharp jabbed my finger. "What now?"

I shook the satchel until the sharp item fell free, and on top of my overalls on the ground, a knife rested with a drop of my blood on the blade. "A knife. Why?"

Pacing, I circled the corral like a horse in training, and panic shot through my veins. I replayed the last few weeks at the house, how Mr. Morning died from a stabbing when I arrived. How the knife in the kitchen went missing.

Shaking my hair to ward off the fear, I bent down, grabbing the knife. Holding it up to the sky, I stared at it. "No, why do I have this?"

Dropping the knife, I tossed my shirts aside, and grabbed the gun. "I have a pistol and bullets. And Mr. Swisher was shot at Della's funeral. I don't understand. I don't know why. Why do I have a gun? And a knife? Did someone pass off the murder weapons to me?"

My questions poured out, becoming shouts, and my arms waved like angry branches. Screaming like a wolf caught in a trap, I shrieked at the moon, at the horses beside the barn, at the house where Ms. Daisy and Hope slept. I even hollered at

158

the porch, at the fence, and at God. "What is happening? I don't have anything to do with these killings. God, I'm a kid. I need to see my life, and I'm afraid someone is after me. Or worse, someone is making it appear like I'm involved, when I'm not."

Realizing my shouts were at a volume louder than a siren on a police car, I gathered up my clothes, shoving them into the satchel. I grabbed a handful of the bullets, and the pistol, and hid them under my shirts.

"Where's the knife? Where did it go?" I felt of the dirt, glancing so fast at specks in the soil, I almost stabbed my hand. Picking it up, I tucked the knife into the side pocket with the flap. "My pennies. I've dropped my pennies." Rummaging the loose dirt like my fingers were a flour sifter, I found the piece of paper. "The note! The one with the names!"

Holding my breath, I froze in place, sitting sideways on the ground, unfolding the paper and reading it again, not sure what to make of the list, not sure what to do. "Clifford Morning. Pax Shaw. Phillip Shaw. Buck Graves. And Samuel Swisher."

Sighing, I shook my head. "Mr. Morning was stabbed, and I have a knife. Mr. Swisher was shot, and I have a gun. Pastor Graves was inside the Methodist Church, unconscious, and someone left him for dead." My anger grew like a forest of trees set on fire. "Whoever burned the church, this person was after Pastor Graves, but he killed my Cody."

Losing my sense of balance, I could almost feel Pax breathing in my face, the smell of whiskey stronger now than earlier. "I am not imagining. I'm not going crazy. I saw the Shaw brothers today. They're here."

I slung the satchel over my shoulder, wadded up the note and stuck it into my overalls, and charged across the corral to the far side leading to the highway. Hoping to wake up from this moment, I wished the darkness wasn't staring me in the face, for I felt like I'd fallen inside of a deep well—without a way to get out.

My legs wiggled, and I need to live, but death knocked on the door. "God, please help me. I'm yours. I am. I need you. I need you."

A breeze rustled the angry trees along with a few happy trees throughout the town. The air turned cooler, and a bank of clouds rushed over the courthouse, over the café, over the treetops. And if I don't hurry, death would swallow me up. "God, break me free. Let me live. Let me find my life. I'm only eleven. I am … a kid."

Climbing over the fence, and standing in the road, I tried to figure out which way led to Hope to the railroad station, or which led to Ozan, where people wade in the water with God. Twirling, I chose one direction, and trekked on, carrying the satchel of death on my shoulders. I found myself with the courthouse to my left and the ashes of the church to my right. "God, help me. These shadows all look the same."

Drip. Drip. Drip. Drip.

The moon hid behind the clouds, the sky cried with me as the rain pelted the ground. I touched my nose, wiping water from my face. "There. Over there's the old jail. I can go there. I can be safe there. I can hide there. I can get …" I choked on my words, "I can get killed there. I met the Shaw brothers there today. I can't go there."

Standing in front of the steps leading to ashes and burnt hymnals, I rushed to the left, to the side road, and charged ahead like a crazy girl right in front of the jail. "Maybe I am crazy. I don't care if you're there. I don't care. I am leaving. I'm never coming back here. I hate it here."

Losing myself in my ugly thoughts and screaming at the horrible-terrible of finding a knife and gun, of being where more people die than those who seem to live, I barreled ahead, storming up near the gate, challenging the ghosts of the jail to a fight. Pushing the gate open, I ran past the twisty tree, past some bushes, and a branch slapped me in the face, knocking me backwards.

Kasplat!

Tumbling like a ball as my heavy satchel pulled me to the ground, I rose up and wiped my brow. Jumping to my feet, I hurried back to the road, rushing up the hill toward the highway. Skidding to a stop, I thought about returning to the Sanders House, and waiting for the O'Malleys. "Naw! I'm extra baggage."

Spinning around, I screamed. "My satchel. I left it by the jail when I got knocked down." Charging back down the road, my PF Flyers carried me to the ugly-thoughts and screaming-fit spot, and I hurried past the gate—

A voice rose up from within the soggy night like a savior of hope. "Where have you been? I've been searching for you."

Peering up from the wet grass, I whispered, "Mahlee?" Wiping my eyes, "Mahlee?"

"Yes. It's me."

Real or Imaginary?

The wet grip of her hand with my slippery fingers made me smile even in the dark, even with the rain. But the anger and love mixed in my heart, with the imaginary and the real, and I couldn't decide if she was there or not. "Mahlee?"

Her matted hair hung in her face, and her shadowy grin lit up the dark skies. "Yes, it's me. In the flesh. What are you doing in Washington?"

"I came looking for you."

"Why did you think I was here?"

My fingers grasped to hold onto the real, and my heart wondered if the imaginary world of shadows was speaking to me. I swallowed hard. "I came here because your papers giving the house in Jefferson to Marion Kane had this town's postmark."

Pulling me up, Mahlee shook her head. "Well, you are a good little 'vestigator aren't you?"

"So you were here?" I backed up, stomping in the raindrops pelting in tick-tocks.

"Do you mean, was I here in my hometown?"

"Yes. In your hometown. I know Ms. Daisy's your sister. I know Della ..." Pausing, I coughed. "Della is ..."

"Dead! I know. I saw the paper in Texarkana when I stopped in at Hobo Jungle to see some of the guys. Her death at Union Station made the news. They were calling it an accident, but I know Morning's involved somehow."

"So you were on your way to where, when you saw this paper?"

"Stop investigating me. I'm here now."

"But you were gone. You left me alone in Jefferson. Alone!"

She squeezed a raindrop from her sleeve, and watched it drip down her skirt to her brown boots. "The rain is picking up. Let's move over there."

Not moving, I pressed myself against her, hugging her waist. "I have missed you. People are killing each other here. Oh, Mahlee! Where have you been? My Mahlee. My mama."

Dragging me to the porch out of the rain, she held me close. "I've looked up and down the rail for you. What were you thinking? Why did you leave Jefferson?"

"Because you left. I had to find you. You're all I have."

"You can't have me. I'm not good for loving, only good for nothing—trouble."

"Like me. We're the same."

"No! We're not the same. You're smart. You have a heart. You are regular. I'm not-so regular. I don't fit in. The rail's a hard life, it takes a heart and plugs up the love. I've lost my heart on the tracks."

"Stop talking like you can't love me. You can. I know you can. I've got in writing on a piano where you carved it for me."

"I love without being there." She glanced at her hands, stepping away from me. "These hands hurt. Kill. They don't mean to do wrong. They don't want to hurt. I'm like my brothers. We're the lost clan of the Shaws. Della and Daisy, they're the good and kind and caring Shaws, like our ma. We got some mixed up blood somewhere. Not sure what made me or my brothers. But it wasn't love."

The love flooding my soul came to a halt. The hope inside my veins froze with my own questions. And my anger at her leaving me behind and not even saying she was sorry sent my

163

mouth into action. "In the ten minutes it took you to carve a love note saying you loved me, you destroyed my heart in ten seconds when you ran away. So why did you go? Why not stay to clear your name?"

"To clear my name? Are you serious? You know why. Talking to Crush and Marion, they told me the law is after me. I had to get out of Jefferson, and quick."

I backed up, gazing into the eyes of the almost-mama who could make me boil with anger faster than water on a stove in a pot. Putting my hands on my hips, I tossed my shoulders back. "You didn't have to leave. You could have taken me with you. You're all the family I have left."

"Have you forgotten, I'm wanted by the police for two murders in Jefferson? Two murders!"

"But I tried to clear it up for you, but the cops won't listen to me. Mr. Clementine killed his own men. He told me right before the train hit his car. You might have had a gun, but your bullets missed them. Clementine did the shooting. He was angry like the trees in Washington. Greedy too."

"There you go making up a story so your story will fit in with my life."

Shouting, I hit my hand on the wall by the front door. "I need you. I have no one!"

"That's why I'm here. To let you know how you need a good home with solid folks. I'm a hard shell, with a hard heart. I love you. But I need you to be safe. You need better."

"You are better. My better part." Stomping, the clouds thundered with my steps.

Mahlee reached for the door to the abandoned jail house. "Inside. This storm followed me from Hope. It's knocked down trees from Texarkana to Fulton, and it's barreling in on us."

"I can't see. It's dark in there."

"Follow me. I know my way through this place." Mahlee opened one side of the double doors. "This old jail became a boarding house but it's empty again. I guess the prisoner ghosts scared them off."

"Prisoners?"

"Ghosts from the past. The prisoners who stayed here left their names carved on the cement posts running from the bottom floor to the top. Folks say they come out and chase people on Halloween. I've never liked Halloween, even before Lizzy Beth was born."

My memory of seeing the note on the piano with the words: Mahlee was here. She has two daughters and she loves them—sent my thoughts to how Mahlee hid her pregnancy, and ran off to have Lizzy Beth. How she had given up Lizzy Beth at the hospital. How my daddy was Lizzy Beth's daddy, but he never knew it.

Shaking my head at how mixed up my life has been, I remembered how my daddy saved Mahlee when I was five from the three men, the now dead men in Jefferson who attacked her down by the coast in Texas. Who kidnapped her in Texarkana and took her to Jefferson. And now, they're the reason we're being pulled apart. And they're doing it from their graves.

Shouting at the darkness, at Mahlee, and the storm. "Why do the ghosts of my past haunt me? Why do I not have a regular life?"

Mahlee agreed, "You need regular. Not me."

"No, you're wrong! I need you." I shouted at her, "But the men in Jefferson are dead and gone, horrible men, who hurt you. They would have killed you or me—Mahlee, you're not a murderer. You saved me. Just like you saved Lizzy Beth and gave her a brand new family."

Mahlee sighed, "I saved her, so I need to save you by making sure you're with a family too. That's why I came back. I wanted to see you from a distance, to see you happy."

Slamming my hands together in a fist, I found myself in the door frame, half in and half out. "So you weren't searching for me, to keep me?"

"I wish it were so. But I'm headed north for the summer. I learned from Crush how you two came here. Seems Marion Kane used him to spy on you. Seems he was going to make you come back home when times got rough. Or they were going to send Pastor Cody."

Hearing Pastor Cody's name sucked the fight out of me for a second. "I'm not Marion's daughter. He has no say over me. Neither does Crush."

"What did you do to his hair? He's got prickly little stubs growing back. You burned his arm pretty bad, his scar is big."

"I know. It was an accident. We were fighting."

Mahlee softened her tone, "You need a family. So you can learn to control yourself."

"I can control myself."

"Then why are you out here late in the night?"

"Because ... because ..."

"I'm the closest Mama you'll get, and I'm telling you to get yourself back to my sister's house and stay put until your cousins come."

"So you knew I was at Ms. Daisy's house?"

"Yes, but only after Crush filled in the blanks for me."

"So you do love me?"

"I do." Mahlee ran her calloused fingers through my hair. "Come in. The storms kicking up and the limbs are snapping."

I held onto her shirt from behind, and stumbled over my feet trying to keep up. "I'm not letting go. You won't get away from me again."

"I'm going into the room on our right. There's a couple bedrolls in there. Saw them earlier. I went through them too. There's matches and tobacco. I even found a gun. And it's loaded."

"A gun? What do we need with another gun?"

Mahlee twisted, "Another gun?"

"I said ... gun?"

Mahlee didn't push me, but the angry trees broke from their roots and the popping and snapping crackled like firewood burning without a flame—they knew I had a gun.

"I can't see. I'm afraid. Hold me close, Mahlee." My cries went to another memory, the one where Pastor Cody gets crushed from the steeple and church bell. "Mahlee, did you know Pastor Cody is ..."

"Dead?" Sighing, Mahlee answered, "I know everything. I know about the stabbing. About the shooting at the funeral. About you being in the mix. About the beautiful niece, Hope Grace. I also know ... I know my sister's life is in danger. And I know Hope needs her mother."

Nodding behind her, even though she couldn't see me, I used her words to make them mine. "I know Hope needs her mama, like I need you."

"Twisting my words won't solve your life. Or give you what you need. You need a proper home. You should be in school. You need to sleep in a bed with a real family."

"I need you!" I raised my voice louder than the last thunder clap.

"You are imagining a life we cannot live." Mahlee corrected me like a mama. "There's a fireplace over here. Let me get some light in this place. It's been too many weeks worrying about you. I need to see you in the light."

"I don't want you to just see me. I want you to want me."

Mahlee bent down, leaving me standing in the shadows, and a flicker of light lit up the almost used up logs.

"How did you start the fire so fast?"

"I ripped off a piece of cloth from one of their bedrolls. Makes for good kindling." Mahlee faced me, her back to the fire. The glow around her shoulders reminded me how broad and strong she was, not frail and dainty like Ms. Daisy.

"Mahlee, I love you. I love you. I love you."

"I love you too, my sweet girl. I so wish life was different. But these cards we've been dealt, we've got to play them or lose."

"I can't lose you. I can't."

Mahlee held her arms out as if to embrace me.

I stood my ground. "No! If you're not going to keep me, then I'm not going to keep you." I touched my shoulder for my satchel. "My bag! It's out by the twisty tree."

"Stay in here. I'll get it." Mahlee rushed from the half-lit room to the foyer and disappeared to the rain soaked grounds out front. Time stood still, and the flickers raced like dancing guns in the light of the fire. The bedrolls on the floor reminded me of—the ones in the bunker.

Bending down, I ran my fingers over one of them. "These are the same ones. Why? Why would they be in the bunker? And now here?"

Looking toward the hall, I waited for Mahlee to return. "Mahlee? Mahlee?" I raised up, moving toward the door. "Mahlee, are you there?" With each second ticking, the ticks turned into minutes, and with each raindrop falling from the heavens, I worried my real was imaginary. "Mahlee? Where are you?"

More Guns to Hide

Through the storm raging, through the wind whipping, and through the rain slapping water on the ground, the faint sound of someone talking stopped me from moving to the foyer.

Whispering, I called, "Mahlee? Mahlee?" I held onto the dream of having Mahlee with me, and spoke in in a soft little girl tone. "Mahlee, I'm here. Are you there? I need you. Where did you go? Don't leave me again."

Headlights shown through the front window and it was as if a shooting star cut through the darkness from the wrong angle. Moving to the edge of the glass, I pushed the curtain open. "It's Officer Tock. What's he doing?"

A call from the porch rang out. "Over here, Tock. It's me. I couldn't sleep, and was sorting through some things. The weather changed from sultry to cool, and the rain showered me, soaking my clothes before I could get back to the house."

Pressing my nose on the window pane, I cut my eyes to the right until they hurt in my sockets. "Who is talking to Officer Tock?"

Running like a horse in last place at the races, Tock tore through the gate and joined the other voice under the awning. "How's your head?"

"Much better. Someone socked me from behind, and whoever hit me, left me cold on the floor."

I knelt to the floor, turning around, and leaned on the wall. "That's Pastor Graves. And Officer Tock. But I don't hear Mahlee talking to them." Sucking in the air, which no longer danced in the light, I got up, and kicked ashes onto the fire, hoping to quiet the flames. But the embers grew brighter, flaring with new flickers. "I've got to get my Mahlee, and get away from here."

The sparkle on the floor grabbed my attention, and the barrel of the pistol begged for me to take it. I wrapped my fingers around the copper-looking finish and stuck the pistol inside the bib of my overalls. "Mahlee doesn't need a gun. Neither do I. But I'll put this gun with the other one when I get my satchel. Extra guns lying around can't be good."

I scooted my shoes across the floor, and turned toward the front glass doors. The chatter outside continued, and the pitch in the men's voices grew with the lightning. They tossed words in the rain water, and I lost track of what they said, but mostly it was because—because someone was in the room with me. I was with someone. And someone was with me. I froze, and held my breath.

Huff-puff. Huff-puff.

The too-close breathing sent me to the corner by the front door, and my hand went to my chest, ready to pull out the gun. My lips quivered, and my neck tightened. "Mahlee?"

A hand wrapped itself on my mouth, and I was being forced to hush, my scream caught inside my throat. My mouth tasted like sour food, and curdled milk, and my ears popped.

The voice with the hand spoke, "Be quiet. Or they'll hear us."

"M...m...m....ah....lee?"

"Be quiet, and I'll let go."

I nodded. My heart skipped several beats, my knees shook, and I almost fell backwards. "What were you doing? I called to you and you could have answered me."

"Hush. Keep it down. I'm piecing together an investigation. Tock and Graves have gambled their money away in card games like your daddy got trapped in."

Snarling, I didn't like how she compared these men to my daddy. "Daddy wouldn't have played so much if he hadn't liked the bottle."

"I know. The bottle brings greed into the hands of the drunk."

"My daddy didn't get drunk. He ... he only drank until he was happy."

"His happy nights landed him in jail, remember?"

"I know. I know." The sad memories of me and Mahlee searching for places to sleep in towns along the tracks crept into my thoughts, and I knew there wasn't enough rain in the sky to wash away the bruises of my past. Or the lonely nights when Daddy slept off the booze in jail.

I tried to remember his smile, his kind voice when he was not drinking, but in the dark, inside of a jail house—memories fade like a fire burning out.

The shadows on the porch screamed with the wind, and Tock hollered, "We have to get the money. Morning's got a stash of bootlegging money hidden somewhere. It's a matter of time before Molasses finds out where he put it. He's working on Ms. Daisy, trying to get her to talk."

My ear glued to the sentence about Molasses, repeating it out loud. "It's a matter of time before Molasses finds out where he put it."

Mahlee touched my shoulder, "Is Molasses helping these crooks?"

Before I could answer, Tock seized the conversation outside, "Don't hurt the kid. We've got him scared. He'll do what we say to protect Silas."

I made a fist, raising my voice a little. "I'm going to give them a part of me. They better not do anything to Silas."

"Hush! They're going to hear you."

Pursing my lips, I sighed, "I should have known Molasses could be bought."

"Be bought? He's been threatened. They'll kill Silas. Or Silas will come up missing. They're a part of the mob in Hot Springs, or they want to be—but they keep losing what's in their pockets at the tables. They dig holes they can't get out of."

Graves bellowed, "We only have a few days to pay Caponnish back. We need to find Morning's money and soon."

"Where's the money we were going to pocket from the offerings at the church?" Tock pressed Graves for answers. "I saw the box on the ground in the ashes after the fire, and it was opened."

"I told everyone the offering money was stolen. Six months' worth of people putting in extra to fix the floors, and the steps. But now, they think it's gone. Not to worry, I moved the money days before and hid it, in a place no one will look."

"Where? Tell me where? It's as much my money as yours. We're in this together. We have to pay our debt."

"Don't worry. It's safe. I had tossed the box in the ground with the money to hide it, with my wife's body. But later, I had felt like someone was watching me, so I dug it up, and hid it where no one can find it. I put the empty money box back in the dirt, in case someone did go looking for it. I guess they did, since it was on the lawn."

Looking up at Mahlee, even though I didn't see her face. "I knew it. He's not a real pastor."

"No. He's a crook, ready to swindle, ready to kill, he's like the devil."

We both grew quiet, and listened to see if their talk of money would reveal where Graves moved the money, but they lowered their voices as if they were worried the angry trees were listening, or maybe they were worried God might be judging them for being gamblers and liars.

I leaned against the wall. "What are we going to do, Mahlee? We need to keep Ms. Daisy safe. She's getting phone calls with threats. They are going to hurt her. Or Silas. Or even Molasses."

"I'm staying, for now, until this is over. We have to go back to the Sanders House. We have to go now. We have to let her know what we know. We have to—"

Kaboom. Kaboom.

I peeked through the curtain, "It's the twisty tree. It's pulled up from the roots and the tree landed on the patrol car."

Graves yelled, "Tornado! It's got to be. Let's go inside before we're blown away."

Tock shouted, "You're right. This is bad."

The door handle twisted with a squeak, and the door opened.

Mahlee yanked me by the arm, pulling me up the stairs … stairs hidden in the shadows. Stairs I didn't even know were inside the foyer behind us.

It was like she could see in the dark when others lose their light. Like she knows her way, when no one else does. Our stumbling and fumbling didn't bother the claps and roars blasting on the roof.

It was like fifty people were playing horns outside—all out of tune and piercing with growls. Like hundreds of people playing the drums with branches for drumsticks, and like the strings to every guitar in the world broke—and all the music turned to destruction and brokenness.

At the top of the stairs, we hovered like mice who didn't want to be seen. Now wasn't the time to show ourselves. Not the time to be visible. I prayed the jailhouse didn't cave in from the storm, and that my chest didn't cave in from the fear. *Slam-bam. Slam-bam.*

The door bounced open and closed downstairs and we listened to the scuffle of shoes in the room by the fire. "What is this? Two bedrolls?" Tock asked questions, like he knew the answers. "I heard they were here, but I didn't know it was true. Someone thought they saw them near the Proving Grounds."

"I don't think they would have gone there. They'll get blown up from the live ammunition left in those woods, and besides, the Army has closed off the land." Graves went into pretend sermon mode. "I'm sure these belong to Pax and Phillip though. What are they up to? They shouldn't be in town. Not after Della's accident."

I tried to figure out how they would know the bedrolls belonged to the Shaw brothers, but the storm wouldn't be still long enough for me to think. The Della comment did make me wonder what they meant though. I did remember seeing the two bedrolls in the bunker. Were they the same ones? I didn't know for sure. And why would they be staying in the bunker where Molasses kept his belongings, only to move here?

Graves gabbed, "If we don't pay the Southern Club, we'll be hunted down. Tock, we're in too deep this time. We can't come up with thousands of dollars. We can't do it without Morning's money."

Mahlee whispered in my ears. "These two gambled as boys behind the cotton gin, playing poker with school kids and the Negro kids. They'd take their pennies, or they'd take a chicken for payment. Or they'd make them do their chores to work it off."

"I never liked either of them. Ms. Daisy doesn't like Tock."

"No, she wouldn't. He's a dirty cop and involved with the illegal gambling in Hot Springs. He's helped Morning with his crimes, and kept him out of jail more than once."

Shaking my head, I quizzed Mahlee. "Wait, how do you know all of this? You've been on the rail for a long time. Years and years. You don't even live here."

"Every so often, I come to see Daisy. Or I write her, and we meet up by the Magnolia Tree by our old place." Pulling me close, Mahlee kissed my wet noggin. "Daisy planned to leave Morning after the baby was born, and Della was coming to stay for a few weeks. One night when he was in Hot Springs gambling, they were going to catch a train to anywhere."

I grumbled, "People are saying he killed Della. Do you think he did?"

"No, he never does his own dirty work. He probably hired my brothers. They're no-good. They hide in the day and play at night. They creep like worms and bite like snakes. They work for Morning. Lots of people work for him."

"I don't. I don't work for him."

Boom. Boom.

I sighed, "What was that?"

"Sounds like something crashed, probably more trees falling. Listen, they're arguing now. They usually do. When buzzards are hungry for power, no one wins. And they end up eating each other."

Graves shouted, "I'll take care of the money problem. Don't push me."

Tock swore at him, "Look! You're not taking me down with you. Tell me where you hid the offering money."

"It's in Della's coffin. No one will ever know it's there."

"So we'll have to dig her grave up to get it?"

176

"Yes, if you want to live—you'll have to visit the dead."

When Life Isn't Pretty

"Mahlee, get up. We must have fallen asleep. I can see you, so it's not nighttime. Get up! We have to tell Ms. Daisy about Tock and Graves." I pushed on my lug of a mama, the best one mama since forever.

She rolled over to her side, and wrapped her arms around her head. "Leave me be."

"Mahlee! Wake up!"

"Where am I? What?" She moaned with a yawn, and stretched like a giraffe. "Shoelace, what happened? Where are we?"

Sitting next to her, I peered down the staircase to the first floor where the double doors led to the freedom, and one side was cracked open letting in the hazy glare of daybreak. "Remember, we're in the jail place, but you know it kind of looks like a hotel."

"Oh, that's right."

"We waited for Graves and Tock to leave, and you nodded off first, and I couldn't help but snuggle with you. I've missed you so much."

Mahlee rubbed her eyes, sitting up. "Let's go see Daisy, and now, before the storm falls in on her. Silas has kept her safe as best he could, but he needs to know what's happening."

"Happening? We can't tell him. Molasses is a part of this, even if he doesn't want to be. He might get her killed."

"We have to tell him. He'll help us. Who else can we trust?"

Standing, I jumped down the stairs holding onto the rail, and Mahlee pounded behind me. I pointed, "Look, there's the gun. They didn't take it last night."

Mahlee smarted off. "They couldn't see the gun in the dark."

Nodding, I picked the Colt up by the handle, and Mahlee snatched it from my hand. "You don't need a gun. You could shoot someone."

"Or you could. You can't hit what you aim at, even if it's a few feet away."

Tucking the pistol in her skirt under one of her shirts, Mahlee sneered at me, and at the bottom of the staircase, I glanced into the room to my right. "A tree busted out the window and the branches of death are reaching for us." I put both of my hands to my neck, pretending to choke myself. *Arrgh!!*

Mahlee slapped my back. "Stop it. You're not funny."

"I am. I can be funny."

"Of course you would think so. You are a little crazy."

"I'm not crazy. You're the one who's crazy. The one who leaves me behind. Who runs off."

"You're a fine one to talk about such things. Where were you running off to—last night?"

"Oh yeah!" I shrugged my shoulders.

Mahlee did one of her mumble talks. "Running is my game. It's part of my name. When you're trapped in the life of empty boxcars, and no one cares, you lose yourself in stares and glares." She turned to me. "Or if you do have a family who wants you, like the O'Malleys who are your cousins. You go home with them."

I glared at her. "But you're my mama."

I remembered my satchel in the yard, and hurried to the front door. "I've got to find my bag." On the front porch, I turned back, and Mahlee wasn't behind me. "Mahlee?"

Peeking inside, Mahlee placed her hand to her face, and then she saw me, putting her finger to her lips. *Shhh!!*

"What is it?"

Whispering, she shook her head, "It's my brothers. They must have come back here after Tock and Graves left. Be quiet. They're asleep. Or passed out."

I glanced into the room where Phillip and Pax lay on the floor like dead men, and my skin went prickly like a snake was crawling up my back, and my stomach soured. Grabbing my belly, I cried, "I'm going to throw up. When Pax touched me, it made me cry, made me spit up in my mouth. I have to get out of here."

Mahlee made a fist. "He didn't do anything, did he?"

"No, he talked like he could."

Mahlee wrapped her arm around my waist, keeping me from falling since I went wobbly in the knees. I stared at them, and their legs were stretched out like the letter V, their arms made a T, and their faces were hiding in the fabric of their bedrolls. We stood like dead trees in a jail foyer watching them—lost in the scary place where men commit crimes, and where we run off.

Mahlee helped me and we tiptoed sideways, making our way to the yard, not shutting the door. Slipping to the side of the building, I sucked in air like my lungs were collapsed, and we charged around a getaway car. "Is this your brother's car?"

"Who knows. The car could be stolen for all I know. Let's hurry and get Ms. Daisy up." We went around the Bonnie and Clyde car parked on the knocked down picket fence, the wheels sitting up against the trunk of a tree yanked up from its roots.

"I have to find my satchel. It's out here somewhere."

"The wind probably blew it away. It's gone. Come on."

"No! I have to get my bag."

Mahlee pointed to the patrol car. "Car's smashed. Too bad Tock wasn't in it when those branches toppled on the hood." Mahlee grinned, "Come on before Pax and Phillip wake up."

"But, I need my satchel." I pointed at the row of trees splintered and laying on each other like Tinker Toys. "Hey, there it is. It's up there beside those limbs."

Mahlee motioned for me to hurry, and she charged ahead of me, down the muddy road, straight toward the spot where my satchel rested. Yelling, I galloped like a horse headed to its stable. "I'm coming. I'm coming."

Slinging my soaked canvas over my shoulder, I marched with Mahlee as we cut across the field, and we ran to the Sanders House.

Mumbling, Mahlee mouthed, "You have no idea what Morning's men have put my sister through. If she'd only moved to Texarkana with Della, we wouldn't have to try and save her now. But she was so afraid of Clifford. He hit her, and pushed her. He caused her to lose her first baby."

I grabbed her arm. "First baby?"

"Stop pulling on me, you almost made me fall. And yes, first baby. It broke her heart and her spirit."

Swallowing hard, I gulped. "Then we have to make sure she's safe. Hope needs her mama." I picked up my steps. "So Della lived in Texarkana? Why didn't you tell me?"

Mahlee shushed me with her finger. "Stop getting all riled up. What I do on my own is what I do on my own. You never checked with me when you were sneaking out for most of the year when we were at the manor with your grandma. Don't go and get snippy with me. We both have secrets."

"But Della was your sister. She's my aunt."

"You did meet her once at the Grim. She worked in the bakery and she let you taste the desserts. She told me you stared at the glass case with the biggest eyes, and she thought you were pretty even with your nose."

"What's wrong with my nose?" I touched my face. "It's my real mama's nose. There's nothing wrong with my nose."

"See, you don't think of me as your mama. You just don't want to be alone. I'm all you have from the rail."

Screaming at Mahlee, I pulled on the strap of my satchel. "I can love two mamas! I can. My real mama is gone, but I could love you like her, if you would treat me as if I was pretty. Or if you'd stayed long enough to make me feel loved." I spewed my anger at her, leftover from her leaving me in Jefferson, leftover from all the times I needed a hug and lap to sit in, leftover from the months she'd disappear and leave me with my daddy who spent too many of his nights in jail.

"Stop whining, I'm here now. I did come for you."

"You came for me, to make sure I went to the O'Malleys." We charged past the corral, to the back yard, up the steps to the back porch, and the sun broke into the day as we barged into Daisy's room.

Mahlee halted over the bassinet where a baby slept, whispering. "Is this Hope?"

I inched next to her, smiling, not happy with Mahlee's treatment of me, but I wasn't going to ruin the love-gaze she was giving her new niece. "Yes, it's Hope Grace. Isn't she pretty?"

Before Mahlee could answer, Ms. Daisy sat up in her bed, yelling at us, her black hair draping her shoulders like silk. "What is going on in here?"

Mahlee ducked to the floor hiding, something she does when people shout.

Ms. Daisy smiled at me. "Shoelace, you scared me. What are you doing up so early?"

"You're not going to believe who I found."

"Oh, don't tell me you saw the polka dotted mouse again."

"No, it's better than a mouse, better than eggs and bacon, and it needs a bath."

Kabam.

"Ouch!" Looking down at my leg where Mahlee kicked me, I announced, "And it's meaner than ever."

Pam Kumpe

When Ugly Isn't Pretty

"Ms. Daisy. I've got something to show you. And you're not going to believe it."

Sitting with the blanket over her legs, Ms. Daisy smiled, "So you've decided to sit at the table and eat breakfast with me?"

"Not quite." I talked to the floor. "Mahlee, get up. Why are you hiding? This is your sister. You do know each other."

Ms. Daisy crawled onto her knees, pushing the covers off, leaning forward, and she peeked over the end of the bed. "What in the world?"

Mahlee grinned, "Hi, it's me. In the flesh."

Ms. Daisy bounced from the bed, her pink gown flowing to her ankles. Her dainty toes rushed to Mahlee where Ms. Daisy knelt, wrapping her arms around her sister's neck. "It's you. It's you. I am delighted to have you here. When did you get here? Oh, Mahlee! Della's gone. And Clifford."

"I've heard. Della was our glue. She kept you going. She kept me going on the rail. She was our link to each other." Mahlee embraced Ms. Daisy with her strong arms and her big hands.

I couldn't help but notice how big-boned Mahlee was next to Ms. Daisy, and how small Ms. Daisy was next to my Mahlee, who towered over most men. They were like sisters who came from different families, but didn't. Brown hair on Mahlee. Black on Ms. Daisy. And me with my blonde hair.

Mahlee interrupted my comparing of our family traits in my mind. "I rode in last night after I heard Shoelace was

184

coming here. I'd gone back to Jefferson to make sure she went home, but I learned she hopped a train, and came here to find me."

I jumped up and down. "It worked. Here you are. And here I am." I put my hands on my hips, making a joke to keep from getting into trouble.

Ms. Daisy rose from the floor, helping the clunky Mahlee up, and they sat on the edge of the bed holding hands. I crawled up behind them from the other side, grabbing Ms. Daisy's pillow and lying down to listen to them talk.

Mahlee hugged her sister, "I'm going to miss Della. I can't believe she's gone. Smartest one on the family. She was saving for her own bakery." Mahlee wiped her face.

"I didn't know what to do. I had first heard she fell and hit her head, then an officer from Texarkana was following some leads, and someone saw Clifford with her. I don't know what to make of it. He came home with her coffin in the truck and by midnight, he was dead. Someone stabbed him on the stairs." Ms. Daisy sniffled, her hand swiping her face, too.

Mahlee squeezed Ms. Daisy. "It's Pax and Phillip. They've done this. I'm sure they're involved."

"But they wouldn't kill their own sister."

"They would do anything for money."

Ms. Daisy sighed, "I hope not. But I'm glad you're here."

Tapping Mahlee on the shoulder, I reminded her about our pressing problem. "Tell her. Tell her about Officer Tock and Pastor Graves."

Mahlee shrugged, "Give me a minute."

Ms. Daisy twisted sideways, "What about them?"

I stood up in the middle of the bed, holding the pillow to my chest. "We were at the jail. We were caught in the storm."

Ms. Daisy put her finger to my lips. "You were out in the storm last night?"

"Yes, I was ... taking a walk."

"After we'd all gone to bed?"

"Yes, I couldn't sleep."

Mahlee butted in, "She was running away, like she does."

Ms. Daisy added, "Like you do, Mahlee."

Mahlee folded her arms and gave me a go-ahead-big-mouth-tell-her-what-you-know stare.

The mattress gave under my legs and I balanced myself, "So we were at the jail. Got caught in the storm and went inside. Mahlee warmed us with a fire. Then Tock and Graves were in the storm. On the porch."

Mahlee stood up, taking the chance to cut me off. "I heard them talking about owing money to the club in Hot Springs. And how they stole the church offering money but need Mr. Morning's money to pay off their gambling marker."

I bounced to the floor, and my thud sent whimpers into the room from baby Hope.

Ms. Daisy rushed to the bassinet, picking up her little girl. "Hush little one. Mommy's here."

Mahlee and me watched the love pour from Ms. Daisy as she changed Hope's diaper and rocked her baby back to sleep in her arms, humming. She kissed Hope on the cheek, smiling at us. "Isn't she precious?"

Mahlee nodded, "She is the prettiest baby I've ever seen."

I inched up next to Ms. Daisy. "Pastor Cody told me I was a pretty baby."

Mahlee pushed me off the side. "Well, this one has the Shaw good looks like our ma, like Daisy got."

Huffing, I stepped on every crack in the hardwood floors, hoping to break my back so someone would think I was pretty, or maybe they would hold me and think I was special.

Unwanted Sidekick

Kicking my satchel, I got my shoe caught on the flap, the bag not budging, and my heart felt trapped in the ugly—and the heaviness of last night sent fear to my veins, and I trembled at how excited I was to see Mahlee, but how fast I changed my mind, and wished her to leave.

Wishing for a mama comes with dreams of perfection, and having no mama and seeing one you want is anything but perfect. To have one like Ms. Daisy, it's a dream come true.

Guns, Bullets, and a Knife

Mahlee was absorbed with Ms. Daisy's steps, and she doted on Hope, kissing her toes as Ms. Daisy placed her pretty baby into the bassinet. "I've got to fix her a bottle in a minute. She's a big eater."

I mouthed, "You better watch out. She'll get big and ugly like Mahlee if you let her eat too much."

Mahlee walloped my behind like a mama would, "Girl, stop acting so spoiled. You know I love you. I can't have you on the rail with me. I'm wanted for murder in Jefferson."

"But you didn't do it, and if you had, it would have been self-defense. We've had this talk. You are a good person. Mostly."

"Not so good. Not so good, at all."

Ms. Daisy strolled to her slippers, and sat down on the bed. "Mahlee, you have a good heart. I know it. I've seen it."

"It's a heart of stone."

I added my words. "It does seem hard at times."

Mahlee frowned. "I would break you and cause you too much pain."

Ms. Daisy shook her head. "The pain of you being gone is worse. So what are you two doing here so early, what's on your mind?"

Mahlee answered, "We need to get you to a safe place. You and Hope. Pax and Phillip are in town. And Tock and Graves are stealing the money of folks in town. You're going to get hurt. I can't lose you too. I can't."

Her pleading with Ms. Daisy made my heart jump like a rabbit hopping from its prey, and I had to tell them about the items in my satchel. I picked up my bag, and poured out my worries. "Remember how Mr. Morning got stabbed?"

They turned to me and answered together. "Yes."

"I think I have … have the knife."

Mahlee wrinkled her nose. "What? What do you mean?"

Ms. Daisy shook her head. "I don't understand."

Opening my satchel, I continued my tirade. "And remember how Mr. Swisher got shot at the funeral?"

Ms. Daisy responded, "How could I forget."

"Well, I think I have the gun. Maybe."

Mahlee yanked my satchel from my hands. "What are you saying?"

Pulling my bag from her hand, I flared my nostrils. "Someone put a knife in my satchel. And a gun. And some bullets. I don't know how they got there. I didn't have anything to do with any murders." My words went wimpy, my tears fell in puddles, and Ms. Daisy held me close.

Mahlee dug in my bag, and turned it upside down on the bed. The knife tumbled to the blanket, along with the gun and bullets that were hidden under my clothes. "How did these get in your bag?" Mahlee's hand went to her side, to her waist where the gun we'd taken from her brothers was tucked inside her skirt.

"I have no idea. When I left last night, the satchel was heavier than it should have been, and then I was digging in it, and the knife cut my finger. See, I have a cut right here," I held out my pointer finger. "And the gun was inside too, and those bullets."

Mahlee shook her head, and Ms. Daisy announced, "It's time to get Silas and Molasses. We need to wake them up and let them in on what's happening, how someone put the gun and knife in your bag, how you two heard Tock and Graves conniving, and how our brothers are up to something too."

I countered her idea, "But don't get Molasses. He's being forced to help the pretend pastor and that no good cop. He could be on their side."

Mahlee gave an order. "We have to trust Silas. He's like family. And if Molasses is being threatened, then we need to help him too."

"But I don't like him. He's bossed me since I got here. He's followed me and cursed me." I lied, but I needed to make him sound hateful, since he was mean to me. Even though we had laughed together just last night.

Ms. Daisy corrected me, "Are you sure he used curse words on you? He's not the type of boy who speaks with off-colored words."

I shook my head, "Well, they were ugly to me. Maybe he didn't use swear words, but he thought them."

Ms. Daisy reached for Mahlee's hand. "I have to let you in on something too. You mentioned the offering money. Well, I have it."

Mahlee squinted, "What? But I heard Graves tell Tock it's in Della's coffin."

Ms. Daisy cleared her throat. "It was. Graves had Big Jake reopen the coffin so he could put some of Della's personal things inside. Jake figured it was suspicious, so he told me about it, and we opened the grave up the next day. And found the money..." She moved to the pillow on the far side of her bed, where Mr. Morning would have slept if he was alive.

Mahlee asked, "What are you saying?"

"I have the money. It's right here. I'm planning on getting the money into the right hands, so they can start building a new church. Tock and Graves aren't using God's money to pay for their sins." She slid a canvas bag from inside the pillow case. "Here it is. Several thousand dollars."

My eyes were wide, my thoughts calculating and figuring, and wondering and confused. We stood there circled around the bed with the offering money, with the knife, and with the gun—all possible clues to the murders in Washington, but I had no idea who might have done the killing.

I couldn't stay quiet. "But they think Mr. Morning has some money tucked away. Does anyone know where he hid things?" I quizzed, using my 'vestigator voice. "If he has money, then it's your money, Ms. Daisy. You could move to another place where you're safe."

Ms. Daisy shook her head. "This is home. Well, it's actually Silas' home, he has the deed. But he's offered to let me stay and raise Hope here, so long as he can stay on in the kitchen."

My heart beat with hope. "I knew Silas was kind, a bigger kind than regular ole kind."

Ms. Daisy smiled. "If all men were like Silas, this world would be a grand place to live."

I agreed. "He's been good to me."

Mahlee broke into our talking. "Shoelace, go wake up Silas. And wake up Molasses too. We've got some decisions to make."

The sisters gathered the items from the bed, putting the gun and knife between the mattress and the box spring, and Ms. Daisy hid the money back inside the pillow case.

I gathered up my clothes and shoved them back into my satchel, and on the last pair of overalls I picked up, I remembered the note with the names—knowing I needed to tell Silas, but I tucked that thought away for later.

Mahlee shooed me out the door to the back porch. "Get Silas. And Molasses. Get them before the town wakes up."

Knock. Knock. Knock.

Running across the side foyer to the front room instead of going to the kitchen house, I peeked out the window to the front porch—and the get-away car from the jail, the black shiny vehicle now sat on the road in front of the Sanders House. I stormed back to the bedroom, "It's Pax and Phillip. They're here!"

Mahlee sent me to the back porch. "Get Silas. And go now!"

Two Guns Are Better than One

Pounding across the grass from the kitchen house, Silas, Molasses, and I rushed to the back porch. The sun exploded from behind the trees to my right, and shining beams of daylight landed on the garden. But it was too bright, too harsh, and too much light. The sun appeared as though it might blow up too. The rooster flew at me with his black feathers flapping, and he brushed my face. "Get away from me."

Molasses turned to me. "Watch out. He's been in a mood lately."

I yelled, "Just get to Ms. Daisy. Don't let her brothers do anything."

With a hammering of Silas' steps, and his giraffe gait, I could see the long gun sticking from the side of his body. "Ms. Daisy? Ms. Daisy? You all right, Ms. Daisy?" He called with a cadence, his breath shallow, his age showing. His suspenders dangled from his hips. "Ms. Daisy? Ms. Daisy?"

Molasses had taken a knife from the shelf next to the hearth. It looked like a butcher knife, but he said it was a James Bowie knife belonging to Skip. His words were, "I may need to keep Uncle Silas from getting hurt."

Molasses stormed behind Silas ready to defend Ms. Daisy, and ready to help Silas. I bent down, grabbed a rock the size of a baseball, and held it with my fist. "I have a pretty good aim. I may need to help both of them." I reached for another rock near the shrubs beside the back porch steps and held it with my other hand.

Silas loved Ms. Daisy and little Hope Grace as if they were kin, like their skin matched, which it doesn't. But it didn't matter, for their hearts were the same. I rushed inside, not sure how I could help or what I should do. I've got two rocks, and I'm ready to hurl them.

Silas had made a phone call from the kitchen where the pie orders come in, and he gave out an order like an Army Sergeant on the receiver. "Bring your gun and come to Washington." He then pulled on his work boots and charged to the gun, and out the door with Molasses and me following him.

Barreling into the main house with Molasses next to him, Silas ordered the room to a halt. "Stop! Everyone be still." He stood across from Pax and Phillip, and Ms. Daisy held her baby across the room. Mahlee was next to her and I hid behind Silas. "You boys better leave before you get yourself filled with buckshot." He held the gun with a shaky grip.

I grabbed ahold of one of his suspenders when Pax took a step forward in his black scuffed work-type boots. "Now, Silas. We happen to come to town to pay Mr. Morning a visit since we learned of his passing. We came to pay our respects."

Peeking from behind Silas, I shouted, "You aren't here to pay your respects. You're here to get paid. Right, Mahlee?"

Molasses broke into the conversation. "Mahlee, when did you get here?"

Mahlee put her hands on her hips, her stance like a guard. "Look at you, Molasses. All grown up, I see."

He held his knife across his chest like a shield, first glancing at me, then her. "Mahlee? I didn't figure you were in town."

"Just got here. Been looking for Shoelace."

Smiling, but still shaking behind Silas, I added my words. "She found me, but Mahlee, you said your brothers are criminals and they're wanted by the cops, and they used to get

194

paid by Mr. Morning to do his dirty work, which didn't mean gardening."

Silas held the shotgun with one hand, and put his other hand over my mouth. "Enough girl. Not the right time for a young'un to talk."

Phillip spoke up. "We've dropped by to check on our sister. Tell them, Daisy. Tell them, how you're happy to see us. How we're family no matter what happens. After all, the four of us haven't been in one room together in years. Not to worry though, we're not staying long."

Pax argued, "But you said we could get some breakfast first. You said we could sleep here tonight. You said we could stay with Daisy since Morning is gone, so we can find ... and get ..."

Phillip touched Pax on the shoulder. "Little brother, we're coming by to pay our respects. Daisy may have a little food for the road. Right, Daisy?"

I stared at the brothers who were wearing blue jeans and buttoned shirts. Pax wore green and Phillip sported a blue shirt. Phillip had on brown shoes, but the black boots Pax wore—sent my mind to last year when the Phantom Killer pushed me from a boxcar. "Oh no! Same type of boots!" I screamed, stepping to the corner of the room, trembling. "You aren't the—you aren't the..."

Falling to the floor, I crumpled and held my knees like Mahlee does on Halloween, like she does when her head gets trapped in places she can't escape.

Ms. Daisy handed Mahlee the baby. "Here, take Hope." She rushed to me, kneeling. "Honey, it's all right. No need to be afraid. My brothers talk a big game, but they're not here to hurt us." She glanced at them. "Are you?"

I mumbled, "But Pax ... he's the one who touched my neck and talked like a sick-in-the-head man."

195

Pax coughed, "I'm not sick. I'm not. I have …"

Phillip shouted, "Pax, shut up."

Pax obeyed like a well-trained puppy. "I'm just playing with her. No need for everyone to get riled up."

Daisy assured me, while helping me stand. "They're rolling through town—on their way to somewhere. I'm sure of it." She held me close, moving me to the sofa on her side of the room.

Pax giggled, "Silly little girl. Your skin so soft. With your hair blonde. You're a nice little girl."

Phillip grabbed his brother by the shoulders. "Enough. She's already afraid of us. Leave her alone." Phillip looked at me. "No one's going to hurt you."

I held a pillow in my lap, scowling, choking on the words backing up in my mouth. Silas put himself between me and the Shaw brothers. "Maybe you two should go. Enough with paying your respects." He clutched the gun aiming for his prey.

Molasses manned up, running his fingers over the blade of his knife. "Yeah! You better get going."

I mouthed, "Go! Leave us alone!" I noticed Mahlee rocking sideways in her stance, and she shivered from seeing her brothers, as if she had a secret about them bigger than I could imagine.

Pax dove for the shotgun, yanking it from Silas' grasp. "Old man. What are you doing with a gun? You could hurt someone with this." He pushed Silas in the side with the barrel. "Breakfast. I want me some pancakes and eggs. And make my eggs over easy."

Silas muttered, "Ma'am, should I fix them their breakfast so they will leave?"

Ms. Daisy owned the room with her charge to her brothers. "Will you go if I feed you?"

Phillip seized the gun from Pax, and handed it back to Silas. "Sorry for our behavior. We're a little tired this morning. A little food for the road might be good."

Phillip's words sounded smooth, but the way they slid out from his mouth, I knew they were deadly like venom from a snake—because if we didn't do what he said, breakfast was the least of our worry.

Ms. Daisy twirled around like the boss of her brothers, and like the boss of the house. "Silas, let's have breakfast. I'm tired of eating alone in the dining room. I have Mahlee. I have my brothers. And I have my baby girl. I have this precious guest, Shoelace too. Pancakes and eggs for everyone." Her excitement made it sound like we were having a party, but the celebration came with unwanted sidekicks and unwanted guests.

Silas leaned on the barrel of the gun. "Ms. Daisy. You sure?" He leaned toward her with a glance full of questions.

"Yes. Breakfast is served in twenty minutes. Let me get out of my gown. Hope needs a bottle, and Mahlee, you need to wash your hands and face. Shoelace, put some water in the wash bowl from the pump out back. Get plenty for Pax and Phillip. They can wash up too."

I jumped up and stood on the sofa. "I don't think they should stay for breakfast. They should leave. This doesn't make sense. They're after your money. Or Mr. Morning's money."

Mahlee jerked her head as if she woke up. "Shoelace, get the water. Breakfast first. The rest will sort itself out." Her words bounced across the room as if she knew something no one else did.

I leapt to the floor giving Pax my evil eye. "I'll get the pitcher in the bedroom. I'll be right back." Hurrying to the side foyer, I hid behind the wall to listen to the rest of the grownup talk.

Silas spoke to Molasses. "We'll get breakfast going. Come with me, Molasses. I need your help in the kitchen."

"I'll send Pax with you to make sure you make our eggs the way he likes them. And I'll … I'll take me a smoke on the front porch." Phillip's words filled up the room like a balloon filled with blood. "Now sweet sister. Don't think about calling Officer Tock. He's not invited to our little breakfast party."

"I'm not calling him. I'm getting dressed and going to fix a bottle for my little girl." The front door creaked, and slammed closed, and I could see through the window to my left to the back porch. Clinging to the wall like wallpaper, Molasses went by first, then Silas, and then the ugly Pax.

Mahlee and Daisy slid into the bedroom as I hid on the other side of the wall-table. I peeked into the bedroom and Ms. Daisy put her hand on Mahlee's arm. "Get the gun under the mattress. And the knife."

Mahlee answered, "I've already got a gun." She touched her waist on her skirt. "I snatched it from Pax and Phillip last night."

Ms. Daisy smiled. "I'll put Hope down after I feed her, and I'll load this gun and put it in my skirt too."

Creak. Creak.

I wiggled on the other side of the little table next to the wall, as Ms. Daisy glanced down at me. "Sorry, I was listening. I had to see what you were doing."

Ms. Daisy nodded. "Just be ready to duck under the table if Pax and Phillip aren't here to eat!"

Eggs Too Sour

Pretending to enjoy my rubbery eggs, I peered at Pax who happened to sit across from me. The dark wood table sat covered in the white China plates with the scribbly etching on the edges. "Phooey! These are terrible. Must be who I'm looking at."

Mahlee sat on my left, and she spit her eggs out too. "What's in these?"

Ms. Daisy stirred her eggs with her fork. "Are they ruined? Maybe the eggs were bad." She put a bite in her mouth, tried to swallow, and gagged. "Horrible. Horrible eggs."

Pax stabbed his eggs and chomped down on the fork with his teeth, making a clanking sound. He pulled the fork between his closed lips, licking the fork. "Best eggs in town. Poured me some of the lemon juice from the icebox in them."

I tossed my fork down. "You ruined our eggs. Hurry up and eat. And go!"

Phillip touched my arm, since he sat to my right. "Tangy. They're a little sour too. Eat up. Everyone eat and let's enjoy this party." He slapped the table and the silverware clinked, and his words dripped like droplets of blood. I could almost see the blood pouring from his mouth to the plate, to the floor, and coating us all with—with death.

Molasses sat next to him across from Ms. Daisy, being forced to eat with us, even though he hadn't taken one bite. "I'll get some more syrup. Anyone need more butter?"

Pax stabbed the table with his fork using it like a knife. "Stay put, boy. We're having a party."

Ms. Daisy scolded Pax. "This is our mother's table. Do you have to ruin everything?"

"Our mother's table?" Pax pulled the fork from the wood. "She wasn't much of a mama. She used her strap on us for even looking at her!" He stabbed the table again and again, until Phillip leaned over Molasses, taking the fork. Pax shook his head. "She wasn't a good mama. Was she?"

Phillip placed the fork next to his own plate. "Pax, the remembering you have isn't the real remembering. Our ma loved us. She did. She made your eggs over easy like you love them, and she packed your lunches for school with notes. We had a good mama, the best."

Pax twitched with a jerk of his head, back and forth as if his remembering got stuck. "She did write me notes. The kids read them out loud, making fun of me. Did you hear me? They made fun of me!"

"Now, Pax. That was a long time ago." Phillip handed Pax a spoon. "Here, eat with this. We're having a party, remember?"

Mahlee sat glaring at Pax, while Ms. Daisy had Silas pour milk into our glasses. "Fresh milk. Hope loves her some milk. Soon she'll be cutting a tooth, next she'll be sitting up."

Ms. Daisy reached to the side next to her chair, between her and Pax to tuck in Hope's blanket around her in the cradle.

Pax tapped the blanket with his spoon. "Pretty little baby. Sleeps a lot."

Ms. Daisy slapped his arm away. "Touch her and you'll wish you hadn't."

Laughing, Pax mocked, "And you, my little sister, what will you do? Remember the shed, remember those times when you screamed? I will tell your secret. Tell how …"

"Stop it, Pax. You are sick in the head. You can't hurt me anymore. I will never let you hurt me again. Or my baby."

Phillip used his smooth words. "Fighting again, you two?" He turned to the table like he tried to keep quiet the family secrets. "So does anyone want more pancakes?"

Mahlee chimed in, and an avalanche of lost words formed sentences. "Pax, you know you did more than hurt her. You stole her innocence. Back then, if I'd known, you wouldn't be alive today."

Pax smirked, "But you didn't know. As for you, there's nothing pretty about you, nothing worth anything."

Mahlee slammed her hand down, not as hard as she could, but firm like she planned to turn the table over. "You can't tell the difference from a bad dream and real life, Pax. You need help."

Pax offered up a bite of his eggs. "You're the one in the family who is the bad dream. You're the one who is crazy. You ride the rail. You're the hobo of the family."

Phillip pushed his chair back. "Stop. Everyone stop. Daisy, we're in trouble. Real trouble. Thanks to Pax."

Ms. Daisy sipped her coffee. "Trouble? I'm not helping you."

"It's a matter of life and death." Phillip leaned on his hands, staring at Ms. Daisy. "We need some money to disappear. I'm sure Clifford had plenty. Can you help us out?"

Pax yelled, "Yeah! Help us out!"

From behind Pax, standing in the dining room door leading to the back porch towered a friend—it was Jake, the man who caught a bullet at the spiritual meeting. He hovered like a giant behind Pax. "Ms. Daisy, I got a call. Heard there's some intruders here. Do you need me to get rid of the rats?"

Phillip's jaw dropped and Pax spun around, and Ms. Daisy pulled her pistol, along with Mahlee, who dug for her gun and they pointed the guns at the brothers. I bent down, and grabbed my rocks, shouting, "It's time to leave, boys!"

Silas backed away from the table, sat the pitcher down, and cradled Hope in his arms. He greeted the giant of a man. "Big Jake, glad to see you in town."

Big Jake grabbed Pax by the collar, along with Phillip. "Time for you two to leave these fine folks alone."

Dragging them down the porch to the back yard, I followed them. "Leave Ms. Daisy alone. She's a fine lady. She's not like you two." At the end of the porch, I jumped to the steps below, lost my footing and landed on my knees on a loose piece of wood. "Darn ole wood."

Big Jake disappeared around the house with the Shaw brothers, and I heard scuffling and smacking sounds. I waited, afraid to go, afraid to move.

Chug-a-lug. Chug-a-lug.

I charged to the other side of the backyard, climbing on the fence of the corral, watching Phillip and Pax drive away, not sure if they'd return. Not sure where they'd go. Not sure what Big Jake did, but glad he did whatever he did.

"Missy. You all right?" Big Jake showed up behind me, with Powder on his shoulder.

"Do you know … do you know you have a polka-dotted mouse on you?"

"If you say I do, I must."

Molasses stormed up next me, shaking Jake's hand. "Well, thank you, Jake. You saved the day."

Slugging Molasses in the jaw, I screamed at him, the anger of the ugly days in Washington boiling over. "Why are you helping Officer Tock? Why wouldn't you tell Silas?"

My questions evaporated into the air since Molasses tumbled unconscious to the ground like a tree blown over by the wind.

Big Jake grabbed my fist before I could swing again. "What are you talking about? Why are you hitting this boy?"

"He can tell you when he wakes up."

"You need a paddling from your pa."

Wishing to run, I mouthed, "I'd take one, but my pa's dead."

Big Jake's frown changed upward, and he wrapped me in his arms, cuddling me like a teddy bear. "No wonder you hit. No one has loved you enough."

I wilted like a leaf broken off from its branch, and hugged Jake back, my arms falling over his shoulders. "I don't have anyone who wants me."

Jake whispered a bellow of words. "Jesus said for the children to come to Him. He's your Father. He wants you."

From behind me, Mahlee's words called out. "I want you, my little Annie Grace. Seeing my sister and her love for Hope has reminded me how much I do love you. I want you. I want you. I'm keeping you. I get lost in my troubles, you bring me hope."

Glancing over my own shoulder, I saw Powder on Mahlee's shoulder now, and he twitched his nose at me. I scrambled down from Big Jake's arms, and raced across the yard almost running into the water pump, and my arms were greeted with Mahlee's outstretched hands. "Mahlee, I love you!"

"I love you too, my little Annie Grace Kree."

"Where's Powder? He was here."

"You and that mouse. Daisy told me how you keep seeing Silas' mouse."

Ms. Daisy stood on the porch, smiling, and Mahlee folded me up like a towel into her arms. She whispered, "I have to make sure Daisy's safe first, but then—we'll go home to your grandma's manor. We'll go home. I love you! What was I thinking?"

Her words rang out like a church bell of joy, but the lingering trouble in Jefferson meant she'd have to face the murder charges—first. My throat swelled with fear, and with the desire to help Mahlee clear her name.

Arggh! Arggh!

Molasses sat up, leaning on his elbow on the ground. "Did the rooster get me?"

Big Jake chuckled from somewhere deep inside and laughter rolled out, and he grabbed Molasses, pulling him up. "Boy, no rooster got you. A girl with a left hook and a swing tougher than my young'uns walloped you."

Molasses turned and scowled at me. "Shoelace?"

I grinned, and Mahlee tapped me on the shoulder. "Stop bothering him."

Rubbing his face, Molasses stumbled to the kitchen house.

"I have to bother him. He has to tell Daisy and Silas how he's involved in the ugly stirrings."

"He will. I've already talked to Ms. Daisy."

"You did?"

"Yes, we'll discuss this and more in a bit."

I shouted at the kitchen house. "Molasses, don't go and hide. You have to fess up. You know about Graves and Tock. You better talk."

Making a Plan to Live

The rest of the morning rushed ahead like clouds floating by and now it's afternoon and Jake and I are carrying limbs to a pile of brush behind the barn. The storm from last night and the almost storm with the Shaw brothers this morning has Mahlee and Daisy whispering inside, and has Silas cleaning his garden, and Molasses pulling weeds.

Torturing Molasses with my calls, I yell at him every time I pass the garden. "Hey Molasses. You better fess up."

"Stop bothering me. I'm working on it. Leave me alone."

"If you don't tell Silas by sundown, I'm gonna ..."

Silas uncurled from the corner by a row of okra. "Tell me what?" He glanced at his nephew. "Molasses, this is not a time for secrets. Ms. Daisy isn't rid of her brothers, yet. They'll be back."

Stopping, I called across the yard knowing we needed protection. "We're keeping Big Jake, aren't we?"

Big Jake tapped me on the shoulder. "You best get to moving with those branches. I took a bullet for you the other day at the revival. Remember?" He rubbed the round muscle where a bandage covered the injury. "I'm not too strong these days. I do have another good arm I can use. But you have two good arms."

"I do have strong arms, but the bullet might have been meant for someone else. I don't have any enemies here. Not yet, anyway. Except Molasses." I giggled, "Besides, I saw you grab Pax and Phillip by their necks this morning. Both of your arms are working just fine. I saw how they tiptoed like dancers, you held them so high."

"I can be strong when it's needed. Cousin Silas knows his limits. He's an old geezer now. He calls, and I come." Laughing, Jake hit his knees with a slap.

Silas yelled, "I'm old, but I'm not deaf."

Jake blasted into a roar. "You are tone deaf. I've heard you sing at church."

Silas accepted the cue, dancing in the garden with a two-step of hope. "Praising my Savior all the day long, don't mean I have to sing in tune."

Molasses and Silas joined in for a garden-sing-along, each chiming off-key like buzzards with a cold. "Blessed assurance, Jesus is mine."

Jake picked up the tempo. "Oh, what a foretaste of glory divine."

Together they all sang. "Heir of salvation, purchase of God, born of His spirit, washed in His blood."

I added my part with theirs. "This is my story, this is my song, praising my Savior all the day long." Turning, I carried a stack of sticks but realized I sang alone, and everyone stared at me. "What? I never said I could sing in tune."

Silas chuckled, "No, out of tune is fine. I never expected you would know the words to an old hymn. You're full of surprises, child."

Tilting my head high. "My daddy taught it to me." Lying to them felt right, but I really learned the song in the missions on times when my daddy sat in jail, and when Mahlee went missing. But she's here now, and I'm not alone.

The hours ticked away as the sun slid across the sky and I helped Jake finish clearing the yard from the branches while Silas got supper in the kettle. Molasses avoided me, moving from sweeping the porch, to carrying trash, to hiding in the

kitchen house saying he was baking pies for supper. Saying
the workers at the tavern café needed four chocolate pies too.
Mahlee and Ms. Daisy spent most of the afternoon inside
the house. They shooed me from the parlor, they sent me on
errands to the kitchen house, and they made sure Jake kept me
busy—to keep me out of their way.

**

Balancing myself on the porch rail, I practiced my circus
high wire act, while listening to Jake snore in the shade of the
tree. His size reminded me of a sleeping hippopotamus, and
his belly wiggled with each snore. Last year, I saw a picture of
a hippo in school in Texarkana, and I'm not sure, but maybe
Jake posed for the sketch.

Creak. Creak.

Mahlee popped her head from the door by the front foyer.
"Shoelace, get Silas. And Molasses. And wake up Jake. We
have a plan. It's a plan for living. A plan for us to get on with
our lives."

Kaplop! Jumping to the porch floor, I jogged to Mahlee,
hugging her waist. "Living is the best idea yet. I'll get them.
Be right back."

Barreling down the steps and across the worn path to the
kitchen house, I slammed the screen behind me as I fell into
the kitchen. "We're having a meeting. It's time to make a
plan."

Molasses dusted the flour on the white apron hanging
around his neck. "I guess this last pie will wait."

Silas raised up from where he stirred the pot of supper
fixings. "This needs to steep awhile. We're having chicken
and dumplings. Skip loved dumplings. I do too." He shuffled
around the table. "Let's see what Ms. Daisy has on her mind."

Outside, I screamed at Big Jake and the horses kicked the fence, but Jake snoozed on. I hurried to him. "Jake, wake up. We're making a plan."

Big Jake grumbled. "I'm up. I'm not asleep. Just had my eyes closed."

Inside the house, humming a tune, I eagerly waited for the news, my fingers twitching.

Silas shook his head. "No singing. This is serious. We've got to move Ms. Daisy and the baby. And soon."

Mahlee put her hands on her hips. "That's our plan. She can come with me and Shoelace to Texarkana. We'll stay at the manor and hide out there. She can start a new life with us."

I raised my voice, with a shrill. "We're hiding out?"

Mahlee corrected me. "No, we're not. She is. Well, I am too, I guess, from the law."

Silas and Molasses circled each other in front of the fireplace and Molasses acted more fidgety than me. Silas moaned under his breath. "Molasses and I talked earlier while making supper."

Ms. Daisy rose from her rocker by the window. "Silas, what do you know, what are you not saying?"

Molasses opened his trap. "It's difficult. I don't know how to tell you."

I bounded around the table by the sofa. "Molasses, tell her. Tell her about Officer Tock. And about Pastor Graves."

Mahlee scolded me. "Shoelace, we're talking. You listen."

Pouting, I sat on the floor Indian style by the door's entrance to the side foyer. "Fine. I'll listen. But this better go the way I want it to, right Molasses?"

Mahlee thumped my ear. "Hush it up. The baby's asleep."

Silas butted in, changing the subject. "First, ladies, tell me how you both had pistols today."

I spouted off, "Mahlee and me stole the gun from her brothers last night at the jail when we saw them asleep. Ms. Daisy has the gun from inside my satchel. We have a knife too. It was in my satchel."

Mahlee pointed her finger at me. "Hush. And now!"

I jumped to my feet, not able to obey. "We heard Tock and Graves talking at the jail, when we got out of the rain. Then I ran away and bumped into Mahlee in the storm. She became the best shadow I've ever been afraid of."

I went on, letting my words fall faster. "We heard them talking about how Molasses is helping them find Morning's stash from his crooked deals. Tell them, Molasses. Tell them how you work for Officer Tock and the no-good Pastor Graves."

Jake stomped across the room, his feet heavy, they thundered on the wood floor. "Shoelace, come over here. Being quiet works better for you if you sit by me."

Moving from the floor to the sofa, I plopped down and folded my hands. Ms. Daisy, Mahlee and Silas were glaring at Molasses, and he sighed, "I have something to tell all of you. I told Silas this afternoon. I don't know where to start."

Shouting, "You might start with how you put us all in danger."

Crimes of Color

Molasses crossed his arms, then held them at his side, clinching his fists. He looked at us with wobbly eyes, his lips quivering. "I stood near the place where Mr. Morning was stabbed. I didn't know what happened at first, because he argued with Officer Tock by the back steps next to the garden. Silas had gone into the house to help with the birth," he glanced at Ms. Daisy, "to see how you were doing, and I stopped to pray for you and little Hope."

I mocked, "You prayed for Hope. You didn't even know her name. Pray? You?"

Silas held his gut as if the words stabbed him. "Molasses, you didn't tell me that earlier. You left out an important detail."

Jake bounded to Silas, helping him to the sofa, and I took the chance to bounce to my feet, to prance up to Molasses. "So all this time you knew who killed Mr. Morning?"

Molasses wiped the sweat from his top lip, only for the beads of water to reappear. "I had no choice. Officer Tock saw me in the shadows by the kitchen door, listening. I didn't mean to listen. I'd stopped to pray and their whispers grew."

I smacked my hands together like a 'vestigator. "And you keep this to yourself about a stabbing. Who does that? Did you pray about that?"

Silas scooted to the edge of the sofa. "Shoelace, enough. This is hard enough on him. As for his praying, the boy's prayed every day since his pa left. Prayed every day for me.

Prayed over his food since he was five. He even prays when he goes to bed. You don't know the Molasses, I know."

"Sorry, Mr. Silas. I didn't mean … to upset you. I didn't know he prayed. He doesn't look like a praying person. He treats me pretty mean so ..."

Silas nodded. "He's a boy most days, but he's learning to become a man. Has to own up to his faith walk. He doesn't always measure up, but he's mine. He's my boy. I'll defend him to anyone—even little girls who have taken advantage of our kindness since she gotten here."

With Silas putting me in my place, my chest ached as if ten knives stabbed me. "I'm sorry, Mr. Silas." Wiping tears from my eyes, I turned to Ms. Daisy, and gave her my sad face. "I didn't mean to take advantage. I didn't. I was searching for my Mahlee, and God sent me here—here to the Sanders House. See, I have Mahlee now. And I have you too, Ms. Daisy, and Hope."

Molasses interrupted me. "Too many wrongs going on. I need to fix mine. Uncle Silas, it's my fault she thinks of me the way she does. I haven't treated her like she's welcome. I tried to run her off. When I found out she knew my pa, I became jealous because she saw him last."

Silas agreed. "But, we need to work this out, and fix what we can fix. The wrongs we've passed on to each other need forgiving."

I tried to hold my tongue, but my mouth hung open. "Molasses, I wasn't your enemy."

Molasses ran his fingers through his hair. "But you did get here the night of the murder, when the birth happened, when everything went horrible, and I couldn't get beyond seeing Mr. Morning die. Then you caught the kitchen on fire, and Officer Tock threatened me. So having you here during all of this wrecked me. I had no choice. Tock gave me no choice."

Ms. Daisy glided her feet on the floor toward Molasses, putting her arm around his shoulder, and her other hand went to his chin. "Sweet, Molasses. You're becoming a fine man, I had no idea you witnessed any of this. Poor thing."

Under my breath, I repeated, "Poor thing."

Mahlee heard me, grabbing my arm. She yanked me to the cloth chair by the window at the other end of the sofa. "Sit here. And this time, I mean it. Be quiet."

Sneering at Molasses, I couldn't imagine his being a praying teenage boy, let alone a fine young man. As for his being a poor thing, he was a poor thing.

Silas urged Molasses to go on. "Tell everyone what you've told me."

"First, let me tell you what I thought had taken place. When Mr. Morning fell by the steps, I figured he'd fallen from a shove. Tock was worried Morning wasn't going to support the evil rogue in Hot Springs."

I couldn't help but repeat his words. "Evil rogue?"

"Oh yeah, you're not from these parts. He's Hot Springs Mayor, Leo McLaughlin and he's being investigated for his shady dealings. Fifteen indictments so far. Tock wanted his payoff for a recent job, and Morning wouldn't give it to him."

I blurted with more questions. "So Mr. Morning does have money?"

Ms. Daisy answered, "He has money. Not honest money, I'm sure. He never left the house without $1,000 in his pocket. I have no idea where he kept it."

Molasses continued, "Tock's afraid he's going down with the mayor since Tock has helped cover for him. He used to be an officer there during the elections last year, then he came here and became a cop. Hiding out, I'm sure."

Ms. Daisy shook her head. "I knew Clifford was in deep, but this is much worse than I figured. I never did like Officer Tock, but you know my husband, if someone needed a job and it was good for Clifford, they'd show up in town. People say he was involved in the scandal of the elections in Hope too. Somehow I'd bet he had something to do with the election problems in Hot Springs."

Jake socked his hand with a fist. "I'd like to find Tock right now. We could settle this behind the barn."

Molasses argued, "No, Tock threatened to kill Silas if I don't come through with the cash. He wants me to spy on Ms. Daisy, to find the money."

Mahlee added her words to the mix. "Molasses, you could have asked Silas for help. He's never let you down."

"I know, but I was afraid of losing him. He's all I have."

Sucking in the compassion I felt for Molasses, I blurted, "You put us in danger. Not just him. But Ms. Daisy, and Hope."

Mahlee stepped closer to my chair, her hand over my mouth. "If you say another word, I'll take you out behind the barn."

Breathing through my nose, I coughed, and Mahlee moved her hand. "I'll be good."

"I mean it. You're acting like a baby."

Squinting my eyes, I puckered my lips, too mad to speak, or to say another word.

Molasses cleared his throat. "I did put you all in danger. Not on purpose. I didn't know what to do. It gets worse. Tock woke me up with a gun pointed in my face one night, when I was sleeping on the back porch of the kitchen house, after Shoelace got poison ivy. He admitted to shooting Swisher, then he handed me the knife he used on Morning and said to get rid of it. Then he placed a gun and some bullets on the porch, and said to get rid of them. He said killing Swisher was easy, so taking out Silas would be easier."

Ms. Daisy asked, "Why didn't you shoot him? You had a gun." She put her hand to her mouth. "I'm sorry. I wasn't there, I don't know how I would have reacted."

Molasses finished with his reasons. "Tock put his hand on his holster, and told me if I did anything stupid, he'd come for me."

I shot to the floor, yelling. "So you could have shot him right then, but you're a chicken. You're a great big awful chicken. You could have stopped some of this."

Silas rose, towering over me. "Enough. You will get a paddling from me if you keep this up."

"Yes sir. But …"

"Shoelace, I've offered you kindness and our home. Try showing some respect." Silas used a deep voice, one with more orders lurking if I didn't obey.

"Yes sir. I'm sorry for not listening."

Molasses' voice quivered. "But Uncle Silas, I am awful. I figured Shoelace was leaving town with Mr. Marion, but she didn't go. And I had put … I put the gun and the knife and the bullets inside her satchel. I figured they'd ride out with her, and I wouldn't have to worry about them again."

I stepped between Silas and Molasses, putting my finger on his shirt. "You? You put the gun in my bag? And the knife? You are awful. You set me up. I could have gotten charged with murder. No one knows me here. I'm a stranger. So you would let me take the fall?"

"I regret it. I do. You were supposed to be long gone with the murder weapons."

Jake pushed himself between me and Molasses, and Silas leaned on the mantel of the fireplace like he might faint. Jake

214

placed a hand on Molasses, and another on me. "What's awful is these men have taken over this town. This is our home. We have family and friends, and our history is here. This could be a place others might visit in the future."

Ms. Daisy agreed. "This home is old. No telling who might stand on the porch or walk through the corral or take a stroll through our old kitchen. We have to fight for what's ours."

Mahlee shook her head. "Daisy, you need to come with me to Texarkana."

Daisy shook her head, "I've changed my mind. I'm not running. Your plan sounded good earlier when we were scheming like little kids, but this is home. This is where I belong."

Silas moved to her, pulling a paper from his overalls. "Ms. Daisy, I've been meaning to give you this, been carrying it around for days. It's the deed to the Sanders House. I want you and Hope to have your own homestead, so long as you'll let me and the boy stay out back."

Ms. Daisy wept, "Silas, you're the kindest man ever. I can't take this from you. Clifford acted like he owned the house, but I've known it's yours. I can't …"

"It's my gift to Hope. She's changing the course of your life. She's given you a future."

Embracing, Silas and Ms. Daisy hugged, and I frowned at Molasses, whispering to him. "You could have gotten me killed or gotten me blamed for the murders. What were you thinking?"

"Nothing. I was too scared to think. Will you … will you forgive me?"

Shocked by his change of heart, I shouted, "Forgive you? For talking mean to me? For hiding who murdered Mr.

Morning? For how you set me up to look like I was involved? Are you serious?"

Silas hit his fist on the mantel. "Both of you. Stop. What's done is done. We are fixing the wrongs. Remember?"

Flinching, I changed my words to pretend kindness. "I will try to forgive you, Molasses. I'm still kind of mad though."

Molasses muttered, "I'm mad at myself too. Silas, do you forgive me?"

Silas assured his nephew. "Son, we will move on. You got caught in trouble, and didn't know how to handle it. We'll figure this out."

Silas and Molasses whispered to each other with low talking, and Mahlee went up to Ms. Daisy. "You can't stay here. Pax and Phillip will come back. They're crazier than me. And Tock is a killer. Not that our brothers aren't, but they're not going to kill us over money."

Ms. Daisy inhaled, "I don't have the answers, but one thing I have is my faith. Living in fear isn't living. I must stay. I'll fight for life. I'll fight for Hope. God will help us."

Mahlee rolled her eyes, "But, Daisy. This is your chance to start fresh."

**

Earlier, Mahlee admitted she loved me and now she's using the love word on her own sister and niece and anyone around her. I scuttled up to Ms. Daisy and Mahlee. "We could stay here. After we clear your name in Texas, we could live right here with Ms. Daisy."

Mahlee switched gears, stomping in her boots. "No good. No good. This isn't how the meeting is supposed to go. Now we're stuck here. I was ready to go, but I can't. Besides, I'm a murderer myself. I killed those men in Texas. I shot them. I can't clear my name. I'm a wanted criminal. I'm no better than my brothers. No better than Tock."

Silas assured Mahlee, and I watched my old Mahlee disappear into her own world, and Silas held her arm. "Sit and rest, Mahlee. This nightmare is looming over you, but the darkness doesn't have to win. We have you. Shoelace is sure you didn't kill those men. And I trust her. Don't you?"

Mahlee rocked a familiar cadence, lost in her own world of mumbling, and her hands went to her ears. "Not sure. Not sure. Got to help Daisy. But I can't help myself. I don't know. I don't know what to do."

Jake clunked over to her. "Mahlee, remember when we were kids, and how you liked swinging in the tire swing under the Magnolia tree, the one by the Blacksmith's shop? You would swing away your worries."

Mahlee mumbled, "I remember. I remember."

Jake unleased more sense to her not-sensible moment. "Remember how I would push you high, and you could reach the sky, and you would soar like an eagle?"

Mahlee put her arms straight out like she was flying, her eyes closed. "In the swing, I became a bird and floated up to God, to the clouds, to places where brothers don't hurt you and pick on you and slap you."

Jake sat next to her. "So let's swing through this trouble. One hour at a time. A day at a time. And soon you will be free. Free to live. Free to soar."

Captivated by the wisdom flowing from Big Jake, I sat on the floor, and Molasses knelt beside me. Jake kept soothing Mahlee, and Ms. Daisy sat in the rocker to my right, and off and on, we all wept, caught in the sorrow of the last few weeks.

Molasses muttered a prayer. "Dear God, forgive me for my wrongs. May we find strength from you. May you guide us and show us what to do. Please, keep my Silas alive, and Ms. Daisy and Hope, and Mahlee and her daughter, Shoelace, and of course, our best friend, Big Jake. Amen."

I added, praying with my eyes wide open, not looking at Molasses, but giving God a better prayer. "God, it's me, please keep my Mahlee whole, and bring her back to me—one more time. Amen."

After nearly an hour, Mahlee replied, stuttering, her eyes bugged wide. "Sorry. So sorry. I get lost in the ugly. And can't find my way out. I get lost in the sad, lost in the broken."

Silas folded his hands to his chest. "We all get lost from time to time. We need to stay with God and walk on his path, and sometimes, we need to walk with each other."

Ms. Daisy hugged Mahlee. "We're sisters always. And always we'll be connected, no matter where we live."

The room went silent, and there was an odd unity of strength rising up as we sat with each other—especially since the yelling ended.

Outside, the day turned gray and nightfall landed. I broke the quietness. "We're sitting in the dark. We need some light." I jumped to my feet, switching on the chandelier which lit up the room.

Waa! Waa!

Ms. Daisy rushed to get Hope across the side foyer, and Silas announced, "I'll check on supper."

Jake remained seated next to Mahlee, who rocked less now, and Molasses rose, wiping his eyes. "I've got to get those pies to the café. I've got one more to bake. I don't know how to handle the worry, so I have to bake or draw. I can't sit for long."

Molasses hurried out back with Silas, and I replayed the 'vestigation of our meeting inside my head. I wasn't over being mad at Molasses, and I was sad for Mahlee, and afraid for Ms. Daisy and for Silas.

Across the room, beyond the front foyer walk-through, in the bedroom where I sleep a beam of light shone through the glass. Muttering under my breath, I stared at the window. "Who's out there with a light? Molasses?"

I rushed to the back porch, leapt from the steps toward the corral, and bounded right into a warm body—not one holding a flashlight, but a gun!

I screamed, "Not you? You've got to be kidding?"

Crush to the Rescue

Stomping my PF Flyers, I jumped backwards. "What? What are you doing here?"

"I couldn't let it go. I knew you were here and I knew this town had two murders, which meant there's a killer. I also knew Mahlee came for you, but I had to make sure she found you. And you found her."

"So you do care?" I shoved the hand holding the pistol away from my face. "Where did you find a gun?"

"It's Mr. Marion's gun, he keeps it inside his chest of drawers."

"So what were you doing taking it? How would you know where to find his gun?"

"I found it by accident, last year. One morning as I waited in his kitchen to ride to work with him to the syrup factory, after the flood, and after my ma and pa died, I came across it in his drawer. I'd had biscuits and syrup with Toby that morning."

"The gun didn't land on the kitchen table for you to find."

"Give me a second to tell you. Toby left for school early to help his teacher, and Mr. Marion got to talking to the paperboy on his bicycle in the front yard. I looked around the house, at Toby's weird blue room, at the pictures of his wife in the hall, and I ended up in his bedroom."

"So you were snooping."

"Maybe, a little. But anyway, the top drawer opened, and his socks were on one side—the pistol on the other side."

Shaking my head, I scolded him. "You have to be nosier than me. I can't believe you went through his stuff. He was good to you. Gave you a job when you needed to feed your brothers. How could you go through his things?"

"Stop with the interrogation. It's not like you wouldn't have snooped. I only saw the gun. I never touched it, until this morning." Crush tucked the gun inside his waist, and pulled his shirt over the barrel. "I brought the gun in case you needed help."

"Why would you think I needed your help? I'm fine. The people in this town might need help though."

"I overheard Mr. Marion and Mahlee talking a few days ago at the orphanage and since they're both loud, all of us boys could hear how the danger brewed in Washington, and Mahlee wasn't sure who killed her brother-in-law or what happened. She had to get you. To save you."

I swallowed hard, "So you came to help me and Mahlee?"

"I did. We are friends. Not on-purpose friends, but friends thrown together by life. I couldn't let you not live. Timmons and Tak love you."

"Your little brothers are special. I sort of love all of your brothers." I stepped away from Crush, looking him up and down, and walking in a circle around him. "Your hair's growing in, it's kind of ugly though."

"It feels good. This weather's so sticky, short hair isn't bad."

"Is the scar on your neck from the fire?"

"Yes, it's a small one. I've got one on my arm too."

"I didn't mean to burn you. You know that, right?"

"I know. I picked on you. You picked on me. It's what we do. I can get you riled up faster than a wild horse bitten by a rattlesnake."

I patted his arm. "I'm sorry." We stood in the shadow of the nightfall letting our hearts heal from our fight. I asked, "But how did you get here?"

"I borrowed Mr. Marion's pickup. He's got himself a new sedan. The truck stays parked in the driveway behind the orphanage. I borrowed it."

"He bought a new car?"

"Yeah, so he won't miss the truck for a couple days, unless he walks across the yard from his house around the garage."

"Mr. Marion's gonna hurt your backside when he discovers it's gone."

"He might think it's stolen."

"But you'll be missing too. He'll figure it all out."

"Maybe, but I'm here to help you get out of this town alive."

"You think you're the answer to this town's problems? You have no idea."

"I came to help you, if you need it."

Pulling him to the ground, I squatted next to Crush, and he bent down. I whispered like the grape vines had ears. "Mahlee and me, we might need your help. Mahlee said we were going back to Texarkana to live in the manor, but we have figure out how to keep Ms. Daisy from danger. Can you believe it? Mahlee wants me."

"But what about the cops? She's wanted for murder."

"I'm gonna clear her name. I bet we can do it together too."

"Talk around town in Jefferson is there's another man who controlled Mr. Clementine, and if we can get to him—we might be able to clear Mahlee."

Smiling at the good news of clearing Mahlee's name, I shouted. "My goodness. I am starting to like you, even if I don't."

Ha! Ha! Ha!

Laughing, we cackled in the shadows, and I shared the dilemma circling the Sanders House and we lost our smiles almost before they finished forming. "I need to fill you in on the rest. Molasses, the boy who hates me more than you do—or more than you used to, he's been threatened by the cop who works here. It's Officer Tock, and he said he'll hurt Silas if he doesn't find Mr. Morning's money. Which is crime-money."

"What? A bad cop?"

"Yeah! And a bad pastor. Mr. Graves is no pastor. He's working with Tock. They're gamblers and they owe someone a lot of money in Hot Springs."

"Hot Springs? That town is known for its bad men and for crimes. People come up missing or dead there."

"It gets even more bad than worse, Pax and Phillip Shaw are here, and they're criminals too. And they're Mahlee's brothers. And Ms. Daisy. We're surrounded by evil."

"We need to call Mr. Marion. This is bigger than the pistol on my waist."

"No! We have Big Jake. He's a Negro with arms like watermelons. He's the strongest man ever. But kind too."

Crush ran his fingers through his stubbles. "I'm sorry about your friend, Pastor Cody. I heard he … he died trying to save you."

"I know. He tried to save me from the church fire, and I wasn't even inside the building. I did bring trouble to this town—I suppose." My eyes watered, and my nose dripped. Wiping snot on my sleeve, I rose. "Come on. You can stay in the barn. I'll hide you out. There's only two horses in there, and the one cow. You'll be fine."

Crush moved to the shadows by the vines, grabbing a bed roll. "I parked the truck down the road, left it by an old house—it's empty. The windows are broken, and the porch is crooked. It has bushes up and all around the house. No one will see it. It's off behind the house."

"The truck might come in handy. We might need it."

Clump. Clump. Clump.

I turned to Crush. "There's the barn. Go over there. I'll come by later. Someone's coming."

"See you after everyone goes to bed." Crush darted to the fence and hopped over it, and headed to the barn, becoming a part of the darkness.

I rushed to the porch steps.

"Shoelace, you can't go wandering off. We've got to stay inside at night, and we have to stay together." Mahlee hollered, using her Mama voice.

"I'm right here." I sauntered up to her, grinning.

"Molasses and Big Jake are taking the pies to the tavern. Ride over there with them. You're safer with Jake, than here with Daisy and me."

"But, if you two are alone, someone can get to you."

"Silas is going to stand watch. He has his trusty shotgun, and you'll be right back. The tavern's a block away."

"I need to be with you."

Mahlee hugged me. "We're together. I'm not going anywhere. Go help Molasses. He needs to see you forgive him."

Scowling in the darkness on the porch, "I don't exactly forgive him. I am mad a little. Being mad at him is easier."

"Then forgive him on purpose. When you stay mad, it only eats away at your soul."

"I'll try. I don't know. I'll try."

224

**

The tray with the pies sat on the bed of the truck with Molasses making sure they remained edible, the meringue dancing in the night's blue light coming from the moon.

Sitting next to Big Jake, I noticed his arms seemed bigger at night, and his body folded in half when he sat in the cab. I laughed, "You barely fit in this truck."

"I can get in, it's the getting out I struggle with." Jake snickered and gave Molasses a glance out the back window when the truck hit a bump. "Sorry, boy. Rough roads in this town tonight."

I turned and got on my knees, watching Molasses baby his prized work. "He's a good baker, isn't he?"

"He is great at whatever he touches. His hands have a gift. He's a painter. A teacher. A baker."

"Teacher?" Plopping back into the seat, the truck pulled up to the back of the Tavern. "What does he teach?"

"He gives of his Saturdays in Bible lessons with the boys in Ozan. He tells a story and draws it on paper for them—like a crayon book with Bible people on the pages."

"No way? He does that for free?"

"He does it for God."

"Oh, I don't do so much for God."

"You might try and figure out what you're good at and see if God might speak to you about how to use it for Him."

"I'm good at 'vestigating and writing poems."

"Then maybe you could become an investigator when you grow up and a writer."

Smiling, the joy at thinking of such a possibility did seem like a good way to make God smile, and a good way to make me smile. "I might become a 'vestigator. I might."

Big Jake encouraged me to be a part of assisting Molasses with the pies. "Let the boy know he's your friend. He's been carrying a burden of worry and fear about his uncle, and has probably felt alone. He could use a friend."

Nodding, I bit my lip. "Yes sir. I'll try." I felt a twinge behind my left ear, but I couldn't get rid of the idea of Molasses setting me up with the weapons, and I struggled to let it go.

Carrying pie after pie to the case inside the restaurant, I moved each one three times to different shelves, until Molasses approved of their location. He conducted the arranging by standing in front of the glass casing as if he might be sketching portraits with pies.

"Right here? Is this the spot?"

Molasses motioned with his hand. "Move the lemon over there. Put the chocolate on the bottom. Swap those two. There. Perfect."

I shut the doors to the pie case, and walked to the side where I could see the pastries. "Who would ever think you could put pies on a shelf and they would look like a painting? I could eat every slice."

Big Jake sat across from us at a table, drinking sweet tea from the cooler and he smirked, "You two are great together. Nice job."

We glanced at each other and I went one way toward the counter where the pitcher of tea begged me to pour a glass for myself, and Molasses went to the kitchen—to check on the supplies.

Meow. Meow.

"Tink? It's my kitty. He's on the front porch." Unbolting the latch, I let the light of the entrance to the restaurant shine a beam right onto my kitty cat. "Tink. I haven't seen you in days." Picking her up, I noticed her coat thick and her belly big. "You're eating good over here. You're getting fat."

Big Jake called to me. "I'm shutting the door, locking the Tavern up. Stay on the porch. Me and Molasses will swing around to pick you up. I'll leave the light on. The more light—the better we all see."

"Yes sir." I cuddled my kitty, and found myself staring across the highway to the corral, to the barn where Crush was waiting for me, and to the Sanders House.

Near the post office a beam of light shot toward the Sanders House. Squinting, I focused on the shadow behind what appeared to be a flashlight, and the light crossed the road—headed to the porch where Silas stood guard.

Screaming, I called with my loudest voice, "Silas, watch out. Someone is coming for you."

Big Jake's truck chugged around front, and I charged to the pickup. "Someone's at the house. I saw a light. Don't let anyone hurt Mahlee!"

Molasses rose to a stance, peering above the cab. "We're coming, Silas."

I echoed Molasses, and jumped into the seat. "We're coming."

Pam Kumpe

When Miracles Slip off

Jake skidded to a stop with dust flying beneath the truck. My lips went dry from worry, and my tongue stuck to the top of my mouth. We barreled from the truck, and were met with the glaring emptiness of the front porch.

I clutched Tink tight, her cries mixed with mine. "Where's Silas?"

Meow. Meow.

Tink shot from my arms and raced up the angry tree, scatting at something on the branch. Peering at the limb, I couldn't see what had her riled up, and then Molasses rushed to the shotgun leaning on the wall by the front door. "Where's Uncle Silas?"

I screamed, "I don't know. Maybe he's ... "

The door creaked and Ms. Daisy and Mahlee came to the porch, and the fear in their eyes made them appear not so pretty, not like art sketches, like leftover slices of pie.

Mahlee held me close. "What's going on?"

Before I answered, Ms. Daisy ran to Molasses, "Where's Silas?"

Molasses rattled confusing words, and he shook his head with each phrase. "Uncle Silas. Skip. Pa. Come help me. Pa, save Ma. She's not breathing. She's gone. It's your fault. It's your fault. And you. You're gone again. Gone when I need you. Now Silas is gone too. I have no one. No one."

The stream of tears poured down his face and the shadows of his past mixed with the present, and he was lost in the pain.

I closed my eyes. "God, let Silas be alive. Come morning light. May he be safe."

Big Jake stood next to Mahlee and me. "The God we adore. The God we worship. The God we trust. We pray for protection."

Molasses heard the prayer, and his words joined Big Jake's prayer. "God, I am weak and I need your strength. Let the guilty pay, but let me stay. Let me win. Let Silas be safe. And let this town find peace again."

We all whispered together, "Amen."

Ms. Daisy folded her arms, sitting on the steps, gazing up at the tree, and I joined her, as did Mahlee—and Molasses and Big Jake stomped around the house in search of answers. We couldn't run—the worry and heaviness forced us to rock together like sad pies on the wrong shelf.

Mahlee pointed. "Is that your cat? I heard that Crush gave you a kitten and Lizzy Beth got the other one."

"I call her Tink. She rode the train with me and Crush. She's eating at the café and eating good; she's gotten fat in the last month."

Mahlee rocked, "I sure miss Lizzy Beth. I'd love to see her. Love to hold her again. But I know she's happy with Ms. Susan, and she's got her a new mama who'll do her good, treat her right, and love her without my plight."

I hugged Mahlee, "She will know you love her. We'll tell her when she's older, how you gave her away—to give her life."

Nodding, Mahlee wept, letting out the tears, which hung inside her body, those waiting to escape, those stuck in her life like a broken faucet.

I whispered, "I love you, Mama."

"I love you too, sweet girl."

Ms. Daisy pointed this time. "What does the kitten see? She's swatting at something in the tree."

Climbing, I hurried up the branch. "It's … it's Powder."

Ms. Daisy responded, "So your cat sees the polka dotted mouse?"

I hollered down from the tree, "She sees more than most." *Crack. Crack. Crack.*

I jumped from the tree, rolling to the ground, and Mahlee and Ms. Daisy stared to the side of the house, as a shadow showed itself to us.

The runaway showed himself. "Hi, it's me, Crush. I'm here to help you anyway I can. I rode in tonight. Heard you talking out here. I have to stay, to help you make a way through this."

Mahlee rushed to Crush, "Boy, somehow when I saw you at the top of the stairs the other day in Jefferson, when I talked with Marion, I figured you to be the type of boy who couldn't stay put."

"I'm here until we can bring you both home."

Ms. Daisy shook hands with Crush. "I'm so sorry for the burns. You are a miracle already. I'm thankful nothing worse happened."

Breaking from the shadows behind Crush on the side of the house, Big Jake pounded onward, not taking a glance at Crush or us, and he went to the fence next to the street on the other side of the house, searching for any sight of Silas.

Hollering at him, I pressed him for more. "Where's Silas? His truck is here. So he's here, right?"

Crush tapped me on the arm. "I saw a light before you drove up. I thought it was you, Shoelace, coming to the barn, but you never came—so I came to you. What's going on?"

"Silas was standing guard in case Tock or Graves, or Pax or Phillip came, but he's gone."

Crush put his fingers to his chin. "I saw Silas a minute ago and he was headed to the kitchen house. I'm sure it was him." I stood inside the barn doors, and he came prancing by like a boy sneaking off for something.

Molasses joined Big Jake next to the fence, coming from the garden area. "I can't find Silas. He's nowhere." He turned to look at us. "What in the world? What is Crush doing here?"

"Hi, I came in tonight."

"So, did you see Silas?"

"No. But I told them how I saw Silas headed to the kitchen. He's got to be there."

Molasses put his hands on his hips. "I came from back there. No lights are on. He's not there."

I turned to my Jefferson friend. "Crush, what did you mean by sneaking off when you saw Silas?"

"He acted like I do when I'm about to do something I shouldn't—he walked with a tiptoe dance, and hurried like he couldn't wait."

Big Jake grabbed Molasses by the arm. "Let's go check again. Ms. Daisy, you best check on Hope. Don't let her out of your sight."

"Yes. You're right. She's asleep, I'll go check on her now." She danced up the steps, giving my kitty one last glance. "Silly cat. Silas sees the mouse. Shoelace sees the mouse. And now you … you better not eat Silas' mouse." Her giggle rang out, not her normal joyful laugh, but a shaky quiver sound like air whistling between dead wood.

Molasses, Crush, and Big Jake stomped to the back yard next to the vines, and Mahlee and me tailed behind them—the five of us charging to the kitchen-house.

At the screen door, Molasses stepped inside, and we fell into the room like pins knocked over by a bowling ball. Molasses switched on the light—and sitting—and sitting at the table by the hearth in the dark was a sneaking old man. Silas smacked on pie and licked the meringue from his lips. And he smiled! "Want some pie?"

He clutched a flashlight with his left hand and a fork with his right, and half of a pie sat in front of him, with a slice on a plate. "I got hungry."

Big Jake reached for the flashlight. "Were you using this?"

"I thought I saw something at the post office, so I walked across the street. Turns out it was a stray dog, a brown one with paws bigger than a wolf. I shooed him off."

Mahlee grumbled. "A dog?"

"Yes, and then I went for pie. Molasses made me my own chocolate pie. I figured I'd eat it in the dark, so if someone came to the yard, I'd know."

Big Jake grumbled too. "We've been searching for you. Calling for you. You had no idea we were even in the yard. Some watchman you make."

Silas sighed, "My hearing isn't what it used to be. I'm fine, really. Sorry."

Molasses announced, "I'm so glad you're here. We may need to put younger ears on duty."

"I had no idea you were rushing around to find me. I was here all the time." He shook his head. "So what are we doing?"

Molasses, who stood frozen, cried like a water fountain. "When you weren't on the porch, I was afraid Tock got you. Or Phillip. Or Pax." He ran around the table and hugged the neck of the man who was like a daddy, whom he loved, and would go to any length to protect—even if he had to set me up to save the only Pa he's ever had.

Gulping back my own tears, I felt sure if faced with the same thing to save my Mahlee, I'd set him up too—and I found myself forgiving Molasses for real, and I cried with them. Real tears. Real forgiveness.

Big Jake ordered Silas, "From now on, keep the lights on. We can't be too careful. You're a target. We should have never left you alone. I'm not sure I thought this through by leaving you on the porch in the first place. We must figure out where Morning might have hidden his money. It's the answer to rid ourselves of all four men. Unless a miracle from God happens first."

In less than thirty minutes, Ms. Daisy used the word miracle, and now Big Jake used it—I'm not sure I believe in miracles, but it didn't mean I wouldn't take one.

A faint scream stopped our excitement, stopped our reunion, and quieted our hearts. Molasses looked at me. "Did you hear a voice? Someone is calling for help."

Mahlee moved to the screen door, pushing it open. "It's Daisy. She's on the back porch. I can't understand her, but she's running to us."

I pushed around Mahlee's skirt, stepping on her boot, and jumped to the ground. "What's wrong, Ms. Daisy?"

Big Jake pounded ahead of me. "Ms. Daisy. What is it?"

Silas and Mahlee came up next to me, and the chill of the night turned to flat out cold with Ms. Daisy's next scream. "Hope is gone from her bassinet! She's gone! Someone has taken her!"

Ms. Daisy collapsed like her bones dissolved, and her skin crumpled taking her to her knees on the steps. In her hand, Ms. Daisy clutched a piece of paper. She opened her palm, and it floated like a broken butterfly to the exact place where Mr. Morning met the knife in his chest—where he met death!

I exhaled, and found no air to take in—for a baby had vanished from the Sanders House. And life had vanished from Ms. Daisy's face—as if a noose hung around her neck.

I ran to the paper, grabbing it, but Big Jake snatched the paper. "Let me see."

He read the note to himself—handed the paper to Silas, while helping Ms. Daisy to her room—then Silas handed the note to Mahlee who let Molasses read it—and Molasses gave the paper to me. Crush read it over my shoulder while I read it aloud, "Twenty-four hours. Take the money to the old jail at sunset on Tuesday. No less than $10,000, if you want your little girl back—alive."

Pausing, I shook my brains between my ears. "It's Mahlee and Ms. Daisy's horrible brothers. It's signed: P&P."

Bad Money Bad Men

Pacing on the back porch, I squabbled with myself. "Six hours. Six wasted hours. It's almost midnight. Monday's almost gone. Ms. Daisy doesn't have ransom money, and she's scared she'll not have it in time. She doesn't even know where to get the money."

I stomped on the porch, knowing I was supposed to stay in my bedroom, but I slipped from the front foyer door to the porch hours ago, and Crush saw me from the kitchen house and he came outside too. No one has come looking for us.

I rattled on, speaking to the mosquitoes, while slapping my arm. *Swat!* "Ms. Daisy needs to escape from this town. This is why she has to go with Mahlee and me to Texarkana. We have to get her baby and get her now."

Arguing on with myself, "Leave her alone, stop talking about her like she's a horse to be stalled in another corral. Ms. Daisy's sick with worry. She can't think straight. She can't function. Or move."

Standing on the railing, balancing on one foot, I shook my head. "We should be doing something. Why haven't we called the police? Maybe we could find some good cops in Hope. Don't they have any connections?"

Plopping to the porch, marching in a circle, I countered. "Oh yeah! Mr. Morning was tied to shady guys there too. Ms. Daisy doesn't know who to trust."

Big Jake and Silas are searching the Tavern for hidden money and have gone everywhere searching for baby Hope. Molasses is standing guard out front now after searching the bunker, and Mahlee has nailed the doors shut after searching her own secret spots in town. No one is getting in or out though, on the side or the front. She's holing up with Ms. Daisy and they've been rocking and weeping.

Crush twisted toward me, holding the ransom note, and he sat cross-legged, mumbling under his breath. The light coming from the cracked dining room door surrounded him with a streak of yellow. "I thought this note was from Officer Tock, didn't you?"

Pursing my lips, I yelled. "I did too. Because he's the one who … who isn't on the list. He's after everyone. I never figured family would steal from family, especially a little baby."

"The list? What are you talking about?"

I searched my pocket, grabbing a rock, a nail, and a dime I'd found, and then pulled out my own secret note—the one I kept from the woods. "This! This is the note with Morning's name on it, Swisher's name, Pax and Phillip, and Pastor Graves. Not Tock! He's taking everyone out to get rid of the other rats. So he can disappear for good."

"You think you've got this figured out, don't you? Where'd you get this?"

"I found it at Molasses' bunker."

"Bunker?"

"Yeah! It's like a fort. But made of concrete."

"Whatever. Tock's not involved in this. Sure he's a criminal too. But with different motives. He wants to get his money and he doesn't care who he takes out. But he wouldn't take a baby."

"He scares me. Ms. Daisy doesn't like him, either."

Crush rose, walking sideways on the steps, up and down, his left leg down, his right leg up, his left shoe down, his right shoe up. Turning around, he went the opposite way, like one leg was longer than the other, a lopsided *gwuf-gwuf-gwuf*, and then he came back the other way again.

"What are you doing? This is serious. You came back to Washington to save me. Maybe you're here to save a baby." I pushed him from his gwuf-walk, and he tripped over his own untied shoelace—brown boots much like Mahlee's.

"Stop shoving me." Bending down, Crush tied his shoe, and the creaking of the board under his foot changed from a high-pitch *eeek*, to a low-pitch *uukk*. Crush whispered, "Did you hear the squeak?"

I hovered over him. "What?"

Running his fingers over the board, Crush pulled on the edge. "This board is loose. Too loose. Someone will get hurt, or trip like I did."

"It's fine. We don't have time to fix a step." I argued with Crush like we were brother and sister, and the way we talked sent me to a place like when Taddy, my best friend and me fought with our words, but loved with our hearts.

I bossed him, "Get out of my way." Jumping to the step, the board broke into a giant splinter, and my foot got jammed inside of the hole. "Ouch! That's not safe."

"I told ya so." Crush stood behind me. "Look at you. You can't leave things alone. You have to tear them up. Even the stairs."

"I tried to get you to quit playing on them, so you could go with me to find Hope. Time's a wasting. We should be helping."

"We're supposed to wait here. Silas said Mr. Morning had an office at the café. Let's see what they find. The money's probably in a safe."

Choking on the worry, I braved words of courage. "It's going to work out, isn't it?"

Crush pulled on my arm. "The baby will be fine. The brothers are using her to get to the money." Crush pointed. "Get your foot out of there."

"I'm trying. My shoe's caught." Squatting, I untied my PF Flyer, and slipped my foot from the shoe, then reached into the hole, jerking on the laces, but something wiggly touched my skin, and I jerked my hand out. "There could be spiders under that step."

"Stupid girl. Move." Crush bumped me with his body, wiggled my shoe, and pulled it from the hole along with paper and paper and paper and paper—flying paper.

I shouted. "Do you see what I see?"

Crush nodded, and handed me my shoe. "Money! It's money. More than I've ever seen. All under this step. Lots of it. Big bills. Not little. But big! This could be the stash."

I rammed into Crush. "Get out of the way. Are you sure? No way. Oh me! It has to be!" I held a wad of bills, more than enough money to pay a ransom and to get out of town. "This is life-saving money for baby Hope and for Ms. Daisy."

Crush hollered, staring at the door to the house—yelling at the house. "Come see. Mahlee, hurry. You're not going to believe what we've found."

I scolded him. "They're in the parlor, and Mahlee's sitting with Ms. Daisy who hasn't blinked or moved all night, except to whimper. They can't hear you."

Crush scuttled over toward the kitchen house. "I'm going to get some paper sacks. We might need several."

Calling to Crush, right before he slammed the screen to the kitchen, I told him where to look. "Silas keeps old sacks in the drawer by his oven mitt, next to the new flooring on the other side of the table. Where we had our fight."

"I'll find them. I'll be right back."

Pud-a-dub. Pud-a-dub.

Looking up to see if Mahlee came, in case she had heard us, I found myself staring into a face I'd grown to fear, one I felt as if I'd seen before—too many times, in real life and in my nightmares. The memory of the Phantom Killer flooded my thoughts—like spiders dangling in front of my eyes. Webbed flashes. Creepy. Like pinchers were grabbing for me. I remembered the mask. And the eyes.

Dropping the money like green snow, I stepped backwards, in my one shoe, and stuck my sock into my other shoe, not tying it. I wobbled sideways, like a lopsided spindly girl who wanted to hide and run. But I could hear my pa calling to me from my past, "Tie those shoes, Annie Grace."

The devil smirked, "Look what I found. You alone?"

Lying, I turned to talk to the garden. "Crush, hurry up, and get the okra. It's a giant one, right by the fence."

"Crush who?"

"He's my ... my brother. He came for me. He'll be here in a second." I gazed into the shadow of the plants, short ones, hoping and wishing for one tall tomato plant to come alive and rescue me from—Pax. He licked his lips like a vulture without wings, and he appeared to have talons ready to clutch, to kill.

He slobbered, running his words together. "I was out taking a walk and saw the light on the back porch, and you—I saw you, my sweet thing. You look like you could use some company."

"Crush, you coming?" I raised my voice to a pitch that sent the sleeping birds fluttering from the trees.

Pax wiggled like a snake, curling and twisting, and touching my hair. "You don't have no brother. You're making that up. If you'll come with me, I'll leave my sister Daisy alone, and she can keep her money. I can go into hiding without money. Even though Morning did hire us to get rid of Della, so Daisy wouldn't leave him and move in with her."

"You're not the only one who wants his money. Seems there's a whole mob of you lawbreakers who worked for Morning." I cringed, mouthing at Pax.

His breath stank, the leftover drops of whiskey fresh from the night, and the odor hung in my nostrils, burning. Quivering, I dashed under his legs like a lizard, but not before he slid his sweaty hand across my cheek. "A pretty girl needs to be made pretty. Needs to be …"

"I'm not yours." Running from Pax, I darted from his grasp, but his hand snatched at my shirt, and he pulled me toward him. I screamed, "Crush! Help me!"

Kaplunk! Kaplunk!

Pax wobbled from the *Kaplunk* on his head and he let go of me, and Crush bellowed from the shadows. "Stop touching her! Don't you hurt her!"

I saw the frying pan walloping Pax on the back of the head, and the drunken man wobbled, and I encouraged more *kaplunking*. "Hit him again!"

The black boots Pax wore staggered sideways as the boots held him upright, and Pax could topple any minute. But those boots! They reminded me of the masked killer's boots in Texarkana, the Phantom Killer who got away. "No, it can't be. He's not here. He's not going to kill me."

I dove at the dizzy boot-man who's huff-puff breathing wavered in uneven breaths. "Get away from us."

"Little girl, tie your shoe. It's untied."

Peering down at my shoe, Pax yanked on my hair, clutching me to his chest, putting me between Crush and the frying pan. Pax offered his deal. "Let me go, and I'll let her go. I meant no harm."

Crush hollered, "Mahlee! Mahlee! Get your gun!"

A shadow rushed from the garden, and Pax and me both jerked our head to see who charged at us. Molasses emerged into the light, pointing a shotgun at Pax. "It's time we ended this, time we stopped with the threats. You need to leave town for good. And with your brother."

Pax released me, but not before he kissed my forehead. "Yuck! Stop!" I wiped the sticky kiss from my skin.

Waving his arms, and backing up, Pax used his slippery words to inch away. "Molasses. You wouldn't shoot me. We've been friends for years."

Molasses held the gun up. "We've never been friends."

"Let me go. Don't tell Phillip. He'll be mad. I'll go sleep it off, and we'll call it even. You have the girl. I'll keep my life."

His swift talking, and even faster footwork sent Pax over the garden fence, around the house to the street, where he dashed into the night—and Molasses never chased him, never pulled the trigger—never moved. He stood frozen like a petrified tree.

I charged at him. "So Silas and Big Jake give you a gun to protect us, and this is what you do? Pax could have killed me, and now, you've let him get away. What were you thinking? I don't get you."

Molasses handed Crush the gun. "I'm no killer. I'm an artist. The likes of Pax and Phillip, they're not going to force me to become someone I'm not. I have prayed for strength and for answers, and shooting a man isn't the answer." Rubbing his eyes, Molasses began to sob. "I'm sorry. I can't use a gun. I don't have it in me."

Crush cradled the shotgun, while standing on a pile of old sacks. "It's all right. I can use a gun. I will shoot someone to save myself or someone else. Let's get Mahlee. We have to get inside, it's not safe outside anymore—not at all. We shouldn't have been out here in the first place."

I knelt by the steps, picking up the money. "But we need to get this inside with us. It's a good thing Pax was drunk. He never saw any of this money."

Molasses came to my side. "Is this Morning's money?"

"Yes. We think so. It was tucked under the stairs." Crush pointed to the broken wood.

"But I found it. I got my shoe stuck and discovered the treasure."

Crush shook his head. "She didn't find it. She fell into the hole."

Minutes later, we had six giant sacks packed with money ready to let Mahlee and Ms. Daisy know what we'd found— the ransom money for Hope was in our hands.

Bahahaha!!

"You thought you'd get away, but now you are mine." The evil, haunting laugh, and deep voice sent chills up my spine.

I stood frozen, as did Crush, and together we glanced around and Crush searched for the shotgun, but it was not there—and neither was Molasses!

A Dollar or More

Darting like bullets to the porch and pounding with our feet on the wooden slats, we rushed to the doorway leading to the parlor, and I crashed into the locked door.

Bam!

"Let us in. Let us in." Screaming together as if we were someone's meal at midnight, Crush and I pounded our fists on the wooden door.

Crush moved to our right, to the other door leading to the chandelier foyer next to Ms. Daisy's bedroom. He yelled with a squeal like a girl, and hit the door with his hand as if he were the strongest teenager. "Let us in. Mahlee. Ms. Daisy."

The boom boom of steps crunching like hammers on the porch behind us came with another squeal, and I twisted my head to see—Molasses with a hand on his neck, and Big Jake behind him doing the holding. Dancing with an exhale of fear busting from my lungs, I cried, "Big Jake? What are you doing?"

The skinny shadow behind Jake held onto a shotgun, and the face showed itself and stepped next to Jake. "What have we got here? We left with strict orders for you to stay put, to stay in the house. We must figure this out, and soon—there's a baby's life at stake—" Silas scolded with a firmness I'd not seen.

Jake finished Silas' words, "What do I find but two boys and a little girl playing in the yard? Do you want to be next? We've had a stabbing. A shooting. And a kidnapping. This is out of control and we can't call the authorities."

Silas ordered Molasses with a wave of his hand. "And you were left to guard the front door, to keep watch and this is what you do? You play like a small boy who can't be trusted to protect folks."

Molasses cowed down, his chin on his chest. "I did stay out front until I heard these two in the back yard. Pax came by and was he drunk."

I joined in, "He spoke with slobbery talk, and he bothered me. Molasses scared him off with the shotgun." I explained how brave Molasses was, but in my head, I knew he was not so brave, but he was kind. He knew when to take a life and when to let it live. I almost thought kindly of him, but knew he'd give me a reason to think of him as ugly before the night was over.

Crush pointed, pulling on Silas' sleeve. "Did you see the sacks? We've found Mr. Morning's money. At least some of it. The money was under the steps, one of the boards was loose."

Adding my reasoning, I explained. "I broke through the step with my shoe, and we found the money. We can meet Pax and Phillip and get Hope back tomorrow, right?"

I danced in a circle around Silas, hoping for a nod, but when he scowled, I moved to Big Jake, who let go of Molasses and took me by the arm. "Girl, you best get inside. We are dealing with the Shaw brothers, unpredictable and volatile, they are. They've been trouble since they were boys. But never, never have they gone this far."

"I don't mean not to listen; I have trouble deciding when its important."

Crush nodded. "I would agree to that."

Silas countered, "I noticed you were right alongside her, disobeying."

244

Crush crossed his arms. "Yes sir. I think after I act."

"He does. I've seen him. He's mouthy, pushy, and bossy."

Crush pointed at me. "You are like a soured bottle of milk sitting too long in the sun—you spew too many sentences. You've curdled." Crush cracked a smile. "But ... you are a friend who not only sticks closer than my brothers, it's like you come with glue. You make me want to fight for living. To not force answers. To trust others."

"Me?" I put my hand to my heart. "I'm not much."

Molasses stepped beside Crush, "She does tend to break you. She's real. She expects more from life. She doesn't give up."

Silas and Big Jake hovered behind Molasses and Crush, the four of them staring at me while the money sat in the yard, and we froze with the awkwardness of hearing two boys only a few years older than me—sound off with cymbals of kindness. They made me think they were friends, but I expect it might be a trap of some sort.

Big Jake broke the silence. "Get the sacks. All three of you. Get it now. And let's get inside."

"Yes sir." I charged first, then Crush and Molasses hurried like deer down the steps, pushing me. I grabbed a sack, Molasses held two, and Crush balanced four sacks in his arms.

In the house, we poured the money onto Ms. Daisy's bed, and no one spoke, no one could breathe, especially after we saw the bassinet. Molasses coughed, and left the room. Crush followed him, and Silas stood and lingered beside it.

I ran my fingers along the edge of the pink blanket, and a light in my head burst with information. I whispered, "Phillip must have Hope, since Pax came here tonight. Phillip's the brother who doesn't get his hands dirty. He's not as slimy as Pax."

I charged to the parlor where Ms. Daisy slept on the sofa with her head in Mahlee's lap, her shiny black hair dangling to the floor. Mahlee's head was bent in half, backwards, her mouth open. Her nose rattled with a deep snore, her wispy brown bangs in need of a trim—and Big Jake knelt near the two of them.

ZZZZZZ!

I closed Mahlee's mouth, and her nose whistled for a second until it caught up with the rhythm of her sleep. I whispered, "Will we find baby Hope? Will we get her back? Why can't we call someone for help?"

Silas assured me with a touch on my arm. "We have people in this here town and around, who have gotten tied up with the devil. Not sure who we can trust yet. Trying to make sense, we are."

Big Jake folded his hands, and Molasses joined him on the floor, kneeling. Silas moved up close, lifting his hands high, and Jake offered up a prayer, while I watched, while Crush wept.

Jake prayed, "Thy will be done. Thy will be done. God, we know you see us. You have plans of good, plans with hope. You see Ms. Daisy. You know her heart. Please. I know your will is for this baby to be with her mama. They will be done. Please, Lord. We trust you. We rely on you. We pray for your will to be done. Amen."

Silas broke out with a whisper of notes, singing with his eyes closed, his fingers reaching, "Pass me not, oh, gentle Savior. Hear our humble cry. While on others, thou are calling. Do not pass us by."

I found my heart in my throat, and my eyes pouring like a river. I whispered, "Jesus, do not pass Ms. Daisy by. Hear her humble cry."

Big Jake climbed up from the floor, and turned to me. "We have to pray for the good Lord to keep Ms. Daisy's baby alive, no matter what it takes." Jake pulled me close. "Shoelace, your shelter is in the Lord. Coming here has put you in the path of the whiskey drinkers and the night prowlers and the gamblers, but there's good folks who live here too. We know plenty of them. And you're a good folk too. You are family."

Silas switched to humming, and moved to the rocker across the room. "We need to count the money. We need $10,000 by tomorrow evening."

Running, I hurried to the bed, and stacked bills, counting each one. Molasses, Crush, Big Jake and Silas had their own stacks going, and the swish-swish became a tune of hope and time ticked ahead, leaving midnight behind. I glanced at the clock. "It's three in the morning." Yawning, I called to Molasses who wrote down the figures when we called them out. "How much? How much do we have?"

Before he answered, Ms. Daisy interrupted the counting party. "What are you doing? Where did all of this money come from?" She wiped her eyes, and yawned.

I scooted up to her, and held her fragile hand. "Mr. Morning hid money under the steps on the back porch. The wood broke and we found it by accident."

Silas corrected me, "Or maybe the good Lord showed you the way."

Ms. Daisy placed a stack of bills close to her heart, and a couple twenties floated to the floor. She asked, "How much? Do we have enough?"

We all held our breath, and I prayed little Hope slept, sleeping somewhere safe. Somewhere, where no one hurts her. Somewhere, off from mean ole men. And that we had enough money to get her back.

Enough is Enough

I handed Ms. Daisy the money she dropped. "Molasses, answer Ms. Daisy. Do we have enough to pay the ransom?"

He tapped the pencil on his pad, staring at the paper on the dresser, scribbling. "We're short. We don't have near what we need."

Crush moved next to Molasses, peering at the pad. "Is this all? We ... we need so much more."

Molasses shook his head. "The money looked like a treasure when it was on the bed, but now, we don't have enough to buy a baby back."

Ms. Daisy rushed around the bed to the side by the window. Pulling the pillowcase off, she yanked on the canvas bag hiding inside, and dumped the offering money on the bedspread. "Here, use this. I can pay the church back. I can ... they will understand. I have to get Hope back. What if they don't keep her safe tonight. I'm sick. I can't stand this." She wobbled like a tree caught in a storm.

I hugged her side. "Sit down. Sit here." Helping her to the edge of the mattress, she ran her fingers through the money, weeping.

Crush squinted, stepping to the end of the bed. "Where did this come from?"

I caught him up. "It's the pretend pastor's offering money, and he stole it from the people. Then he hid it in Ms. Della's grave, and now Ms. Daisy has it."

"How'd she get it?"

I explained, "Big Jake thought Pastor Graves was up to something when he had him open the coffin after the funeral, so Jake checked it out." I smiled, giving Jake a glance of approval. "You'd make a good 'vestigator."

Jake gave me the look of no he wouldn't. "I'm a farmer. Always been a farmer. Like farming. Don't need to investigate nothing. Unless it helps someone."

Silas counted the money as I did, while the already re-sacked money got moved to the wardrobe closet behind Ms. Daisy's frilly dresses.

I danced around Molasses as he put the final numbers on the paper. "Hurry up. How much? We must have enough."

Molasses nibbled on the eraser on his pencil. "We're short. We still need about $3,200 to make the ransom. Maybe a little less or more, I'd say $3,500 to be safe."

I hollered, "No! We can't be short. If God showed us where this money was, then why isn't there enough?" Stomping, I collapsed on my stomach across the bed, hitting the mattress like curdled milk pouring itself out.

A hand on my arm touched me with a softness only a mama could give. "Shoelace, we'll figure this out. Our brothers aren't going to hurt Hope. They're crazy, but not baby killers." Mahlee sat next to me, stroking my hair. "You need sleep. We'll think better in the morning. Everyone, let Daisy have her room, and we'll meet again at sunrise. Maybe we have something we can sell."

Ms. Daisy careened to her dresser; Molasses stepped aside, and she opened the top drawer. She pulled out a long paper. "Silas, this deed you gave me on the house, I noticed it's for the café too. I can go to the bank in the morning and get a loan. I'll put the property up to get the rest of the money. If we pay Pax and Phillip off, they'll leave town. I'll pay them—and get my little girl."

She wobbled again, and this time Molasses propped her up. "Careful Ms. Daisy. Careful."

He helped Ms. Daisy to the bed, and she crumpled the paper in her hand, sobbing. "I'm so sorry, Ms. Daisy. We'll get her back."

She pulled on his arm. "I can't believe my own brothers would go this far. I can't do this."

Mahlee curled up with her, moving Ms. Daisy's feet under the covers, and she handed me the deed. I handed it to Silas, who handed it to Molasses, who passed it to Jake.

Mahlee motioned for everyone to leave. "Everyone, give us some time to rest. We'll load up and go to the bank in the morning."

Jake placed the deed with the money in the wardrobe. "Better safe in here than left out for someone to take."

Silas picked up the shotgun from the corner. "I'll take the first watch on the back porch. I heard the front and side doors have been nailed, so only one spot to guard."

Molasses put his hand on the gun. "I'll take the second watch."

Crush placed his fingers around the barrel. "And I'll take the third."

Big Jake grinned. "It'll be sunrise in three hours. That's an hour each. Crush and Molasses, get some sleep in between. I'll keep watch from the front porch."

Mahlee reached for something under the mattress. "Jake, take my pistol. You might need it."

Molasses cringed, "Too many guns in this house. I don't like them."

I headed to the back porch, but Jake grabbed my arm as if I was his child. "And you, go to bed. Stay inside. No more sneaking out."

I nodded, "Yes sir. But I think I saw headlights outside through that window. We should check and see who it is."

Jake used a deeper voice. "Bed. Stay put. I'll see who it is."

**

Mahlee and Ms. Daisy snuggled like little girls beneath the sheets, and they kept the lamp on in the room—we had a lamp lit in the parlor and foyers too. I lingered by the bed, hoping Mahlee would invite me to sleep with them. I hummed, and I rocked on my feet sideways.

She threw the covers to the side. "Get in. We need you safe with us. And we need you to be quiet."

Sliding onto the sheets, I snuggled next to my Mahlee. "I'm ... I'm sorry for all this trouble. I'm so glad you're here though. Do you think we'll get Hope back?"

Mahlee patted my head. "Enough. No more talking. You didn't make our brothers mean. Or Mr. Morning. You happened along when the mean and the ugly in folks spilled out. We'll get Hope back. We will."

Ms. Daisy sniffled, and the bed shook. Mahlee rolled over, putting her back to me, and she held her sister. "Oh Daisy, I wish I could take this pain from you. I so wish I could."

Sitting up, I listened to the air in the house as my tears dropped to the bedspread. I stared at the bassinet, and the floors expanded, creaking, and the roof twisted as if to say it was tired too. I heard someone whispering. "Did you hear that?"

Ms. Daisy sat up. "It's nothing. Just an old house saying goodnight."

"I bet it's Crush. He's not guarding right now. He must be in my bedroom."

Mahlee sat up. "Want me to go with you?"

"Why? The house is all locked up. I'm not scared." I shuffled in my sock feet, still wearing my overalls, not taking any chances. I might need to be dressed if we had to run for our lives. "Crush, is that you?"

Rounding my way to the front foyer, I stopped when I heard him talking to someone, a muffled sound, not like his out loud voice. I leaned on the wall, taking in the conversation, but not understanding what it all meant.

"Yes, we need it by tomorrow. I know. It's the worst thing to happen. We ..." Crush paused his words. "I've got to go; someone is coming. I will explain later. We're going to the bank in Hope in the morning. Bye."

Jumping around the wall, I caught Crush hanging up the phone. I whispered in a deep tone. "Who were you talking to? And so late?"

"I can't tell, you're not good at keeping secrets."

"I am too."

"You are not."

"I'm gonna tell Mahlee you were on the phone."

"See, you can't be quiet for nothing."

"I can too."

Creak!

Molasses stuck his head inside the foyer door from the back porch. "Big Jake's having pie. He's starving. I carried him a piece out front. He said to tell you your headlights are gone. So do you want some pie or not?"

I swallowed hard. "Sure, I'm not sleepy anyway. Pie would be good."

Crush stormed past me. "I love pie too."

Mahlee showed up behind me. "You, my little one. Bed. Either with me and Daisy, or in your bed. No pie for you."

252

"Fine. I'll go to my room." I slithered to the bed, got under the bedspread, and held the covers up to my neck. "Night, Mahlee."

"Night. Go to sleep." She hollered from the other side of the house. "Stay put."

Crush and Molasses disappeared to the kitchen house, Silas stood guard out back, and Mahlee and Daisy went to sleep. Crush probably ate my piece of pie—and I was awake with worry, awake with the sadness surrounding the farmstead. My eyes were stuck open, and I felt a little afraid in the big ole bed.

After staring at the wall, my eyes tired, the minutes ticked, and the pillow felt soft under my head, but then out the front window facing the street, a light shone through the blinds, and it looked like headlights again.

I sat up, and something moved on the windowsill outside. "Powder, is that you?"

I raced to the window, peeking from behind the shade, freezing like a dead girl. "Powder? You're showing yourself again. I wish you'd let everyone see you."

He twitched his nose, scampering out of view, leaving me staring at—two shadows who stood by the angry tree. "No! What are they doing?"

I was glued to watching Officer Tock, who held a gun on Big Jake, and my feet were glued to the floor, unable to move—I noticed Pastor Graves shadowed them off to the side. He had a plate, gobbling down Big Jake's pie!

Some loud talk, some pushing, and they made Jake go with them. Tock climbed into Jake's pickup and Graves followed them in his truck. I pressed my nose on the window. "No way! They can't take Big Jake."

I had to follow—I had to help Big Jake, the giant who prays, who takes a bullet in his arm, who has so much wisdom, who likes pie, and who is kinder than most people. He prayed God would not pass Ms. Daisy by, so I must not let him pass by—especially since I'm family.

Yellow Creek Secrets

Under my breath, I sighed. "This blasted front door! It's nailed shut with this board. Darn ole Mahlee!" Spinning around, I tripped on my shoelaces as I'd slipped my shoes on. "I better tie these now. Got some chasing to do, and I've got to use a window to get out of this house."

Creak. Creak. Creak.

"Shoelace, what are you doing? I can hear you talking and walking. Sleep. A little sleep is needed. If you wake Daisy, I'll blister you." Mahlee scolded me from two rooms over.

"I'm turning out the light in the parlor. I can't sleep with so much brightness." Switching off the lamp by the rocker, I whispered. "I'm off to bed. I am so ... so tired."

"Hush! Get to bed."

I dashed to the window by my bed, ripping the blind in my rush. Pushing on the levers, I slid the window up. "There, it's open." I kicked the screen loose, and I tumbled to the damp ground. "The lights headed toward the mercantile store, past the Presbyterian Church."

Jogging fast like a bear set loose from a trap, I barreled up the street, following my gut, chasing the wind, circling corners and going one way, then the other. Minutes turned into too many, and I panted, afraid I'd lost their trail. I leaned on a sleepy tree with leaves draping down like an umbrella. "What's that? Are those voices?"

A gust of wind sent the limbs in whips around my head, and they pointed toward the cemetery. Looking toward the hill where the dirt sloped downward to the tombstones, I parted the spindly limbs. "I'm not sure. You think I should go there?"

A branch pushed me from behind. "Stop it. I'm going."

Stomping in the dust, the sadness of being too tired weighed on my shoulders, and being alone in the dark sent my heart to pounding. At the top of the hill, I skidded to a stop. "There they are. They're parked at the arch leading to the cemetery, and they've left the headlights on to see. To see what?"

Creeping like a wolf ready to get its prey, I hid behind one tree, ran to another, crouched behind a bush and jumped into the back of Big Jake's pickup—into the bed. Peering over the side, I listened to the shouting, to the ugly words from ugly men.

Graves stood short, lower than Big Jake's shoulders, but he ordered Jake to keep digging. "You're dragging. Stop taking your time. You're stronger than the two of us. Get Della's coffin uncovered. We need to get ..."

Tock slapped Graves on the shoulder blades. "No need to give yourself away, Graves. We don't need to tell this Negro what we're doing. I'm an officer of the law. I have the right to investigate the belongings of the dead."

Graves swung around, like he wanted to swing the fist he held behind his back, but he shouted at Jake instead. "Get to digging, boy."

Jake stuck the shovel into the ground, pushing the bottom with his foot. "I'm no boy. What you're looking for, isn't what you're going to find."

Tock kicked a pile of dirt. "What does that mean? We're here to get the money. The money you hid in the coffin. Graves? What does he mean? It is here, isn't it?"

Graves shuttled up next to Jake. "Of course, it's here. Don't give yourself away, Tock. No need for this boy to know about your plan to steal from church folks."

Tock pulled his gun from his holster. "Hurry up and uncover the top of this coffin. We've been digging for an hour. Get it done. I should shoot you, boy. And be done with it. I could do this faster."

Jake mumbled. "Almost got it. Just a little more, Boss." He swooshed the shovel and tossed dirt onto Graves' shoes.

Graves shook his leg. "Get to the coffin."

Jake pulled the shovel to his side. "Opening a coffin once is terrible, opening it twice lets the ghosts out."

Graves whined, "Stop with the ghost stories. We've got to get out of here."

Tock hollered at Graves. "Jump down there and open the latch. Get the money so we can get out of here. I don't like cemeteries; things are dead here."

Big Jake echoed his words. "They sure are. And some of them wake up when the town sleeps."

Graves mouthed, "Stop saying that. These coffins are full of dead folk. Nothing's gonna get us here." He fumbled in the hole, next to the pile of dirt, and all I could see was the top of his head.

Tock pushed Jake aside and hung next to the grave. "What is it? Why haven't you got the money?"

"My gosh! I'm covered in maggots and the smell. This is sickening. I'm gonna lose my supper, and the money ... the money is gone."

Tock pulled Graves from the top of the coffin and stood him upright. "What? You put it in there yourself. You said so."

"I did. I had Jake help me." He grabbed the shovel from Jake's hand. "Where is it? Did you come and get the money?"

"No sir. Not me. I don't have your money."

Cringing, I knew Jake knew the truth about the offering money, but he protected Ms. Daisy. Then Jake spoke and got himself into trouble. "You can't find what doesn't belong to you."

Tock pointed the gun at Graves. "So you let this Negro take our money? If we don't pay our marker, it's over for us. Do you hear? We're as good as dead."

Graves danced with his words. "I know. I wouldn't go to the trouble to come out here if I knew it was gone. Jake had to take it. He's the only other person who knew I put something inside the coffin."

Tock hollered, "You've wasted my time with this tonight. Looks like I don't need you anymore."

Pffft! Pffft!

I shook. The trees rattled and the bushes quivered, and Graves went to his knees, holding his stomach. "What? You … can't shoot me. I'm the one holding the money."

Tock pulled the trigger again. "You're holding death. That's all you've got."

Pffft!

My hands flew to my ears, and I slumped into the bed of the truck, knowing Graves died. I peeked over the side, in time to see Graves tumble backwards, landing on Della's coffin.

Tock turned to Jake whose eyes bugged with fear. "Do you want to live or die? It's your choice. Take me to the money, and you'll live. Or you'll meet your maker with Graves."

Jake clutched his hands, and reached for the shovel on the ground, and the wind picked up, sending a whistle through the trees. The ghosts stirred, and it's like the tombstones opened up with things that were dead and they were coming alive.

Tock stepped closer. "Do you hear me? Are you deaf, boy?"

Jake stepped back. "I'm not a boy. Time for someone else to meet the Maker."

Hoot. Hoot. Screech. Hoot.

Tock twisted his head when the owl sent its chirping screech into the wind, and owls from all over the hill must have heard the first one—for the screeching grew into a shrill pitch of chirps and hoots.

Jake swung, almost in slow motion at Tock, and I jumped from the pickup, running toward him like lightning—for his swing meant certain death for Tock.

Wallop!

"Officer Tock! You're unworthy to wear the badge."

Tock shot his gun into the air, high above Jake's head.

Pffft!

The blow to his head sent Tock stumbling, and he lumbered, leaning on a tree. "You will never leave this cemetery. You are as good as dead."

Big Jake glanced at me, when I yelled, "Big Jake. Don't kill him. You're not made like them."

Tock swung his arm my way, pointing the pistol at me. "A little girl who wants to die has joined us." Tock grinned and blood poured from his lips, and he pushed with his free arm against the trunk to stand up. "Maybe if I shoot a little girl, this Negro will give me the money."

That's when the hoots rose to a piercing noise and when all the ghosts held me, and when I tumbled, sure I'd been shot—because the night became a blur with my screaming and Jake's shouting. "Never! Not ever! You will not hurt my family! She's my little girl!"

Blinking, I lay on the ground, and tried to see. And two ghosts circled me with arms dangling, two white and two brown. I moved, trying to stand, trying to focus.

The dark ghost called to me. "Shoelace, are you shot? Did he hurt you?"

Before I could answer, the white ghost held me. "No! God don't let her die."

Breathing a regular breath, I sighed. "I'm not hurt. I'm not shot, either." I gazed into the eyes of the ghosts, and I saw—two friends, two alive friends—Molasses and Crush, who were smiling at me.

The owls stopped hooting, as if on cue, the ghosts went back to their graves, and the winds felt cool on my face. I shot to my feet. "What are you two doing here?"

Crush announced, "We followed you, and we've been here listening and wondering what to do this whole time. We saw it all. We know the truth."

Molasses stepped up to Jake as he walked over to us. "Jake, what are we going to do? There's two dead men over there."

"I've got to do what the Lord tells me. And He's telling me to let the living bury the dead."

**

Jake made me wait in the cab of his pickup while Molasses and Crush helped him show Ms. Della respect by filling her grave back in. Then they put Tock and Graves in the back of the pretend pastor's pickup—tossing them as if they were toothpicks, broken, wobbly and lifeless.

Jake came to the truck, and opened my passenger door. "Crush is driving my truck. You ride with him. Molasses will ride with me in the other truck."

"Where are we going?" He tossed the shovel into the back of the truck, and I saw the gun stuck in his waist. "Are we gonna die?"

"No, you'll be fine. But if we don't do this, I might die." Jake sighed, an exhale of sheer exhaustion. "Not so many years back, my cousin, Tuggle, was hanged in Hope for hurting a white woman."

I sighed, "Did he do it?"

"He said he didn't, and the woman wasn't clear on whether it was him or not. The deputy did find blood on some clothes at his place. A mob of men lynched him from the water tower. It's only been about 25 years or so ago, and I was a young'un myself. Things ain't changed much since."

"What are we going to do? You're saying no one will believe you were defending yourself. You think they'd hang you?"

"I reckon they might. Or I'd go to jail."

"I could tell them. Crush too. And Molasses."

"Plenty of witnesses won't change the color of my skin." He scratched his head. "So you follow me down the dirt road west, and we'll head to Yellow Creek, where we'll leave their truck and them behind."

"Why? Why there?"

"There's an alligator there, bigger than two of me, some say he's 300 pounds. They call him Arkie, so if I leave the windows down on the truck, Tock and Graves might come up missing—all together."

"Oh no! We can't be a part of this."

"I need to make it look like an accident. I can't go to jail. I gots my Auntie Etta to care for, and my five boys."

"You have five boys?"

"Yes, youngest is five. Oldest is twelve. My wife, Jettie, she's the toughest on them. I'm the one who can't get a thing out of them."

I found myself agreeing with Big Jake, especially when I saw pictures in my mind of him hanging from a water tower. Weeping at the ugly, I sat in silence in the seat.

Crush hollered over the running motor. "Hold on. We've got to catch up with Jake."

I held onto the door's handle, not sure what was next, and worried about Arkie, the alligator—hoping he won't eat us or kill us. But one thing's for sure—Jake is worth saving, he's good folk—and he's a pa I'd love to have—if God would let me.

Answer the Call

"Where am I?" My whisper felt like an echo of horror with flashbacks of Tock and Graves jumping in twitches beneath my eyelids. Sitting up, wiping my eyes, I stretched my arms, and focused on the window to my left. A bent blind, a window now pulled down, the screen on the outside back in place.

But the sun did shine like sweet lemonade ready for the drinking. And boy, did I need a drink. My mouth felt like cotton.

Under me, the mattress let my tired body mold into the cushion of softness, yet, my legs ached, my head pounded, and my lips stuck together—like someone poured sand in my throat. "Where is everyone? What happened last night?"

Swinging my socked feet to the floor, my PF Flyers sat next to each other, and my overalls gave off a smell of dirt like swampy water, like death. I swiped my hand over the fabric, and stood up. "I'm filthy. Dirty. The night left its stain on my clothes and ... and on my heart. Where is Big Jake? And Molasses? And—"

Thud.

"Ouch! A shovel? The shovel?!!"

Running from my room, I charged to the parlor. No one. I darted into Ms. Daisy's bedroom. No one. "They wouldn't leave me here. They wouldn't leave me alone."

Pounding my feet across the floor, I dashed to the back porch, the singing birds chirping a shrill of music, of wishful hope. "Where is everyone? Mahlee? Mahlee? Something terrible happened. Something I know about. Something I can't erase from my brain. It's stuck like glue to my forehead. I need you, Mahlee."

At the end of the porch to my left the dancing voices met the song of the singing birds, and I peeked into the dining room. "Molasses? Crush?" The two teens sat beside each other like different colored book ends, and they were stained with mud and with green swampy water.

Molasses smiled, "You finally got up, I see."

Crush motioned to me. "Come eat a bite. It's oatmeal with raisins."

Not answering, I looked around the room. Ms. Daisy sat on one end of the table holding a cup with both hands. A slight tremble in her fingers sent the coffee to the saucer. Her face taut, her eyes swollen from crying.

Mahlee reached for the cup. "My sweet sister. We're going to the bank. We'll get the money. We will get Hope today. You'll see."

Big Jake sat on the opposite end of the table facing Ms. Daisy. He leaned on his elbow, the blood on his shirt trapped in the fabric, revealing the stains. He turned to me. "Little Missy. Sit. Your night was long. Your courage longer."

Inching over to Mahlee, I hugged her from behind. "I love you. I thought you left me, again."

She turned to me, giving me a hug. "You've only been asleep for an hour. Big Jake carried you in from … from the terrible horrible you witnessed last night. You poor girl, my life has rubbed off on you. This is why me, being your mama, is frightening. I'm the horrible to go with the terrible. You need better. You need a stable mama."

Screaming, I stomped, my sleepy body rebelling at the last few weeks in Washington. "No, you're the best mama ever. Ever."

"You wish I was a good mama. I do too. Somehow, wishing don't make it true."

Holding her neck with a clinch of fear, "You are who I want. I want you."

Mahlee lifted my chin. "We are together. I will be with you. I do love you like my own. I worry about you though."

"I want to be with you forever."

Silas showed up at the door to the porch, "Time is getting away, Ms. Daisy. I've got the truck running. We best be going to town. The bank opens in a bit."

Screeching chairs slid across the hardwood floor, and Crush smacked on his last bite of breakfast, pouring milk down his throat. I grabbed a piece of toast from someone's saucer, and drank the rest of Ms. Daisy's coffee as she moved to the porch like a snail with a broken shell.

Silas helped Ms. Daisy on one side, and Mahlee held the other arm. Silas encouraged her. "Ms. Daisy, in a few hours, your little baby girl will be home. She'll be home for good."

Big Jake patted my head. "Molasses is riding with me. You and Crush can ride in the back of the truck if you want."

Trying to smile, trying to act normal, we all moved according to the plan, and the plan didn't allow for crying, didn't allow for me to ask questions, or for me to breathe. Didn't allow for Ms. Daisy to mend her heart. Nor for Big Jake to deal with the heaviness of the horror from last night.

But I could tell—everyone knew that Officer Tock and the pretend Pastor Graves wouldn't be bothering anyone ever again.

I nodded. "I'll ride with him. I have to get my shoes." Racing to the bedroom, I charged through the door to get them.

Jing-a-ling. Jing-a ling.

Hollering, I called to anyone who cared. "Phone's ringing. Phone's ringing."

Jing-a-ling. Jing-a-ling.

Moving to stop the noise, I picked up the receiver. "Hello."

The tiny voice asked, "Who's this?"

I quizzed the person. "Well, who's this?"

"This is …"

Click.

The phone went dead, and I shook my head, hanging up the phone. Galloping to my shoes, I pulled them on, and the phone rang again.

Jing-a-ling. Jing-a-ling.

I reached around the wall to the table. "Hello. What do you want?"

"Who is this?" The small voice rattled with a nervous sound.

"You called the Sanders House. Who is this?"

"This is … Jake, Jr."

"Jake, Jr. As in Big Jake's … son? How old are you?"

"I'm five. Almost six. My brother Jett dialed the number for me. He's eight. But he's too scared to talk. I'm looking for my pa. Me and my brothers can't find him. Our ma is sad cause … cause Auntie Etta is missing. No one has seen her. Have you?"

"No. I haven't seen your auntie. I'll get Jake. He's outside. Hold on." I placed the receiver on the table, running from the back of the house because the blasted front door is nailed up. Rounding the house, I rushed to the truck, and Silas with Ms. Daisy and Mahlee drove away toward the highway. Big Jake turned around and followed, stopping long enough to wave at me, and he rolled his window down. "Get in. We've got to go."

Swallowing hard, I considered telling him about the phone call, but going after the ransom money became more pressing. "I'm coming. I'm coming," and I leapt over the picket fence, and dove into the bed of the truck.

Molasses glanced at me from the cab like he was worn out from this horrible spring of 1947, but it's almost May now. Summer is ahead, and I'll be home in Texarkana with Mahlee before you know it.

Crush scolded me. "You need to stop making folks wait for you. You aren't privileged, you know."

Mocking him, and putting my back to the cab of the truck to keep the wind from whipping against my face, I smarted off. "I am privileged. Privileged to be alive after last night."

Crush sighed. "We can never tell anyone about last night."

"I know. Tonight ended bad, but the ending for Jake would be worse. No one would believe he killed a pastor and a cop in self-defense."

Crush agreed. "Molasses and me saw it all though. We know. We know the truth."

"And God saw it too. He knows what happened." Reaching for my throat, "Do you think the alligator's for real?"

"Doesn't matter if he is. But if he is, it matters."

"Why? What do you mean?"

"If the gator gets them, everyone will think they had a wreck. Jake ran their truck off the road and into the marsh. So it could make it look like … like it matters."

Shaking my head, I blinked my eyes. "You confuse me. This whole thing is confusing. I'm afraid I'll tell someone by accident."

"And who's gonna believe a hobo girl who chases criminals like your Mahlee?"

"Mahlee's not a criminal. She's not. I'm gonna clear her name. I am."

Arguing the rest of the way down the highway toward Hope, we bounced with the truck on every bump, the dried dirt acting like rocks when the tires rolled over them.

I pointed, "What happened over there?"

Crush and me moved to the right of the bed. "Looks like they had a celebration. History was made there." Balloons floated above the airplane hangars tied on by ropes, and streamers waved in the air from the fences.

"History? You think there's something special about this part of Arkansas?"

Crush laughed, "You're so hard headed. Everyone knows this is the airport where the Army used to test bombs for the war." He pointed at the land on the other side of the truck. "There's thousands of acres of testing ground over there. It's the Proving Grounds."

Slapping his arm, I mouthed, "And how would you know? You've been talking to Molasses, haven't you?"

He chuckled. "Yeah! A couple of days ago, the Army gave the airport to the city of Hope. They had an air show here."

"How would Molasses know?"

"Silas told him."

Wrinkling my nose, we sat down, not saying another word on the bumpy ride into town.

**

At the bank, Jake parked to the left of Silas, and Mahlee and he propped Ms. Daisy up as she held onto the deed in her hands. They disappeared inside the doors, and Molasses and Big Jake paced on the sidewalk, while Crush jumped to the ground. "I'll be right back. I need to go inside and tell Silas something."

I dove over the edge of the truck, ready to dart inside the bank too, but Jake grabbed me by my overall strap. "Not you, little Missy. You stay out here. This is work for the grownups."

"Crush isn't a grownup. He's not even out of high school."

Molasses shook his head; his words were hidden deep inside like the alligator from the swamp had chomped off his tongue. "You're a kid. You should listen to Jake."

Snarling, I stomped. "I try to listen. It's hard though."

Jake pulled me to his side. "Crush is the answer to the call. He's the one God sent to us."

"God sent Crush to do an errand?"

Big Jake said, "You could call it mission work."

Trying to figure out what Jake meant sent my brain to mush since my thoughts were jumbled. Smacking myself in the head, I stammered. "Jake, I forgot to tell you."

"Forgot what?"

"At the house, when I went inside to get my shoes, the phone rang. Twice actually. First time, the person hung up. Then he called right back, and it was Jake Jr."

Stepping back from me, "My boy, Jake? He doesn't know how to call someone on the phone."

"He said Jett helped him."

"Girl, what did he want? Are my boys okay? My wife, Jettie?"

"Yeah! They're fine. It's ..." Scratching my head, trying to remember Little Jake's words, I sighed. "He asked about Auntie Etta. No one has seen her."

"What? She stays with us. We stay with her. We stays together."

"I don't know. I'm sorry. He called when we were leaving. I don't know. She's probably out … somewhere with … another auntie."

"She don't drive. Her eyesight's going. She trusts everyone. Thinks the best. Takes walks and gets lost. She could have wandered off. I've got to get back to check on her." He stared a hole through the bank door. "They'd best hurry. I gots only one auntie. I need to get home and see about her."

Boom. Boom.

The door at the bank flew open, and Mahlee barreled from the swing glass, her arms waving. "Oh me! Oh me! Oh me!"

Right behind her came Ms. Daisy, who held her shoulders straight, her eyes seemed clearer, and the bun on the back of her head appeared to sway with a breeze of its own. She clutched her purse, tapping it with her fingers.

"You okay, Ms. Daisy? Did you get the money?" I ran to her. "We have enough?"

Ms. Daisy flapped the owner papers for the farmstead in front of me. Her voice rattled when she spoke. "Yes, and we can keep the house and the tavern. We didn't need a loan from the bank—we have someone watching over us."

I danced around Ms. Daisy and Mahlee, and found myself moving to Silas when he did the jitterbug out the door. "What is it? How did we get the money?"

"It's a downright miracle. Downright, wade in the water with Jesus, miracle." The old man who walked with a slight bend in his back rose to a new height, like a young tree reaching for the sun, strong, hopeful, ready to conquer.

270

"So we have enough?" I kept waiting for one of them to answer me with details, when the door flew open once again, and from inside the bank, Crush appeared holding the hand of a man larger than life. A friend with a bank account larger than three banks—most likely. "Mr. Marion. What are you doing here?"

He wrapped his thick arms around me. "My sweet Shoelace, I got a call from Crush. Seems your family needed a little help. Crush has been saving for a home for his brothers, and for himself—for a day down the road. He's saved every penny he's made at the syrup factory, and I gave him a little advance to go with his money."

I cocked my head at Crush. "You?! You called Marion on the phone, didn't you?"

"I did. I'm going to be working for him for a long time now. But your cousin, Hope, she needed rescuing."

I put my hand to my heart. "My cousin? Yeah, I have a cousin."

Crush smiled. "I know you'd do it for Timmons or Tak, or any one of my brothers, if you had any money."

Hugging Crush as if trying to pop him like a ripe watermelon, I wept with alligator tears. "You'll go down in history for saving baby Hope. For rescuing her and getting her back home to Ms. Daisy."

Crush peeled me from his body. "We need to get to Washington, and we need to figure out what to do next."

Marion shook hands with Big Jake. "Seems you're the one fighting this battle for this family yourself. I could always use a good man like you in Jefferson at the factory."

"Thank you, but I'm a farmer. Always been one."

I grinned. "Yeah! He's a farmer. Always has been."

"Oh goodness. I'm so weak." Ms. Daisy's words tumbled from her lips and she wobbled, and Mahlee helped her inside the pickup.

Silas urged us on. "I'm not sure Ms. Daisy is going to be strong enough for this evening. She needs rest. I need to get her home."

I rushed to take Mr. Marion's hand. "So you're coming with us to the Sanders House?"

"I am. I've got my new car and it needs to be driven." He pointed across the street. "See, it's sky blue. A Cadillac. It has white leather inside, and a white steering wheel. You can ride with me."

Crush argued. "She's covered in dirt. Looks like a pig that wallowed in the mud. She needs a bath. And you're giving her a ride in your new car? And you won't even let me drive it."

I laughed, "I've seen how you drive. Remember you hit me?"

"Hit you? You ran into the side of the truck. It wasn't my fault."

Laughing, Mr. Marion and I walked across the street, and I heard Big Jake holler from the window of his pickup to Silas. "I'll be back to see you after I check on Auntie Etta. She's missing. And I've got to figure out why."

Molasses rode with Big Jake, and I rode with Mr. Marion. I prayed for the sunshine to light up tomorrow, and that Hope would make it back to her mama. And I prayed with my eyes closed in case that would help.

Sisters Forever

"Do you see what I see? Where did they come from?" Leaning on the dash of Mr. Marion's car, I squinted, wondering if my sight blurred from lack of sleep, wondering if what I saw was inside the corral. Or was I having a dream?

Pointing, I asked him again. "Can you see them? Do you see them?"

Smiling, he answered, "Yes, Annie Grace Kree, I see them."

Plopping sideways in the seat, I rolled my eyes. "Why did you call me by my given name?"

"I love the sound of your name. Just like I love the name of your sister, Lizzy Beth. She will be proud to know you are her sister. I hope you'll come see her. I've heard you and Mahlee will move into the manor in Texarkana."

"Yes, we're moving home." I rose to the edge of the seat, staring at them, counting them. "One. Two. Three. Six. Seven Ten. Eleven. Twelve."

"You missed the white one in the corner of the corral. He's beautiful, isn't he? He has a gold mane. I bet his eyes are blue."

Mr. Marion turned from the highway past the corral, and parked behind Big Jake, who parked behind Silas. Turning around in the seat, I blurted. "So where did all these horses come from?"

"The deputies are here. The Arkansas State Patrol has come to Ms. Daisy's aid. They insist on meeting Phillip and Pax at the jail, but I expect Ms. Daisy will have a say about that—so they're waiting in the barn out of sight—for now."

"What? We have cops in the barn?" I exhaled, knowing all the melodies of spring were blooming, and soon, Hope's rescue would be underway.

"Everything in its time. What lies ahead is unknown. But every effort to save this child and to bring her home will happen."

Hugging Mr. Marion who turned the key off in the ignition, I squealed. "Thank you for coming. Thank you for bringing the waves of the ocean to us. It's as if we're riding the ripples to start a new life, to get our lives back. To find our smiles."

"We best go see what the plan is. We're meeting with the deputies on the back porch at noon." He looked at his watch. "About thirty minutes from now, you'll see the blue and gray uniforms of the men who are here to save a life."

We got out of the car, and Mr. Marion headed to the front door. I yelled, "No, we can't go that way. It's nailed shut."

"I'll go around." Mr. Marion wobbled, and ran his hand along the trunk of the angry tree. "This tree's smiling at us. See those branches up there. It's a grin. Like a welcome sign for Hope."

Glancing up, I squinted, the sun blocking my view. I put my hand over my eyes, shielding the beam of sunshine. "They are smiling at us. I see it. I do." My own grin broke out from behind my face, after being locked in for weeks.

We strolled like soldiers ready for battle to the backyard, and I went to Ms. Daisy's bedroom where she rested, where a damp cloth covered her eyes. I stood to the side taking in the delicate moment between two sisters.

Mahlee sat on the edge consoling her. "We'll get Hope in a few hours. Then you'll get your life back. And I'll get mine. We'll be friends for life. Sisters even longer."

Ms. Daisy reached for the cloth, moving it from her face. "Mahlee, you will be the best mama to Shoelace. You're so loved by that little darling."

I stepped into the foyer, out of sight, for she hadn't noticed me listening. Whispering to myself, I repeated her words. "...so loved by that little darling."

The tears ran freely from my eyes, and from the side foyer door, Crush lingered like a nosey teenage boy who gets in the way, but whose heart is bigger than Arkansas. I stared at him. "What are you looking at?"

"You. A girl who'll get her life back. I'll get mine in Jefferson. You'll get yours in Texarkana. Do you think we'll be friends? Or will we ever see each other again?"

"I do have a sister in Jefferson. I bet I come see her someday. I would come see you. I would love to see all the Crush boys too. And Toby."

"I would like that." He slugged me. "You're not so bad, you know."

"I know." Moving past Crush, I stepped to the back porch, with him on my heels. "Stop following me. We might be friends, but I don't need a shadow."

"Whatever."

We both stopped at the rail, listening to Silas and Mr. Marion talk, straining to understand, wishing to get closer. Big Jake came up, making a few arm motions, and his voice strong, but his words dropped off before I could make them out. The meeting around the water pump was a reminder they were pumping out a plan to give life to this house, to save a life.

I whispered, "Crush, did you hear what they said?"

"Some of it. They're going to let Ms. Daisy ride with Silas in her truck, and she'll have the money."

"But I heard Big Jake say something about his pickup too."

"Yeah! And Mr. Marion's taking his truck. I told him I had it parked over at the café."

"So where will the deputies be? Will they ride over on their horses?"

"I'm sure. They'll come and surround the jail, and take out the Shaw Brothers if they have to."

Molasses stepped up behind us. "I hope they can capture them. I hate all this killing."

Sighing, I agreed. "I know. Pastor Cody loved to tell his hobo friends we're here to love the Lord with all our heart, mind, soul, and strength. Killing folks off isn't love, it's not."

Molasses added some wisdom. "I thought this was all a mirage of my mind at first—a nightmare, but it's been the roughest and saddest two months."

"I didn't mean to bring all this with me."

Molasses added, "You didn't bring anything, except your knack at creating a mess. Mr. Morning's business dealings were criminal, and they were filled with low life men, and he was caught in a love for money and the corruption. All of that killed him, not the knife."

Quivering, I reflected on the others on the list. Mr. Swisher must have been one of Mr. Morning's men. And Officer Tock and Pastor Graves were too. Their lives were lost in the marsh, their greed like leeches on their hearts.

We all inhaled together using up all the air in the county, and one by one the blue shirts and the gray slacks appeared from inside the barn. The first officer made his way through the horses, and opened the gate to the yard. The freckled man with red hair called to Silas, Marion, and Jake. "Time to finalize our approach. My men are ready. We're ready to end

276

this for Daisy Morning, and to help her get Hope safely home."

The matching shirts and slacks lined up in a half circle around the water pump with the three most perfect daddy-men I'd ever met listening and talking. I hovered, leaning over the rail trying to catch their conversation, but Crush and Molasses were mumbling a plan of their own behind me.

Molasses whispered in a lower than normal tone. "We can hide in the back of the truck. We'll need to lie down and hide. If they see us, they'll make us stay here."

Crush nodded. "Yes, you and me. We should ride behind Mr. Marion. He's older, slower, and rounder. He won't ever see us, or even think to look for us in the bed of the truck."

I put my hands on my hips. "What about me? I want to go."

"Me too. I want to go with the three of you."

We twirled around and Crush, Molasses and me were facing Mahlee who stomped her boots. "I'm going with everyone to the jail. I know my brothers. I can talk to them if need be. So, Shoelace, since I know you won't stay put, you and me—we'll get in the back of Big Jake's truck. In case we're needed."

I shook my head. "You're going to let us do this? You're going to get in the back of the truck with us?"

Popping my backside, Mahlee corrected me. "No way! You, Crush, and Molasses will be here at the house. Do you hear me? We don't need any mishaps."

Stomping my feet, I rushed to the end of the porch and twirled around. "I can't stay here. If you go, I go."

"Listen here. I'm your mama. What I say goes. You have to start listening to me."

Crush mouthed. "You're the one who wanted a mama. Now you've got one."

"Shut up, Crush. I'm not listening to you."

Mahlee moved to me. "I want you alive. I can't take the risk of something happening to you. Do you hear me?"

"Yes, I hear you." I sat on the steps watching the horses in the corral, the ears of some went straight up, the ears of a few shot backwards like they heard something.

Waa. Waa.

Crush bounded to where I sat, kneeling beside me. "Did you hear that? It's like the sound of a baby crying in the wind. The sound of a baby calling for her mama."

I rose to my feet, trying to listen, but the men planning their rescue sent words in my left ear, and I couldn't make out the crying with my other. "I thought I heard it, but now I don't."

Molasses danced between us. "You want to hear the baby, and you're starting to imagine her cooing or crying. I thought I heard her last night, but the leaves on the tree rustled with the breeze. I pray we get her back. I pray this more than anything."

I exhaled. "Me too. I hope we can get Hope to her mama."

Molasses put his arm on my shoulder. "Hope to Hope."

Crush nodded. "Yes, we're hoping for Hope."

**

The afternoon twirled like an hour glass, spinning like a top, and seemed to be stuck with glue on one side—stuck in slow motion. Some of the deputies rode off on their horses toward the cemetery. A few more headed off toward the courthouse. A group of men rode down the highway, stirring up dust with each clop of the horses galloping.

Leaning on the rail, I counted the horses remaining. "There's five. No wait, three. Those two belong to Ms. Daisy."

Crush marched to the fence. "This white one has stared at us all day. He must like to stay outside. Not sure why he keeps turning his head to look at the barn though."

Silas tiptoed across the porch from the other end, and I followed him when he went inside where Mahlee and Ms. Daisy waited—they were sitting in the parlor now.

I hung behind in the foyer, trying to stay out of everyone's way. I had gotten too close to the deputies doing their planning and Big Jake had shooed me off.

I had pretended to fill up a bucket with water from the water pump, but Silas sent me away with a firm, "Shoelace, that can wait."

Then I chased the rooster through the yard, and Mr. Marion used his bossy voice. "My dear little one. We grownups are talking. Do you mind?"

Now I'm holding up the wall, and wishing for the time to move faster—so we can rescue Hope.

Silas interrupted my thinking. "Ms. Daisy, we've decided you should stay here with the children. We don't want to risk your life. We will take the money. We will get Hope for you."

I peeked around the doorway. "She needs to go. It's her baby."

Mahlee shot me a glance. "Shoelace, this is not your decision to make."

"Yes ma'am." I sat in the rocker by the window, biting my lip.

Ms. Daisy moved to the edge of the sofa, still holding onto her purse, and the other money sacks were stacked on the table by the end of the sofa. "I'm going. Mahlee and I know our brothers. I can talk them down from this. I can make this work."

Silas knelt in front of her. "We have the deputies. They're all over town now. We can get Phillip and Pax, get Hope, and save you."

"Nothing is going to happen to me. I have to go. You can't stop me." Ms. Daisy rose, Mahlee rose, and Silas stepped back.

"I will drive you then. I figured you'd have to go. So we had a plan with you in it too."

He reached for her as if to embrace a child who was lost and scared, and Ms. Daisy fell into his arms weeping. "What if I don't get her back. What if they did something to her? How have they fed her? Or changed her diaper? Or held her?"

Mahlee consoled her. "A wet diaper we can fix. A hungry tummy we can fix. Holding her, you can fix. I'm sure she's ready to come see you as much as you long for her."

Sobbing, I rocked the wooden chair so fast, it toppled forward and I landed on the floor. "Sorry. I'll go outside. I'll get out of the way."

Racing to the yard, I hurried past Crush, past Molasses, and darted between the last few men who were headed to their horses. I climbed the fence, sitting on the top rail, and the white horse kicked the dirt, snorting. He inched up to me, and I held out my hand. "Come here, boy. Come."

A blue shirt called to me. "His name is Powder."

I wrinkled my nose. "No way! Powder? He is pretty. I have a pet mouse." I stretched the truth, since I didn't have a mouse, but I wanted one. "His name is Powder too."

The man with slick black hair combed over his head sideways, smiled. "Is he white?"

"He's part white. Part not."

280

"So he has stripes?"

"No, dots!"

The man chuckled, "Well, I've got work to do. I'll be the one holding the baby when we ride back. Powder will be the hero horse of the hour."

"I hope so."

The man stuck his foot into the stirrup. "Me too."

He rode off with the other two deputies, and I turned around in time to see Silas with the shotgun, to see Crush holding a pistol, and to see Mahlee sticking the other pistol in the waist of her skirt.

Molasses paced by the garden, his hands folded, praying.

I leapt from the fence, and barreled to his side. I joined in, "I'm so confused, God. I know you talk to others. But I have trouble hearing you. I've ended up here. I don't understand. I do know you gave me Mahlee, but why, why would you let two men take a baby? Why?"

Molasses turned to me. "You always pray with your eyes open? How come?"

"In case God comes. I don't want to miss Him. I prayed with them closed in my last prayer though."

Molasses held my hands with his. "He's in your heart. He's saying to trust Him. To hold on. And when you don't know what to pray, do this."

"Do what?"

"Do this."

I repeated myself. "Do what?"

"Say, I know your plans are for me, Lord."

"Your plans are for me, Lord."

Molasses cleared his throat. "Lord, You are near me. You see me. Your goodness is ahead. Thy will be done."

I muttered. "I hope you're here. I hope you see me. Do you have a good thing ahead for me?"

Molasses shook his head. "Thy will be done, Lord. May we keep our eyes on You. May we rest in Your embrace. May we ride like a stallion into the canvas of the life you have for us."

I coughed. "So what is it you want me to do?"

"Pray without ceasing. Trust God. Keep your eyes on Him. He is with us, even now."

I wept, not sure why my eyes kept leaking—I had no idea how the rescue might go, or end, and the sun lowered behind the trees.

The time was at hand. We were loading up, and if I was going with them—if Crush was going—if Molasses was going; then we had to jump into the back of the pickups—and we had to do it now!

I told God my "Amen," and I ran around the house, as did Crush and Molasses—and diving, we slid into position, not sure what was next—but I was next to ... next to Mahlee in the bed of the truck.

She slapped my arm. "What are you doing here? I told you to stay at the Sanders House."

"I can't stay behind. You know that."

"Then stay low. Stay quiet. Don't say a word."

When Bullets Fly

"Phillip? Paxton? I'm here." Ms. Daisy's words shook on each letter and she leaned on Silas calling to the jail, and I watched for the door to open, but nothing. No answers came from inside. Silas held her on his right, and steadied himself with the shotgun.

Mahlee jumped from the back of the pickup, joining her sister in front of the truck. "Phillip? Come outside. We're here to get Hope. Pax, show yourself."

Peeking through the back part of the cab window, I listened to the birds chirping, and watched the leaves dance on the trees. The croaking of the frogs became a competition at the pond behind the jail. It hurt my ears. Their noise wasn't music to Ms. Daisy's heart, or mine, it was just screeching sounds growing with each croak.

To my left, Mr. Marion situated himself in front of his truck, his belly sticking out like a watermelon, his hands on his hips. On my right, Big Jake towered above all of us, as he plopped his hippopotamus body upright on the hood of his pickup, his left hand grasping a pistol.

Mahlee hurdled the rickety white fence, causing me to stand up in the bed of the truck. I screamed at her. "Phillip's on the balcony. Up there. I see him."

The silver suit bopped to the rail, and Phillip talked with his hands. "Mahlee, Mahlee, Mahlee. Stop right there. Where's the money."

Glaring up at him, she shook her fist. "Where's our baby?"

Phillip smirked. "She's safe. I get the money. You get her."

Mahlee charged up the steps to the left of the balcony, the ones I hadn't noticed before now, and my feet were determined to help my mama. I found myself bounding up the stairs behind her, my face hot, my mouth dry, my words stuck in my throat.

At the top, Mahlee dove at Phillip and his hand slipped inside his jacket. "Don't think for a second I can't take you out, big brother." She charged Phillip like an attacking bear, scratching and screaming, hollering and pounding, the rolling fierce, the noise sending birds fluttering.

Big Jake flew up the stairs, pushing me aside, causing me to bounce off the wall, sending me flat on my back, and shaking my head, the *Pffft Pffft* zinged in my ears.

"Mahlee! Are you … are you?" I jumped on top of the pile, and a hand swiped my face. "Ouch!" The force sent me rolling across the balcony, and I careened into the rail, stopping with a kaboom to my head.

Phillip fell to the side. Mahlee rolled off her brother, and Jake grabbed the gun from Mahlee. "Run. Go back to the trucks." He pointed the barrel at Phillip. "Where's Hope? We get her. You get the money."

Screaming, I shot to Jake's side. "Don't shoot him. He knows where the baby is. We have to know where she is…"

My words evaporated in the air when Mahlee rose tall for a second, then reached for my arm, yanking me harder than a jerk of kindness. She collapsed. "Shoelace, don't forget to tie your shoes. I … I love you."

Feeling the weight of her body, I balanced myself, and Jake reached for Phillip who curled up and bounced to his feet too—diving into Mahlee like a hammer—pushing her to the rail—away from me. The splatter of red on her side beneath her right arm filled up her tucked-in blouse with blood. "No! You've been shot!"

"Phillip! Tell us where the baby is …" Mahlee stretched her arm toward her brother. "Daisy needs her baby."

Jake held Phillip by the collar, and had one pistol in his overall pocket, the butt of the gun sticking out, the other gun was next to Phillip's temple. "Tell us where Hope is."

"Never! Never! Not until I have the money!"

Mahlee lunged at Phillip, they spun around, and Phillip pulled the gun from Jake's pocket, holding Mahlee in front of him, her back on his suit. He pointed the gun at me.

Jake pointed his gun at Phillip, and I glanced down to see Silas holding the shotgun up, ready to shoot Phillip if he could get a shot at him.

Phillip hollered, "Now, get me the money, little girl, or Mahlee's a goner."

"I will get the sacks. The money is down there." I shot to the rail. "Silas, I'm coming for it. Let me get it and we can get Hope."

Marion latched himself next to Silas with Crush and Molasses frozen like trees beside them, the four of them wobbly, moving in herky-jerky movements, and Crush and Molasses picked up the sacks. Marion called to me. "The boys will bring the money up."

Phillip scooted to the rail, keeping Mahlee between the aim of the shotgun, and between Jake and his gun. Jake inched closer, ready to fire at the first chance. Phillip shouted down at Marion. "Let them hand off the sacks to the girl."

Mahlee shook her head. "Shoelace, don't do it. He's gonna shoot you. You get near him, and he'll do it. If you give him the money before we get Hope, he's gone. And we may never find her."

Phillip fired his gun at Jake, the bullet piercing Jake's hand, the gun falling to the balcony. Without thinking, I dove for the pistol, and Phillip kicked it away, sending it behind him and Mahlee. Jake towered with blood dripping from his palm, glaring at Phillip, but not attacking since Phillip had a death grip on Mahlee's neck.

Silas hollered, "Boy, I've known you since you were a wee one. This is no way to end your life."

Ms. Daisy hunched over on the bumper, her arms crossed, as if she couldn't watch her family go through this horrible terrible.

Phillip laughed. "End my life? I'm gonna live. Today I'm rich!" Phillip mocked Silas, and I raced down the stairs and back up, balancing the sacks, carrying them, and plopping each one beside Phillip. "Here's your money. Where's Hope?"

Phillip shoved Mahlee into me, her mouth dripping with blood, and the push sent me stumbling to my knees. She cried, "Stop Phillip. We don't have the baby." She then collapsed as Jake caught her in his arms.

Phillip bounded to the door leading inside the second floor of the jail, dragging two money sacks with him.

I popped up, and shouted at him. "Don't forget the rest. Remember, you're rich."

Phillip barreled at me, pushing me backwards toward the rail, and Jake pulled on my arm, trying to hold onto Mahlee and me—at the same time. Mahlee mustered up enough strength to grab my foot when the rail snapped, and my head dangled over the balcony.

I screamed. "No! Stop!"

I couldn't see what happened on the balcony, but the scuffling and screams, the thuds and the booms left me with someone holding onto my hand to keep me from falling to the ground.

Behind me, down low, Ms. Daisy shouted. "No! This is not happening." I could see Molasses and Crush watching—see them readying to catch me, and time stopped. The birds perched in trees didn't fly, and the sun went down while darkness fell. The shadows of death and night hung over me.

In the trees to each side, I caught glimpses of horses, with blue shirts and gray slacks on them. "God, come now. Hurry."

Craaack.

The snap of wood told me the rail was giving way, and a body flew by me, one wearing a skirt and brown boots, and a bloody top. "No! Mahlee! My Mahlee."

In seconds, I was flung back to the balcony, and Big Jake hugged me. "You okay, little bit?"

Not answering him, I charged down the steps, rushing to the limp body on the ground—and Mahlee's pistol lay beside her. Kicking it, I shouted. "Get the gun away from me. I never want to see another gun. Never!"

Crush picked it up, and stuck the gun in his waist. Jake hovered over me. Ms. Daisy too. Silas wept. And Molasses knelt beside me. "Is she …?"

Silas placed a hand on Molasses. "She's gone."

I bolted at Silas, hitting his stomach. "She's not dead. She's fallen harder than this before." I glanced up at the balcony, and I stopped swinging my fists, turning back to Mahlee, falling across her body. "No! No!"

Someone pulled me off. "Shoelace, we need to … need to …" Mr. Marion wrapped me in his arms, and over his shoulder I saw the horses galloping from behind trees, and circling the jail, disappearing to the pond behind the jail.

Ms. Daisy cried, "They've got Phillip cornered. He's caught. But … where's my baby?"

The deputy with the white horse rode up, and I hollered at him. "So where's the baby? You were going to save her. She's gone. Mahlee's gone. I can't live without my Mahlee."

Storming from the yard, I made up my mind, and headed for my satchel, ready to leave, sure to hide from everyone—by catching the next train. "I have no one. No one! I have to leave! I have to leave! I have to go now!"

Crush called to me. "Wait up. Stop running."

Molasses echoed Crush with a call to my heart. "Shoelace, you have us. We're family."

I kept running, bounding down the road, racing through the back door at the Sanders House. Grabbing my satchel and my engineer's hat, I halted by the water pump on my way out of the yard.

Waa! Waa!

Crush bumped into me rounding the corner of the house, and Molasses puffed to a stop. Together they asked me. "Do you hear the cry? It's a baby! It's a baby!"

Rescue Me

"Leave me be. I'm leaving. I have no reason to stay. Nothing is here for me. I can't be here. I can't." I shouted, circling the the two bookends who had followed me from the jail.

Crush whispered, "Stop. Listen. I hear her."

Molasses covered my mouth with his hand, holding my arm with his free hand to make me stand still. "Listen. I hear Hope. It's her cry."

Muttering, I slapped Molasses on his back, and he moved his hand from my face. "Stop bothering me. Did you see what happened? Mahlee fell to her death because of me! Me! It's always me causing people to die! I need to leave before one of you is next!"

Crush corrected me. "Phillip was the cause. Not you! He did this to his own sister. And she—she tried to save you."

Molasses wiped his face from sweat or was it a tear. "Your Mahlee held you from falling. She had you! She saved you for your future."

Waa! Waa!

Sobbing, my chest heaved in and out, my breath fast, my sadness caught in my veins, stopping up any reason to live. Sighing, I looked toward the barn. "The crying is coming from the barn. I hear it too."

We inched in small steps, and I longed to run away; but the Mahlee who saved me from the balcony would want me to be brave, to do the right thing. Not that I have any idea what the right thing is, since I got here.

Sniffling, I stood on the bottom slat of the fence, gazing toward the barn door.

Molasses slipped into the corral, crawling between the slats, as did Crush, who pointed at the limb above our heads. "There's Tink. Look at her. She's creeping along, ready to get something."

I mouthed. "No, it's Powder. She's going to get the mouse."

Molasses planted himself in front of me, pointing his finger. "You're seeing things again. There's no polka dotted mouse."

Crush tapped Molasses on the shoulder. "You better look up. I see him. He's white and black polka dotted, and Tink is chasing him into the loft of the barn."

"No way! He's for real!"

Wiping the flood of tears breaking free from my sadness, I shook my head. "I told you so. He shows himself when he knows we need to see him."

Molasses touched my arm. "I'm sorry about Mahlee. I am, she was good to me and taught me how to bake."

"My Mahlee? To bake?" I rattled my head sideways. "Not her. My grandma taught her how to bake cakes last year. She made some dry ones at first."

"She must have forgotten, because the Mahlee I know— she's swift in the kitchen. Good with an axe too. Stronger than most of the men in Washington."

Wishing to see her, wishing for her to come running, I nearly lost my will to stand. "I don't know how to live without her. I don't."

Waa! Waa!

The cry called to us, and we marched into the barn, as if we were sneaking around on someone's property—instead of Ms. Daisy's farmstead, which is her place, thanks to Silas.

Up in the loft, I saw a shadow, and I put my finger to my lips. *Shhh!* Whispering, I bent down and got inside one of the horse's stalls. "Up there! It's Pax! Pax is holding a gun, sitting on a bale of hay."

Crush pulled a gun from his waist, Mahlee's gun. "I can shoot him, if I need to."

"I told you I don't want to see any guns. They kill people I love."

"No they don't. Guns don't kill. The person holding the gun is the one who shoots it." His words were firm, and he put the gun under his shirt and tucked it back into his pants.

Molasses whispered, "I'll be right back. I'm going to shimmy up the rope by the loft. I can see if he's alone."

Crush and me nodded, sat down on the straw, and my shaking and shivering kicked in, and the sadness of seeing my Mahlee staring at the moon, not seeing it, sent me to crying, again. The tears were salty in my mouth, the blood stains on my overalls damp, fresh, too much to look at.

Crush gave me a boyish, awkward, I-don't-know-how-to-help-you hug. "God, put Shoelace back together again. She's torn into pieces."

I put my shoulder on his, and wished to fall asleep forever, wished to hide, wished to disappear, wished for the pain to leave my heart, and mostly I wished for Mahlee to return. This is a nightmare. But I knew it wasn't. I saw her face. I saw that she was gone. Gone for good.

Molasses crept back to us. "You're not going to believe it. It's Pax all right, and he's got Ms. Etta!"

I shushed him. "Quiet down, he'll hear you."

Crush rolled his eyes. "Ms. Etta? What for?"

Molasses folded his arms as if he held a baby, and he cut a grin. "Hope is alive! She's up there with them. Pax must have taken Ms. Etta to keep the baby. She's tied by the ankle to a post, and he's probably waiting for Phillip to come for him."

I stood tall, rising up with hidden strength I didn't have. "We have to get Hope before it's too late. We have to."

Molasses placed his hands on his hips. "Hope was here all along. She was right under our noses. They knew we'd never search for her here."

"Search for who here?" The whiny, squeal of a voice coming from the loft edge, pointing a gun at us repeated his question. "Who are you searching for, my three little intruders?" Pax mocked us, his chatter sloppy, his words mushed together, his wobbly stance a sign of drinking early tonight.

I whispered to Crush. "He's drunk. He'll miss me. I'm running for Hope. I'll go up the ladder, grab the baby, and toss her to you out the loft window."

Molasses argued, "This is a job for a boy. You're a little girl."

"I have nothing to lose. Let me do this, or I'll die myself."

Crush shook his head. "You could die doing this too."

"I don't care. I have to do this. You have to let me. I'm fast. I'm small. I'm used to darting around the drunks of the night. I can do this."

Pax called, holding onto a post and his one foot slipped, his gun tumbling to the ground in the barn, landing right next to Molasses, who picked up the pistol. "I don't like guns."

I snapped my fingers. "Now, let's get him. We've got his gun. He's coming down the ladder, and I'm going up this way." I bounded onto the stall fence, swung my feet to the stack of hay on the side, and climbed to the loft, running to Ms. Etta while Pax disappeared below.

Ms. Etta screamed, "Oh me! Oh me! He put the gun to my throat, threatened to shoot me and little Hope. Tied me up. Hit me. Cut me with his knife." She showed me her wound on her arm. "His knife is stuck in the wood of the post over there." Ms. Etta rambled fast, her words slurred, and she reached for her ankle, untying the rope. "Is he gone?"

I shook my head. "No! He's weaving between the stalls down below, but he's dropped his gun. Molasses picked it up."

"No! Don't let my Molasses get hurt."

"He's not going to get hurt." I hoped my words were true, but so far I've not been good at knowing who was safe and who wasn't. Looking around, I asked. "Where's Hope? Where is she?"

"She's over there between those bales of hay. On the blanket. Her diaper is soaked, she's run out of milk, and I can't keep her from crying. She wants her mama."

Sobbing myself, I uttered the same words. "I know. I want my mama too."

I jumped over the hay and saw the sweet pink face, and cuddled Hope up. She was the prettiest bundle of wet clothes and spit up. "Hope, your mama's gonna be so happy to see you."

Creak.

"Happy to see who?"

I spun around, holding Hope close to my chest, and Pax shadowed me, but behind him on the ladder peeking into the loft was Molasses. "Stop Pax. Let Shoelace and Hope and Ms. Etta go."

Pax twirled around, ready to attack Molasses and Molasses fired the gun.

Pffft!

The silver suit tumbled sideways, and he wobbled like a horse with a broken leg. "You've shot me in the knee. I can't walk."

Molasses yelled. "Hurry, Shoelace. Hurry."

I ran to the loft window, ready to toss Hope down, when I saw how far the drop was, and creeping behind me was Pax, who yanked the knife from the post beside me. "Little girl, this is now how this ends. I'm not letting you leave without leaving my mark on you."

I swallowed hard. "You are not in charge of me. God is. I'll show you a thing or two." Jumping over his swipe at my leg, I glanced out the loft window—as the most beautiful white stallion rode up with a deputy in the saddle. "Sir! I've got the baby! We've found her."

He pulled on the reigns. "Lower her to me. I can catch her. I've got her."

Leaning as far as I could, I let the bundle tumble into the large hands of the deputy. When I blinked—he favored Pastor Cody, but in the next blink, I thought I saw my daddy, and then in a split second—he looked like Jesus—bright with a light surrounding him, with scars on his palms, with a crown of thorns on his head.

I shook my head, crying, "No! Pax has cut my leg."

From behind me, I heard Molasses holler. "Let her go. She's my sister. I'm not letting you hurt her."

I twirled around in time to see Ms. Etta, the rather heavy woman, give Pax a swift kick in his gut. "Pax Shaw, you're not getting away with this. Not if I have to push you off this loft. This is the last day you'll ever hold me hostage, or hold a gun on me."

Owwee!

Pax moaned, holding his stomach, and lay on the loft floor.

Molasses pointed the gun at Pax. "I've got him, Ms. Etta. Go for help. Go get help now." And Molasses held Pax in check, ready to shoot if necessary.

Crush came up the ladder, running to me. "Is it bad? Your leg is bleeding through your overalls."

"No, it's not too bad. Might need some stitches. Might need them for my heart too."

Crush held me until the others came, until the rest of the deputies rode up on their horses. "You'll be better soon. You might have tears for breakfast. And tears for supper. But the Lord will ride in to comfort you."

I whined, "Where did you hear such a thing?"

"Mr. Marion had a saying about breakfast and supper tears. You will get better. Some days will be sadder, but you will hold onto the good memories before long."

My tears ran like blood from my eyes, and I grew weak, the blood from my leg gushing like an artery was busted. In the background of the night, I heard people talking, and heard myself mumble, wishing to run to Mahlee, to save her. I wanted to hide and to stare at the moon until the sadness went away but someone carried me inside the house.

Someone said Pax would go to jail for a long time, and Phillip got caught with two sacks of money behind the jail.

Big Jake went to the hospital to get his hand fixed up, and Silas suffered a small stroke from the stress. Or so someone said.

Molasses tossed the pistol to the ground after Pax got arrested, and Crush swiped the gun, putting it inside his suitcase. Or so he told me.

Baby Hope is with her mama, and Ms. Daisy couldn't be happier. Mr. Marion talked to a reporter from the newspaper, and Tink is snuggled on my bed asleep.

I can't cry anymore—I can't feel anything because at sunset tonight, I left my heart in front of the old jail—and I gave it to Mahlee to hold, until I see her again.

Epilogue

Sometimes memories are the worst form of torture, but having a few good memories of the Sanders House will live in my heart for years to come. Sitting on the steps, I'm waiting for Mr. Marion and he's hurrying Crush along inside the house. He told me to sit, to not wander off.

The month of May has brought out a million mosquitoes and my arms are covered in red dots. We put my Mahlee to rest next to her kin at the cemetery a couple of weeks ago. I've gone to talk to her every day, and said goodbye for real this morning. I heard the owls hoot too, when I walked away from the tombstones, and the ghosts of the rail flew by as if Mahlee won't ever leave me—in my heart.

She's next to Della, so they'll have each other. And they'll be with their ma and pa too.

For now, my search for a mama is over, but Mahlee brought me here and she came for me, like a good mama would. She showed me how much she loved me, and we have Hope now. A baby who is safe with her mama, who will know what having one is like—and who will feel the hugs and the love—like I felt when Mahlee reached for me on the balcony. When she saved my life, with a little help from Big Jake.

Crush showed his true self here too. He offered his own money to save a baby. I believe God sent Crush to save me, and to save Hope. Now Molasses was here to save us all, because when it came time to stop a killer, he shot him in the knee.

I'll never look at alligators the same though, and I will carry that secret with me—until alligators die off.

Creaaaaaak.

Turning, I stood on the second step on the front porch and Jake moved outside, holding a claw hammer, having taken the nails from the door so folks can get inside.

Ms. Daisy left them nailed for days; she couldn't sleep at night, and Ms. Etta is staying for a few more weeks until things settle down. Silas and Molasses have moved into the front bedroom to be closer to Ms. Daisy too.

Jake walked up and tapped my hat. "Nice engineer's cap." He sat next to me, his long legs stretched out. "I'm gonna miss having a girl around. Them boys of mine can be a handful, but you—you bring a spark every family needs—you're a firecracker."

I rocked, holding my knees. "I don't feel much like a firecracker."

"Your fire is inside, it will rise up. You'll find yourself." He squeezed me. "You will become the girl who fights for joy, who brought our hope back to us."

"You mean, little Hope?" I wiped my nose. "Crush did that."

"No, little missy. I mean hope, the spark to fight for life." Big Jake handed me a nail. "Take this. Nail hope to your heart. Never forget, God is with you."

I removed my cap. "Thank you. I'll remember."

"You've reminded us of what is real, and how we need to be there for each other. To show our kindness. To act like family."

Smiling, I felt peace rushing through my body for the first time in days—a river of new tomorrows awaited me.

Crush showed up behind us, and made his way to Marion's car. "Come on, Shoelace. Marion said we're running behind."

I rose, twirling in a circle for one last glance at the Sanders House. Ms. Daisy moved to the porch. "I'll miss you. Come see me." She held Hope like she was fine china, and she smiled. "I love you, sweet thing."

Charging up the steps, I kissed Hope on the nose. "You're the luckiest little girl, I know."

Silas stepped from the side of the house holding a shovel. "Bye Shoelace. Next time I need someone for chores, like painting or replacing floors, I'll call you."

Running to him, I hugged his thin body. "I will always remember you. You're as nice as Skip."

Silas kissed my head. "You're the bravest little girl ever. Skip would be proud of you."

Ms. Etta bounced to the porch from the foyer. "Now! You need to hug me too. After all, you're the little girl who brought hope to us."

"I didn't do much. I got in the way—mostly."

Daisy blurted, "You have done that for sure. I'm so thankful though, that you got in the way."

Ha! Ha! Ha!

Laughter rose up on the corner of Carroll Street, and I could stay in this moment forever, on this street corner. I realized the best family I could ever pray for gathered around me. And they loved me like mamas and papas. Like brothers and sisters.

I hadn't seen Molasses today, except at breakfast, and afterward he rushed down the road without a word.

Marion pounded between everyone. "Let's get on the road. Time's getting away. We have a long drive."

"Bye, everyone. Bye." I hopped into the pickup, rolled my window down, and waved to my family. "See you down the rail someday."

They waved with a fierceness, which made me want to stay. Sighing, I hugged my satchel, and watched Mr. Marion's car inch away from the side of the house. "Are you sure you want to let Crush drive your new car?"

"I'm sure. I need to ride with you. I have something to tell you."

Spinning in my seat, I gave a final goodbye wave out the back window and plopped into the seat, swinging my feet. My heart ached since Molasses didn't make it back in time to see me off. "What do you need to tell me? Is it about the O'Malleys? They do want me, don't they?"

The wind whipped through the open window and my pigtails slapped my face, and the buckle on my overalls was unhooked. Clipping it back, I glanced in the side mirror on the truck, and we were being chased by Molasses on a horse. "Stop the truck. It's Molasses."

Marion slowed the pickup down, stopping on the rough dirt road, and Crush drove on down the road—oblivious to our pulling to the side.

Molasses pulled on the mane of the horse with one hand, his bare feet bouncing on the side of the horse. "I've got this for you. I did it this morning. I want you to have it."

"What is it?"

"Unroll it, and see."

I reached for the scroll, unfolded it, and a charcoal world was canvassed on paper. "Oh my! This is the best! That's me. You. And Crush. We're standing in the loft. And we're saving Hope."

Molasses hung onto the horse. "You saved me from me. I will always remember the girl who hitched a ride to Washington, and who burned up the kitchen."

"And I will always remember you, my new brother," I glanced at my pale skin, "the brother whom I favor, whom I love."

Mr. Marion chuckled. "You both look a lot like your mother."

Together we both said, "We know."

I handed the engineer's cap to Molasses. "This used to belong to Skip. He gave it to me. He would want you to have it."

"No way!" Molasses slipped the cap onto his head. "Thanks."

"You're welcome. It's made for you."

**

Down the road, Mr. Marion patted my leg. "I need to tell you something. I'm not sure how to—"

"Yes sir. What is it?" I folded the drawing into a scroll, putting it on the floor.

"Well, you're not going to the O'Malley's." Sighing, Mr. Marion wiped his brow. "It's Lizzy Beth, your little sister. I have to get you to Jefferson as fast I can."

"What's wrong? Is she sick?"

"I'm not allowed to say. I'm only allowed to bring you to her."

"Tell me. Tell me, Mr. Marion."

Screeeech!

Mr. Marion swerved the truck, missing the man in the middle of the dirt road, who lumbered across the highway in front of us. "What is he thinking? I nearly hit that man."

I crept back into the seat after tumbling to the floorboard, and I peeked over the dash. "Archie? My Archie?"

Mr. Marion raised his hands in disgust. "He could have gotten himself run over."

Archie slopped to the passenger side, smiling a grin from ear to ear, looking inside the cab through the opened window. "I could use a lift, sir." He tipped his brown hat. "Hi there. If it's not my little friend, Shoelace."

Mr. Marion offered his manners. "Hop in, sonny. You could have waited until I stopped. I saw your thumb. We're headed back to Jefferson."

I scooted to the middle of the seat, gazing up at Archie. "I thought you were working with the circus."

Archie hopped into the truck, his suit coated with dust, and he swiped his lap clean, reaching into his jacket. "Here's a handkerchief for you."

"Thank you. I always seem to need one." Holding the white hanky, I put it to my nose. "It smells like honeysuckle."

"Watch out, you'll sneeze."

Achoo!

Wiping the snot and tears from my face, I stuck the handkerchief into my overalls pocket. "You always show up at the oddest times."

Archie nodded, "I guess it was time for me to show myself."

Marion grabbed the wheel. "Hold on. Let's get you to your baby sister."

Archie waved his hand, and pulled out another item from his other pocket, whispering to it. "She's right here. She needs a friend. So show yourself."

I unfolded Archie's fingers, and a twitching nose and two beady eyes stared at me. "No way! Powder? You're here! With us?"

Powder scampered into my hands, and I kissed his teeny ears. "I can't wait to show Lizzy Beth. She's not going to believe I have a spotted mouse."

Mr. Marion gave me a glance. "Hold on. If we get to Jefferson after dark, the ghosts of yesterday may change their mind about your future."

"My future?"

Archie gave me one of his riddles. "We all have a future, and we will spend it somewhere. The question is ... where is the future? And where is somewhere? And does anyone care?"

Discussion Guide

1. Molasses Jones became jealous when he discovered Shoelace knew his pa on the rail. Have you ever felt slighted in life? Ever wished for the perfect family?
2. Crush argued with Shoelace and taunted her, but their fighting often revealed a struggle within, for each dealt with losing their parents. Have you faced times when the struggle felt heavy? Have you trusted God for strength to persevere?
3. Ms. Daisy lived in bondage to a crooked man, and her depression hung like death over her. The reminder of her past was trapped in her present. Do you sometimes find your past sneaking into your day? May you lean on Christ for joy and peace.
4. Silas Jones' life was built on his faith in God and he expected those around him to live with integrity. Have you built your life on trusting God? What can Silas teach you about living a peaceful life?
5. Officer Tock, Pastor Graves, Phillip Shaw, and Pax Shaw were set on getting money that was not theirs. They pursued riches at any cost, and lost their way. Have you ever lost your way? If so, run to Christ for redemption.
6. Big Jake towered over everyone and could break someone in half, and yet, he loved God with all his heart, soul, mind, and strength. He made hard decisions and faced them, in part, because he was Negro. Have you found yourself caught in a world

where the color of your skin divides? If so, what can we learn from Big Jake?

7. Shoelace searched for her rail-mama in hopes of finding a family. Her pursuit would end with heartbreak, but not before she knew how much Mahlee loved her. Have you shown love to someone important in your life? If not, why?

8. Tin Can Mahlee lived a tough life on the rail, and her choices put her in danger, and her life became chaotic. She wasn't afraid to shoot a gun, and feared she'd gone too far by killing two men. Have you made bad decisions? Is your life chaotic? Is it time to settle down?

9. Pastor Cody left footprints of love and of Christ on Shoelace's heart. His words, his walk, and his life will forever go forward. She will never forget him. Shoelace will hold his friendship close to her heart. What will others say about you when you're gone? Will you be a person who has left a Godly mark for the Kingdom?

10. Marion Kane became a father image for Shoelace, and he's standing on the foundation of God, as a leader, and is guiding her. His ways are not of hate, nor sin, nor of deceit. How can we walk with such grace? Is it time to pass on the hope found only in Christ?

But in your hearts revere Christ as Lord. Always be prepared to give an answer to everyone who asks you to give the reason for the hope that you have. But do this with gentleness and respect.
I Peter 3:15 NIV

Pam Kumpe

Washington, Arkansas
Sanders House / Barn
Old Post Office / Cotton Gin
Jonquils

Annie Grace Kree Chronicles Series

1 Untied Shoelace
2 Unknown Soul
3 Rescue of Undaunted Spirit
4 Unwanted Sidekick
#5 Coming 2017
#6 Coming 2018

Other Books by Pam Kumpe

See You in the Funny Papers
A Scoop of Inspiration
Things I Learned in Jail
In the Lick of Time
My View from the Bridge
A Goat with a Tote

www.pamkumpe.com

Leave comments on my Facebook page.
I'd love to hear from you!